Praise for

AVAILABLE LIGHT

"An extraordinary first novel...fluid and self-assured."
— *Boston Globe*

"*Available Light* is wildly funny, weirdly accomplished, and compulsively quotable...sheer stylistic razzle-dazzle."
— *Chicago Tribune*

"*Available Light* is a quick-flashing tale whose action is as wild as its language is carefully controlled...an impressive and delightful book...*Available Light* makes your mind jangle with associations—the sunshiny arm in arm with the perverse, running for cover and giggling like crazy." — *New York Magazine*

"Brings real energy back to the novel. An extraordinary book. It's outrageous and funny, about the never-ending sexual battles we stage, but very serious indeed." —Maureen Howard

"Its language and wit will make you laugh out loud. A book about generations, guilt, and the maddening drive for the ownership of babies." — Grace Paley

"This first novel reads like anything but. The voice is so warm it glows at the edges, and the pacing is sure and consistent... *Available Light* is funny, literate, fabulously verbal, and completely accessible. It deserves to be read on a sunny spring day."
— *Village Voice Literary Supplement*

AVAILABLE LIGHT

Ellen Currie

WSP

WASHINGTON SQUARE PRESS
PUBLISHED BY POCKET BOOKS NEW YORK

This novel is a work of fiction. Names, characters, places and incidents are either the product of the author's imagination or are used fictitiously. Any resemblance to actual events or locales or persons, living or dead, is entirely coincidental.

A Washington Square Press Publication of
POCKET BOOKS, a division of Simon & Schuster, Inc.
1230 Avenue of the Americas, New York, N.Y. 10020

Published by arrangement with Summit Books,
A Division of Simon & Schuster, Inc.
Library of Congress Catalog Card Number: 85-26239

ISBN: 0-671-63205-1

First Washington Square Press trade paperback printing February, 1987

10 9 8 7 6 5 4 3 2 1

WASHINGTON SQUARE PRESS, WSP and colophon are
registered trademarks of Simon & Schuster, Inc.

Printed in the U.S.A.

*To
Ann Lynch
Currie*

AVAILABLE LIGHT

Kitty

◆

I waited and waited and waited for Rambeau to leave me. But would he, no he wouldn't, damn well wouldn't budge. Then one morning he was gone. I knew he was gone because both sets of car keys were on my chest and so was Rambeau's flea-chewed grudge-holding little sour dog. The keys were to Rambeau's car of course. My car had better tires.

I was depressed by Rambeau's leaving me. I'm always depressed when they leave me. (I'm depressed, as a matter of fact, before they move in, which is why I persuade them to do so.)

Rambeau was a gambler—if a man who never, ever wins can truly be said to be gambling. He had a lot of red hair on his shoulders and a little on the top of his head. He was a pretty good cook—a good cook, to be fair about it; a sweet-voiced man; an inept and relentless teller of dialect stories. He was housey—he liked to wax and polish, liked to run the vacuum cleaner, liked to iron. He really liked to iron, most particularly ruffles. There's no sound like the sound of a fine man bashing away at an ironing board. I must say I missed that, after Rambeau left me.

Rambeau wasn't, strictly speaking, employed. He played a little hockshop saxophone, nothing too demanding. He never played the thing for me, even though I asked him. But I believed he could play it. Sometimes, when he'd pawned it, he wore the neckstrap. I thought he was missing his saxophone and I suspect I found that touching. It also made me jealous, but that's the way I am. I have an awful character.

Eileen, my sister, the living vigil light, had all kinds of theories about Rambeau, every one of them gaudy. She thought he was hooked into some kind of racket; she thought he was a wanted man; she thought he had an enormous trust fund; she thought he pushed dope in schoolyards. It really did upset her that he didn't bring his friends home. Eileen says it isn't healthy for your children or your lovers not to bring their friends home. But that was all right with me.

Rambeau and I went into this knowing it wasn't permanent. We were just marking time. We were waiting for the real stuff, the good stuff to start. And so we were careful; we weren't too confiding, and we made a point of believing each other.

If he told me he earned enough playing club dates in Queens to cover himself at poker and blackjack and the track and the fights, I believed that. If he'd told me he painted holy pictures holding the brush in his toes, I'd have believed that too.

At the time Rambeau moved in, each of us was so grateful to the other for not being the last person we'd lived with that everything was roses. We knew it couldn't last. But it did. It lasted.

Eileen, my sister, when things go wrong for her, which is always, says, "I can't handle this, I can't deal with this. This is the sort of thing with which I cannot deal and so

I'm just not handling it." And then she digs out her rosary. Well, I couldn't handle/deal with Rambeau's running off, and my rosary and I are on very distant terms.

It wasn't *Rambeau*, naturally. How could it be Rambeau, an interim attachment, a man who gambled, had hair on his shoulders, liked to iron, wouldn't play his saxophone for me, stole my car, abandoned an unprepossessing dog? It wasn't really Rambeau, it was just that Rambeau's absence left a man-shaped hole in my life. An aperture that hope kept leaking out of.

And I missed him in bed. He wasn't a one-man orgy, but he was chummy in bed. Allowing for the baby talk, the chewing gum, and the fact that he wore his drawers, to keep, he said, the mystery. And allowing of course for the goddam dog. He had a companionable snore, Rambeau.

Oh I like men, God help me. Not that I'm a siren on a rock, I just like them, the way some women like cats and some others hate spiders. I tried to explain all this to Eileen, but she tends to go a bit dim on you in areas. Sex, to Eileen, is basically what you do to avoid an argument.

Once Rambeau put some real estate between us, I realized what utility he'd had. I never ate a decent meal anymore. Not that I'd actually eaten that many first-class meals with Rambeau, but he saved me first-class leftovers. Now I was back to tofu and Tab. Now I was back to gnawing on my kneecaps, alone in my bed, hungry and remorseful. I wished I'd let old Rambeau take that Chinese cooking course he wanted, I wished I hadn't boggled at the cost of the cleavers and the knives.

Another thing Rambeau did well was swap domestic particulars. I like that. It's boring, but it's family. He'd natter on to me about the carrion smell that haunts my elderly freezer, or the price of veal, or what the smartass plumber said to him and what he said back as opposed to what he should have said and why he didn't deck him. And I told

Rambeau a whole lot more than anyone could care to
know about my dreary trade. There was something about
Rambeau. He was a kind of kin.

Eileen, my real kin, came and stayed with me two nights.
A considerable sacrifice for her, since she and Gordon live
wrapped around her expensive thermometer, trying to
strike while the ovaries are hot. And Eileen doesn't like my
house. It's a gate house and the big house, the main house,
is empty. That makes Eileen nervous. She likes action in
all three rings at all times. She thinks of the big house as
abandoned, whereas I think of it as waiting for a tenant.
But to speak the truth for once, it makes me nervous too.

It was nice, having Eileen there in my little house,
though not as nice as Rambeau. Oh, nice, nice, as if nice
had to do with it. Eileen is a far nicer person than Rambeau, any way you look at it. I told her so, sitting with her
in my kitchen, eating hot chocolate chip cookies as fast as
she could bake them and drinking the softest, reddest wine
that nasty Rambeau bought with my nice money. Eileen
said of course she was nicer, I was nicer than Gordon, too.
And we sat there, drunken sisters, facing one more ancil-
lary verity.

I told Eileen I hated Gordon because he'd had pieces of
the lining of her uterus strewn all around the city of New
York while he himself declined to have a sperm count.
Eileen told me she hated Rambeau because he let me keep
him. "But he *didn't* let me keep him," I said, and I howled.
"He's gone, he's gone, he's *gone*." Of course the dog had
to woof and wail; it barked so hard it levitated and peed
down its leg on the kitchen floor.

"What kind of man deserts his dog?" Eileen said in that
tragic way we have.

"What kind of man deserts *me?*"

"Oh, you," Eileen said, "you, you drove the bugger out,
that's you. You fear commitment. You were afraid he'd
jump and so you pushed him."

Well of course she had a little tiny point there. I'd been after him to go. What kind of man was he, anyhow? A gambler, a man who put his dollar down on me a little while, and lost it. I can't get involved, not really involved with a man like that—I've got a life coming up. I'm just stretching my hamstrings before I take the run.

Of course I've been doing that a while now, but I'm a staller, that's my nature, I stall. But Rambeau? Ho, I'm giggling in my cuff. Rambeau was a stall. A stall, like my psychology major, a renowned, a time-honored stall. My dance minor, a staller's stall. My job, a stalling-around-till-the-cosmos-gets-your-number kind of job, a shallow, not a serious job, a stall.

Not that my job is easy. I'm a photographic fashion styl-ist. I round up the clothes and so on for the models and actors in print ads and editorial features and television commercials. Once in a while I do a soap. I'm supposed to know what people wear when and why. I'm supposed to pull it together, give it a *look*. Improvise a pair of sandals out of a piece of rope. Know what's chic, what's stylish, what's "in" or about to be. In practice, I fasten belly bands around male models in shirt ads to make sure their shirts stay tucked in. I tape down actresses's nipples. I iron quite a lot in the way of business, pick lint, flatten collars or turn them up, tie bows.

It's the kind of job that, when you first start out, stomp-ing around Saks dragging twelve-hundred-dollar tea gowns behind you, halfway plays at being a job at all. And early on you don't so much mind, blow-drying sweat stains in actors' armpits. Not that I mind that specifically. Good for me, keeps me keen, keeps me in touch with the basics. It's just that what I really want, what I want in the marrow of my bones, I want to write some poems.

After the wine and cookies booze-up, Eileen and I went to bed. I let her sleep in my very bed, in the space vacated by Rambeau, and there she lay, abusing him. My little family: Eileen and the goddam dog. There was a lot of fallout from this dog. Not just hair, and fleas, and what Eileen assured me were flea eggs, but affliction. There was an interval of misery surrounding that dog; a cloud of suffering, a fog of woe. And I admired it, the dog. You accidentally put your hand on it, it bit you, no questions asked.

Eileen talked and talked to me; I love her voice, a light, condoling voice, it's just like mine. We have only one voice between us, one spread thin. She was thinking of awful things to do to Rambeau and we were laughing. She was laughing to keep my spirits up and I was laughing so as not to let her down.

"You could have him arrested," Eileen said. "Charge him with grand theft auto. Charge him with dog neglect." She tickled me to try to keep me laughing. I was getting tired of hearing Rambeau picked on. It impugned my taste, for one thing.

"You can trace him through the papers that came with his car," Eileen said.

"No papers came with Rambeau's car."

"Lots of papers came with Gordon's car." She said this in a married way and it bruised my tender feelings.

"Including a death certificate," I said. Gordon's car is a mean red Porsche and neither one of them can really drive it.

"Oh, you know how *men* are," she said. She said that to me, my sister.

The dog and I commenced to cry and Eileen lost her patience. She turned around in bed and pinned me. "Destroy that dog," she said. "Get rid of it. Take it to the vet. Get over this."

Well, even though I can't bear the dog, I don't want it listening to this stuff. The dog is the relic of a romance. The dog is half deposit and half hostage. What's more, it looks like my father and would make a vicious ghost.

"I don't *want* to get over this."

"Kill the dog," says Eileen. "Finish Fido. He's got himself

a woman who wouldn't have his mutt. Kill the dog, I'd do it, bye-bye bowwow."

In the morning, the dog put an eggshell in my slipper, well before I thought to put my foot in it. I don't know if the dog meant this kindly, but I chose to take it that way. I had been interviewing, auditioning, so to speak, a Rambeau replacement, and one glossy little television producer had asked me away for the weekend. But I don't know, I didn't want to do it. I didn't, this is very strange, I didn't want to leave the dog.

Eileen returned to her husband and the grim pursuit of fecundity, and the dog and I settled down to feeling lousy. We hung around the house, letting gravity attack us. Rambeau's plants went droopy, his neglected avocado pits shriveled or festered according to their karmas; a thin and varied compost filmed and furred and felted itself on my tables, my chairs, my rugs.

The miasma that lingers under sinks in even the best-run establishments spread through the house. The house, I felt, was missing Rambeau. It wanted its windowpanes rinsed in ammonia water, its carpets sponged with vinegar; its refrigerator yearned for an open box of baking soda, its cupboards for tiny tins of saffron and glass tubes sheltering vanilla beans.

The dog and I were unequal to all these demands. We tried going out for walks, but the dog wasn't much of a walker. It is no easy thing to carry a dog that bites. And then too, the dog and I didn't stray far from the phone—in case it should cry out and require our assistance.

The only people who telephoned were Eileen, losing interest, and persons wishing to employ me. But I no longer cared what America wore to the laundromat. *Women's Wear* piled up, along with my gas bills, my light bills, a valentine from the revenuers and other printed matter I couldn't get my head around.

I somehow didn't fancy a nice little outing to the A&P.

I'd have had to tie the dog to some lamppost. I couldn't telephone for foodstuffs because I knew I might be hogging a wire at the very moment Rambeau called. I know about that kind of thing—chance, destiny—you can't let them get a handhold.

There was nothing much in the house to eat but dog food and garbanzo beans. The dog didn't care for the one or the other. I felt like calling my mother up and telling her I wasn't hungry. That always got her attention. That and sucker-punch love affairs like the one I'd had with Rambeau.

My mother, Our Lady of the Perpetual Cardigan, is forty years out of the slums of Belfast, pink and white and tough as a boot. She's said to be charming, and indeed she's been charming, I've seen her be charming, I've seen it myself. But I've seldom seen it really close up. We call my mother Mick, or The Mick. We call her that to defuse and defang her, but it's no use whatsoever.

"Hello, Micky," I said to my mother. "It's me, it's not Eileen." This is a standard opening, because I do sound so much like Eileen, and, in my mother's view, if she had to have two daughters, better they should both have been Eileen.

"Is he still living with you?" my mother said, a not unfamiliar salutation. (What she really said, or squalled, was more like "Izzystillivinwidyez?" because she knows this poor old boggy widder woman dialect goes to my very heart.)

"Who?" I said. My sister and I pretend to be virgins. We pretended to be virgins before we knew what virgins were, we elaborated our pretenses once we had that information, and so long as our ma is breathing in and out we will be virgins still. My mother declines to leave Queens for a visit to my house in Westchester and Eileen never gets pregnant, so the poor bitch has no proof either way.

"What's-this-his-name-is," my mother said, "is he still living with you?"

"No," I said. "He's gone."

"Oh, Sweet Divine," my mother said. "I'm passing no remark. I know every wheel and turn of you, I know you all roads and directions. To think that any daughter of mine." And so on, blahblahblah et cetera.

"Ma, I'm so unhappy," I said to my only mother.

"Oh, well, now," she said, softening, "there's nothing to roar and cry about, no nothing, you'll do rightly."

"I will?" I said, I was cozying up, my mouth was all fixed for some sweetness.

"Och aye," she said, "you little hooer, you wasn't new when he got you." And thwack! she'd hung up the phone. Well what did I expect, I ask you—the old cow's in cream and the pasture's in parsley and mind you stay out of the sun? That's never been her way, she's Big Queenie Thumbscrews.

My head was full of Rambeau—not really Rambeau, you understand, but something Rambeau represented—and my closets were full of his clutter. The thought of my simple goodness in having, albeit whining, cleared space for that man made my throat tight with tears.

I couldn't stand the sight of his stuff and I couldn't stand to dump it. He'd left behind the neckstrap of his saxophone. I wanted to hold it for ransom, I wanted to give it away to Goodwill, I wanted to make a noose of it and hang myself and the goddam dog but it was useless for all these purposes. I was very, permanently hurt that he never played his saxophone for me. Not that I can quite imagine how or where I'd look while Rambeau played his saxophone for me, but I'd wanted him to do it and he wouldn't.

"You never hear the music," Rambeau said, "all you ever hear are the six beats up front. Uhone and uhtwo and

uhthree and uhfour and uhone and uhtwo." And he'd give
a sort of downbeat and he'd grab me.

"Come on," I'd say, "Rambeau, play for me."

"I'll play alto clit," he'd say, or "I'll blow tenor vulva," or
"I'm a mean, mean man on the vagina—you got to catch
these chord changes." Well, I thought he was funny and
I thought he was cute but that's no way to talk to my
mother's daughter.

I tried to get the dog to take an interest in the neckstrap.
Love it, hate it, play with it, chew it up, do something.
"Uhone and uhtwo and uhthree and uhfour," I said cheer-
ily to the dog, shaking the strap at it. "And uhone and
uhtwo." The dog just sighed and sulked at me, and I sighed
and sulked at the dog.

I had to go to my mother's for dinner, and I had to bring
along the dog. The bloody creature wept and ranted if I
left it all alone. Or, to be accurate, I assumed that it did.
We hadn't spent much time apart since we fell into each
other's custody.

I wasn't keen on introducing Rambeau's dog to my
mother, or my mother to Rambeau's dog, but I hoped it
might confuse her. "Confuse the enemy!" was one of her
cries; she was full of cries and exhortations.

I couldn't seem to rake together anything to wear. I
wanted sackcloth. I wanted ashes. I couldn't lay my hands
on those, though some of my items come close. And I
wasn't looking good. Even for me.

My ma hates my nose. It's a little blunt, and once she
smacked me for it. She considers my ears and neck two of
her major strikeouts and it was years before a tiny ground-
swell of opinion convinced me that my ears and neck are,
in point of fact, quite nice. She thinks of my eyes as one of
her better efforts, though not quite up to the standard she
set when she knocked off Eileen's complexion. There is no
space between my two front teeth. My mother and her

sister, dead, and Eileen all have such a space. My mother managed to convey to me her honest suspicion that a woman of our blood without that split can't be pretty, can't be good, can't be—legitimate. As a child, I practiced keeping my upper lip well down over my failure. This makes me look, I fear, as though my unsatisfactory nose were running. My mother doesn't buckle, though—my old ma will go down fighting. When I am in her company, her thumb, without announcement, intrudes into my mouth. Her tough old thumbnail pries between my two tight-fitted teeth. And since there is no space there, it tries, quite painfully, to manufacture one.

The only things I could bear to wear were things that Rambeau had recently ironed. And so I couldn't bear to wear them. I put on an old holey tee shirt of his and over it I tied his pale blue evening shirt—he bought it in a thrift shop, seventy cents. It was tucked and floppy, with a long dudey collar. He used to wear it on club dates and I used to sleep in it, we liked it. I put it on and took it off again. I held it in my teeth and tried to tear it. I threw it on the floor and stamped on it. I yelled at the shirt. I think I would have burned it on the bedroom floor. Burned the house down. But—if Rambeau came back—of course he wouldn't—if Rambeau should happen to come back, he'd need a roof over him. I had a fireplace, but burning his shirt in a fireplace would only make him laugh.

I put on a white sort of thing. I am a maiden outraged. I put on a cheesy red sort of thing. I am plenty woman, baby. I put on a black mournful thing. My neck was too short, my nose too blunt, my ears stuck out, there is no split between my teeth and I haven't my sister's complexion. I took a long look at the dog. The dog could've used a wash and brushup but the dog wasn't getting it from me. I put on a top and a bottom that recalled my knee-blistered years with the Little Sisters of the Jilted. I snapped a lead on the dog, disengaged its teeth from my wrist and went to spend the evening with my mother.

"And where is Doctor Ass-in-Pockets?" Our mother asked Eileen. "Will he grace us with his presence or is he home having your courses?"

"No," Eileen said. "Yes." Our mother doesn't miss a lot. When Eileen bleeds, her husband sulks. He's not fit to speak to during Eileen's periods.

"You look like the Wreck of the Hesperus," Mick then said to Eileen. "You in that drabble-tailed skirt, and it dragging after you in the muck and the mire."

"Too long?" Eileen asked me.

"A half an inch," I said. "Three-quarters."

"Just you step out of it now," Mick said, "and I'll see to it this minute."

"I don't want to step out of it," Eileen said.

"Step out of it," said Mick. And of course Eileen stepped out of it, and our mother whipped it away to take a razor to its hem. This left the upper half of Eileen dressed in silk shirt, suit jacket, real pearls, Cartier ear plugs, tank watch, plain wedding ring, engagement diamond the size of a kidney bean—flawed—and a certain superfluity of Youth Dew. The bottom half of her wore sheer-to-the-waist pantyhose—the kind you don't pick up in supermarkets—and high-heeled snaky sandals. Eileen always makes me think of the ladies in that poem of Louis MacNeice's whose "knickers are made of crepe de chine, their shoes are made of python Their halls are lined with tiger rugs and their walls with heads of bison."

When our mother took away Eileen's skirt, she took away her starch and burnish.

"Why," Eileen said, "why am I letting this happen?"

"And you, miss," our mother said to me. "Were you pulled through a hedge assways?"

"Yes, I was," I said. "I was pulled through a hedge assways."

"Don't turn your word on me."

"I'm not," I said. "I happen to have been pulled through a hedge assways, emotionally speaking, and I'm trying to see what self-pity will get me in this house."

"Not much," Eileen said.

"Your two eyes are sunken in your head," my mother said. I have only a foster-parent or curatorial relation to these eyes, they are understood to be of Mick's workmanship.

"Well," I said, "I'm sorry." I was sorry. It was wrong to abuse the eyes. They were the only sort of heirloom we'd ever have in our family. I felt it was good of Mick to let me have the use of them.

"Peel off them hidjus rags," she said. "I'll rinse them out for you."

"They don't require to be rinsed out, thank you."

"When you get arrested in Belfast," Eileen said, "they take away your shoes. That way you can run, but you can't run far."

"Peel them off," my mother said. "They're glazed with dirt, they'd stand alone, the filth of them."

"Oh, knock it off," I said. "Oh, button up. My clothes are perfectly clean and well you know it." In fact, they were, but underneath them I was naked. My unwashed underwear was all around my house, festoons of grubbiness and wreaths of squalor.

"Off," our mother said. "Now off, I say."

"Off, off," Eileen said, stamping and clapping, "take it off, for godsake, or we'll have no peace."

I was in a rage at my mother. I felt she had a chair and a whip and a pistol. I pulled my clean clothes off me, and as soon as Mick saw me naked in her living room, she began to keen. Some of it was the ritual yowl and yammer, but some of it was real. Our mother is old, she was old when we were born, she started living her hard life very early. She is cursed by her sense of the possible. She has no sense of the probable at all.

"Our mother is thinking you've gone to the bad," Eileen said.

"Will you talk to her," I said, "will you just reason with her."

"Our mother is thinking that only sluts and slatterns venture out into the world without their bloomers and their shifts," said fastidious Eileen.

"Oh, shut up, you," I said. "I'll tell her a thing or two about some of your fetish underwear; I'll tell her about your red satin teddy, the one with the garters and the matching gloves."

"Oh, shut up, you," she said. "I love your purple clodhoppers, what are they, something ethnic?"

"It goes beyond me," our mother said to Eileen, "it's well beyond my ken, how you can sit there wrapped in a blanket while your sister shivers in her pelt."

Eileen had a corner of an afghan figleafed in her lap. "Oh, why do I come here?" Eileen said. "I could be home shampooing a rug." She balled up the afghan and threw it at my head.

"You," my mother said to me, "have a belly on you like a poisoned pup."

"I have no such thing." I wrapped the afghan around me. Of course I looked a fool.

"You'd think she was in the family way," she said to my sister in ghastly play. "Now tell me, what do you think?"

"If she gets pregnant before I do, I'll open every vein in my body."

"How can you be so petty?" I said.

"It's easy," Eileen said, "it doesn't inconvenience me at all."

Peril sparkled in my mother's eyes. She could see disaster and I could see her seeing it; I was pregnant, I'd been ditched. Next she would be worrying would the kid turn out an idiot. I was neck-and-neck with her, worrying too. All this despite what I said before—you could snap her on the rack before she'd admit that either of her daughters, even the married one, had ever been what she calls "interfered with."

"It beats the life out of me what anyone wants with a kid," Mick said. "I certainly don't want one."

"If I was eighty, I wouldn't want one either," Eileen said.

"Now don't be so ill-natured," our mother said to us nicely. We were getting to the stage she liked, it was back near the place where we started. She knocked the gloss off us, she disarranged us. When we seemed young and wobbly again, I guess we had more future. It was only mother love. We tried hard not to mind it.

"Kitty," my mother called from the kitchen, where she was basting a hen, "tell us about your lover man, I hear he done a flit."

"You should have brought Gordon," I said to Eileen.

"You should have brought the goddam dog."

"I'm getting out of here," I said. "Tell her I was running toward the river."

When I got to Rambeau's car, there was a man sitting in it. I knew the man couldn't be Rambeau, but all the same the wet went out of me. My mouth was like cotton cloth and I had no juices anywhere. Of course the man was not Rambeau, it was small old frowsy, dusky Mr. Conrad, held prisoner by Rambeau's dog.

Mr. Conrad and I are poetry workshop groupies. So far as I know we have only that one thing in common, though Mr. Conrad does seem lately to be pressing for more.

Well, to be truthful, Mr. Conrad and I have two things in common. We are poetry workshop groupies and we are the two worst poets in any given group of twelve. Mr. Conrad tends to apostrophize his womb and I take a whisk broom and dustpan approach to my dreams.

We are obsessive and we are bad. Neither of us has ever thrown a poem away. We move commas around, change line breaks, sometimes cross out adjectives and sometimes reinstate them. Then we type up clean copies and have them Xeroxed. Then we read aloud these endlessly refurbished bits of verse. At poetry workshops—the Ninety-second Street Y, the National Arts Club, the New School, many places. While we do this, the workshop—nine or ten halfway decent poets and one official one—stares at its hands. After we do this there is a long silence. Once, someone said that Mr. Conrad's "syntax was nice" or I think it was "rather" or "quite" nice—that meant, I believe, that he had temporarily gotten a grasp on the agreement of tenses.

Mr. Conrad is said, by himself, to know any number of languages, but English, strictly speaking, isn't one of them. However, he can rip off a length of vowels and consonants and plunks and snorts and interesting mouth noises and then say: "Pushkin." Or "Dante." And all of us in the workshop, even the official poet, feel elevated and a little shy.

Eileen thinks Mr. Conrad is really pretty dodgy. She thinks he's a decadent old coot who gets a kick out of doing shtick. I find him, perhaps try to find him, childlike or elfish with just occasional grotty spots of ancient European whatsis peeping through.

Mr. Conrad is my only fan. Real poets all over town have stormed at me. Who can blame them. "Dreams are not poems," they rage. "And poems are not dreams. *Poems* are works of *art*." "Oh, I quite agree," I say, arranging my peculiar clothes around me. "Oh, I quite see that." But I give them a fierce look, which I hope unsettles them. Fierce looks come easy to me; I take after Mick in that way.

I do see their point. If there's one thing in the world I cannot stand, it's listening to people's dreams. They make me want to caw and claw my armpits; I cannot listen to them, I don't even try. But as Mr. Conrad would say, "That is notwithstanding."

I got behind the wheel of Rambeau's car. Rambeau's car was a 1967 Mercedes limo, modified by various doting owners. It was the five-passenger model, he always used to say, not the seven. I don't know why he thought that was funny. He told me he had won the car in a crap game, and possibly he had. He used to call it his light classical wheels, and the sunshine hearse, and another mouth—he wasn't the sort of person to give an automobile an actual nickname. But the car amused him and he indulged it. He used to buy it treats: Greek tassels for the mirror, and an ancient lap robe of some flat fur he said was dogskin. In the refrigerator armrest he installed the occasional rose, and sometimes dog food, sometimes caviar, sometimes apples.

The car was always clean, and shabby genteel. But it was a cranky car, no matter what you did for it. I couldn't drive it very well and neither could I park it except three feet from the curb with its hind end hanging out. And the car was subject to seizures. Its seats would refuse to adjust, its windows would fling themselves open or closed, you couldn't get into its trunk. "Hydraulics," Rambeau said, but Rambeau didn't know—I've seen Rambeau lost in wonder at the operation of a toaster.

Mr. Conrad shared the shotgun seat with the dog. He was most unhappy about this arrangement. They were eating something, which was pleasant for the dog, since nothing much had entered or left it for some time. They regarded me, my Ishmaels, my hairy exiles, neither with nor without approval. Under my coat, I may remind you, I was wearing an afghan sarong. No odder than most of my wardrobe. I get expensive, eccentric clothes cheap and dress in the wrack of fashion. Experimental colors and beadwork, that's me. Pantaloons and queer boleros, things that jingle and clack; or floating panels, drifty scarves, frocks the Queen Mother rejected. My old ma says I look like a tinker and I expect she's right, but really it's partly a uniform, partly a disguise. Once someone described my clothes as witty, but what they are, they're another one—a stall. Mr. Conrad likes them.

"No," Mr. Conrad said, not to me, "Hungarian is not

nice. Rumanian is nice. Polish is also not nice. Slavic languages, not nice. Russian is not nice. German is hammer-hammer but not so bad though not nice. French is nice. English is nice. Portuguese I like very much."

"I want you to stop following me around like this," I said severely to Mr. Conrad, who had been turning up a lot in the shrubbery. But I didn't really know if I wanted him to stop following me around. I think I wanted him to stop following me around provided he didn't start following around someone else.

The three of us gloomed through the windshield. The car parked in front of us had a doggie in it too—plush—and a baby's seat. Also two squash rackets, a net bag of onions and a big box of Tide. All of these objects, of course, appeared to me to be lit from within. I know it's just because I'm mean and crazy that I seem to have spent all my life sitting in the wrong car.

"Rambeau," I said, only to be saying it, only to be hurting, "Rambeau and I have parted."

Mr. Conrad clutched his left shoulder pad and gave a dying sob. He and Rambeau had gotten a bit matey. I thought it was unwholesome, but Rambeau liked him. They used to spend whole evenings together, drinking toasts, Rambeau said. Once, Rambeau said, they drank all evening to the blue devils that danced in my eyes. Well, I knew he was having me on, but it had the Mr. Conrad touch. It made me want to scurry to confession, but I liked it.

"A lobster dinner," Mr. Conrad said. Mr. Conrad had high regard for the healing or annealing properties of a lobster dinner. Largely, I was beginning to suspect, because he never ate one.

"Rambeau stole my car," I said. "And left me this monstrosity. He also left me this dog."

"I am considering making an offer of money to you," Mr. Conrad said. "For this automobile. Also, I like also to buy this dog." Mr. Conrad was trying to flatter or intimidate the dog.

"No dice," I said.

"Some derangement of the senses," Mr. Conrad said. "A lobster dinner. I am calling this dog Bela. So smart, Bela. A gorgeous animal. I'm not kidding. And so nice."

Well, I couldn't see it myself, but who knows. "Mr. Conrad," I said, "I want you to come home and meet my mother."

Mr. Conrad wuffed and chuffed but of course he was delighted. "I must ask you not to do that," Mr. Conrad said, ducking his head and butting the air. "You have no way of knowing what you do to me when you do that." Mr. Conrad always said to me something along these lines. Rambeau loved it. "I must ask you," Rambeau used to say, "not to do that. You have no way of knowing what you do to me when you do that." "That" might be blinking or scratching. Or swallowing or yawning or blowing my nose.

"No, *no*," Rambeau used to moan and wince, clutching invisible shoulder pads, "what you *do* to me, what you *do* to me when you *do* that."

"The coast is clear, Mr. Conrad," I said. "If you'd like to make your move."

Mr. Conrad's habitual expression of deep, resolutely controlled disapproval did not lighten.

"Why he fucked off?" Mr. Conrad asked

"Well," I said. "It was a very difficult relationship, I think you knew that." I was pleased at the way I brought that off —"difficult relationship" in a measured sort of voice, suggesting that I was on top of it.

"Oh, Kitty," Mr. Conrad wailed, "why you can't be nice, I'm not kidding."

"I am nice," I said. "I am nice enough for everyday practical purposes and I never represented myself as one bit nicer than that."

"Rambeau is hell of nice guy," Mr. Conrad said.

"Well he was and he wasn't, Mr. Conrad," I said, trying to suggest dark mysteries.

"*Hell* of nice guy," Mr. Conrad said.

"Yes and no, Mr. Conrad. Yes. Actually, he was."

"Hell." Mr. Conrad accidentally put his arm around the dog, which instead of going for his throat appeared to recline on his knee. I will say I felt conspired against.

"I'm sorry you're so broken up about it, Mr. Conrad. I suppose, really, you were more his friend than mine."

Mr. Conrad looked into the dog's nose holes. "Why," he asked them, "she couldn't be nice?"

"I am operating at the peak of my niceness potential," I said, "I told you that."

"I could something tell *you*," Mr. Conrad said. "Is too bad you don't speak Hungarian."

"It is," I said. "I've often felt that."

"You have no intermission, Kitty," Mr. Conrad said. "I could tell you in Rumanian.

"You just told me in English."

"Running up and down, running up and down. Like cat in mat," he said.

"Rat in cage," I said.

"Like dog for sheeps in Australia. Not running just at head of sheeps, not running just at heels of sheeps, running all the time on top of backs of sheeps."

Well of course the life I'd had with Rambeau was all in candy-box colors now. I couldn't have told you one single thing that wasn't perfect—and I know it wasn't perfect. Despite what Mr. Conrad said, I'd worked really hard at not crowding Rambeau—I mean, I could have eaten him with cream. But I kept my distance. I gave him so much room toward the end that we hardly ever saw each other in daylight.

"You such nice little girl," Mr. Conrad said, relenting, looking up at me, for even sitting down I'm two heads taller than he is, "so gorgeous, I'm not kidding." Mr. Conrad put his curvy thumb to his curvy nose and fanned his fingers. "Feh!" he said. *"That* for Rambeau!"

I was really touched. My two eyes filled right up with tears. I put my hand out to Mr. Conrad and of course I hit the dog. And naturally, it bit me.

Rambeau

◆

"You play sax, right? I saw you, so I know. Not here, though, right?" This very young, fat, glowering pretty girl had been trying to pick him up for twenty minutes.

"Right," Rambeau said. He wanted rid of the girl, but he was a silent man by nature, and his sort of short answers never seemed abrupt.

"The first porno movie I ever saw, there was this saxophone player in it—with a black mustache and wearing black socks," she said, "that's all he had on him, though, just black socks. Right?"

"Right," Rambeau said. The other players at the blackjack table were restless. Her chat annoyed them. The dealer was waxen with righteous displeasure. Rambeau didn't care about that. Rambeau was spiritless; he felt bruised and elderly and untutored in the wisdom of the world. He couldn't think of a way to get shut of the scowling, foxy-faced young fat girl that wouldn't do damage to her feelings. Hurting people's feelings, Kitty's excepted, was beyond him for the time being.

The girl made the little crook with her finger—hit me—and looked at the cards she'd been dealt. "Atlantic City sucks," she said. "Am I right?"

He looked at his cards. They made no sense to him. For the first time in his life, he'd held cards in his hands and been bored. For some days, he'd been trying to suggest that he was deaf, in the hope that people would stop talking to him.

"I grew up in casinos and on campuses," the angry little girl said. "They suck unless you're coked out of your brains. Vegas sucks. Yale sucks. You know Vegas?"

"Shhh," Rambeau said. "You better hush now."

"I know where you're coming from," the girl whispered, "I know what you're saying. You're a card counter, right?"

"Right," Rambeau said, although he was no such thing. He tried a showy focus on the cards, making rabbit nibbles with his mouth, tapping his foot, pretending to be a card counter. He felt trapped. Oh where were the sweet, the simple girls—the girls whose wants were few, the girls whose jaws were wired.

The casino in the afternoon seemed trashy to him, and he was a man who loved casinos. There was no time in them, no clocks, no natural light; the air was queer, filtered, still, spiked with oxygen to keep the gamblers awake and greedy. Ordinarily, he savored the monitored cool gloom, the bright wheels and green tables, the disingenuous slot machines—apples, plums, stars, bars. Now the place looked sad. The girl kept talking. He was betting against the conversation instead of against the cards.

He lost the last of his chips and stood up. The fat girl stood up too, she rubbed against him.

"Yesterday I made it with the drummer," she said furiously. "Today I'm gonna make it with you."

"Oh sweet Jesus," Rambeau said. He walked away, moving fast, fast enough so that people looked at him; the girl clung close. He reminded himself of a cat he'd seen, dodging under hedges, trying to scrape off a pursuing robin. The cat had not been successful and neither was he. He ducked into the men's room—the light was unkind. He saw the thin red hair that filmed his skull, the hollow eyes; he looked wan and watchful, like a croupier. He slammed his palm against a sink and strode out again. He couldn't see himself hiding in a toilet, hiding from a little, crazy fat girl.

The fat girl, stalking, jumped him, linked his arm. "I'll do anything you want," she said. "I mean, you know, fantasies, *weird* things, freaky."

"All right," Rambeau said. He blamed Kitty for this, for all of it. "You can watch me take three aspirin and eat a fried-egg sandwich."

"That's the most incredibly sensuous thing I've ever seen, what you just did," the girl said.

Her name was Dorinda; she said to call her Drindy. She sat on the edge of her bench in the bar and dazzled at him, watching him chew and swallow. There was nothing like it for taking away the appetite. His lips, his teeth, his tongue, his gullet were self-conscious.

Rambeau thought about the drummer, a pale and worried little man. He wore a short, clubby pigtail, like a bullfighter, and had a brood of children. A widower, he mother-henned them. He drove unconscionable distances to superintend the banding of their teeth. He telephoned them constantly, at every break and sometimes, frenzied, in the middle of a set.

There was grease at the corner of Rambeau's mouth. He dabbed at it. The fat girl, Dorinda, fell backward in an eye-rolling swoon. He wondered, secretly, if there *was* something incredibly sensuous in the way he ate a fried-egg sandwich. Trust Kitty not to tell him, if there was.

"The drummer," he said.

"You get off on that?" Dorinda said.

Her bare toes were climbing his calf. She was so short and her breasts were so big that she lifted them and laid them on the table. Although it was March, she was wearing a thin, fine cotton blouse, wonderfully embroidered. It had been starched and beautifully ironed. The blouse was the only thing about her that specifically interested him. Although he found all women touching and exotic. And in some measure, menacing.

"Like to hear about Irving?"

"*No*," he said. He wanted to hear about Irving.

"Bondage," she said. She did her eye roll and her swoon.

"Bondage," Rambeau said wisely. He thought of binding Kitty. Swaddling her in ropes. Rolling her in a rug, like Cleopatra. Cuffing her wrists and shackling her ankles. Why had Kitty turned him out? Why had she abandoned him to this world at once so familiar and so strange where everything dislodged itself and found its mooring somewhere else? He thought of a redheaded cocktail waitress, a tormenting girl called Cherokee. There was no comfort in thinking of that girl either.

"I should advise you," Dorinda said. "Since I was sixteen, I been more or less dysfunctional."

"Dysfunctional," he said. He ordered himself another double bourbon and the girl another root beer. He had no head for alcohol and got drunker, faster, cheaper than any man he'd known.

"Don't drink too much," Dorinda said. She looked into his eyes and took away his glass.

He took it back again. "I'm slightly dysfunctional," he said. "But I'm not working till tonight."

She looked into his eyes and took away his glass. "Never mind tonight," she said. "We gotta do it."

He attempted to take the glass back; she fought him for it. "Be sensible," he said. He felt himself accompanied by Kitty's spirit. "I'm not going to do it. I don't want to do it. In fact I couldn't do it if I tried."

He was right. He tried and he couldn't do it. He couldn't do a thing. Dorinda was not a bit nice about it; Kitty would have been. "Let me alone," he was moaning, "someone will hear us, you're hurting me, don't *do* that." This girl he had hoped was a fraud and a frost, had big moony buttocks and big moony breasts and hundreds of tongues, fingers, toes. *"Please,"* Rambeau found himself whimpering, "I've been drinking, it's not fair."

He longed for Kitty's familiar flesh; for Kitty who was tender and admiring, or ingenious and sly, or innocent and hungry but always, he thought, placidly inexpert. At the thought of Kitty, his blood at last was summoned to his groin and he turned to hide himself, to deprive this awful, greedy fat girl of his bounty.

Dorinda was by now on her knees on the floor. She had dusted the room with his underpants. She had dusted the tops of the window frames, dusted the tops of the doors. She had polished the mirrors with his shirt. She had rolled back the old flowered rug and was scrubbing the boards of the floor. The brush, the bucket and sponges were Rambeau's, the plastic jug of green Top Job. These were the symbols of a clean new life.

"Not a bad room," Dorinda said. "I don't mind it." She had put the blouse on, nothing else. She was shaped like a marshmallow, her bare skin was pearly. Her hair was a black, curly thicket, reminding him of Kitty's, although Kitty's hair is white, and has been since she was a little girl. I only want Kitty, he said to himself. The knowledge appalled him. It's Kitty I want, just Kitty.

"Come over here, Dorinda," his voice came issuing out of his throat, entirely unbidden.

"Listen, don't sweat it," Dorinda said. "I think I just as soon do this, to be honest with you."

"I like to wash my own floors," Rambeau said. "Dorinda," he said pitifully, "my head hurts."

"Tough it out," Dorinda said. "I'm busy, do you mind?"

"Look over here," Rambeau said coyly. "I think I may have something for you. A poor thing, but mine own."

"Sex is boresome," Dorinda said. "I don't hardly even like men. I D'd in Marriage Adjustment. I'm doing something here. I'm trying to *wash* this *floor*."

Rambeau put on his new Azuma kimono. There was a dragon on the back that he somehow hadn't noticed, buying it. There was a dragon on the front, too. He didn't feel comfortable about displaying all these dragons to Dorinda. He was a little sore at her.

The room he'd rented was a dingy shrine to girlhood. The wallpaper burgeoned with soapy-looking blossoms. The white-painted Frenchified furniture was ugly, borax, but had charmed some child. The mirrors were spotted with stickers—a rainbow, a unicorn. The closet door was pasted up with rock stars and Snoopy. When first he'd moved into the room, its atmosphere of dismal cheer and the general teariness of the landlady had made him think that the girl who'd slept in it was dead. But dead she was not; she'd won a scholarship to Princeton.

"Dorinda," he said gently, "I'm going to take a shower now."

"Oh all *right*," Dorinda said, grumpy. She threw down her scrub brush and scrambled to her feet. He understood her intention.

"No, no," he said. "I'm taking a shower *alone*."

She rolled her eyes and fell into her swoon. It was her all-purpose gesture, more flexible, he thought, than many.

"Do you have any money, Dorinda?"

"Plenty," she said. "Need some?"

"You have a place to stay? You can't stay here."

"Was staying at the Boardwalk with my folks."

She looked young to him and naked. And despite this unpleasant news about her family connections, orphaned.

"My parents, they don't dick around with me," Dorinda said. "Not since my sister punched her own ticket. They want to go to some ratfuck convention, it suits my private purposes, I go. See a little action, you know what I mean?"

"I think so," Rambeau said. Tomorrow she'd be saying to the bass player, "You want to hear about Rambeau? Do you get off on that?"

"My old man's a geneticist," Dorinda said. "Genetics

sucks, right? My mother's a psychographologist. She can diagnose your hangups from your loops. My mother likes the slots, my father likes the tables."

"Put your clothes on," Rambeau said. "Go home now."

"No," she said. "Don't walk on my clean floor."

"Dorinda," Rambeau said, "it's been very interesting having you." Or not having you, he thought. Thank God. "But it's time to go now."

"No."

Implacable black-eyed stubborn fate, surrogate for all the wronged and wronging women of his days, she stood confronting him. She held the scrub brush with which she'd cleaned his dirty floor.

"I like it here," she said. "I'm staying."

"It doesn't work that way," he said. He sat on the bed in his dragon-cloth robe.

"Sure it does."

He felt like a fugitive tracked to his hideout, an animal trapped in its lair. Her breasts were motherly and milky, her blouse was something Kitty would wear. She was young enough to be his daughter, not too young to be his wife; she was a punishment, she was a penance.

"I am a man with a load of troubles," Rambeau said.

"Oh for shit's sake," said the girl.

Rambeau felt his destiny accumulating around him. He was very tired. When he rented this room, he had thought to spend some time in it with the girl called Cherokee. He couldn't do that if Dorinda was in residence.

"Oh, well," he said. "What the hell."

"Why are you staring at *me*?" she said. "I'm just a regular-looking pregnant woman."

"No, no," he said. "No, no. That's impossible." Terrible, missionary pulses beat in him; he had felt them with Kitty, felt them with Cherokee, hoped not to feel them ever again. "No," he said. "I can't do it. Go home, Dorinda."

She crossed to him and laid his boneless flat hand on her

potbelly. It was potty, but all of her was potty. Maybe she was pregnant, maybe she was not. "Well, you can't feel much yet," she said. "But after a while they kick."

"Why is this woman happening to me?" Rambeau said aloud. He was sure she was pregnant. She would have curious eating habits; he would get fond of her and she would break his heart. She would be strenuous in bed and surly out of it. He would get fond of her child and *that* would break his heart. She would not make interesting remarks nor love him—those things Kitty had done. It was dreadful, but peaceful, in its way, envisioning life with a woman who could be counted on not to love him, not to say anything he had to pay heed to. This is your fault, Kitty, he said in his mind, it's your fault this woman is happening to me. He noticed that Dorinda was caressing his head. His neck went limp beneath her hands, his head fell forward on her platter of breasts.

"Know your piano player?" Dorinda said. "He likes to dress up in costumes."

Kitty

◆

There's just no way to figure out my ma. I've brought
people to her door—perfectly okay, well-cast and rehearsed people—and she's given me a look that grabbed
me by the ankles and dashed my brains out against the
wall. But that night she took to Mr. Conrad and the dog
right away. I may say that she thought it was his dog, which
was what I had in mind. She seemed to think they were a
set, and indeed they did look similarly orphaned and forlorn. "Ah, the poor, wee articles," she crooned at them,
and began to pet and cosset them and generally stroke
them up. Before long, she is dimpling and twinkling and
they are dimpling and twinkling back. She gives the dog all
the chicken's white meat and Mr. Conrad both the drumsticks, which puts Eileen and me out of temper. We are,
after all, the daughters of the house, and besides that,
spoiled.

I hadn't seen my ma so perky earlier. She beamed and
reared back and recited. She loves to quote, my ma, she
does it all the time, you can tell she's quoting by the little
hooks in her enunciation and also because what she says is
so peculiar. This is what she said: "Little Jerry Hall / he is
so small / a rat could eat him / hat and all."

I truly think that might have stunned a lesser man, but Mr. Conrad was ready for her. "You catch me unshaven," he merrily rejoined, right out of the middle of his little hairy face. "Pushkin." If he said that's Pushkin, it's Pushkin so far as I know.

This exchange, a numbing one to me, was worth a hearty laugh to them. Eileen and I were nervous. Me, because Mick's little love bouts tend to leave her steaming; Eileen, because Mr. Conrad once enwrapped her in a long, unintelligible memoir of Transylvania and ever since he's made her think of sprigs of woodruff, moonlit crossroads and splinters of the true cross. "You have conceived?" he says to her, most courteously. "Not really," she says, and she's peeved.

Soon, of course, the conversation turns to me, despite precautions to the contrary.

"My daughter Kitty's fancy man has left her," my mother confided to my friend.

Mr. Conrad looked attentive but it was going past him. Which suited me.

"A horn tooter," says my old ma. "A card sharp. A red-headed man who first-footed me on New Year's Day and I had no luck for the whole year after. Rambeau," she says. "He called himself."

Mr. Conrad does a token grab for his shoulder pad. "Hell of a nice guy," says Mr. Conrad. "I'm not kidding."

"Card sharp and horn tooter," Mick repeats with emphasis.

Mr. Conrad, wet finger to the wind, jumps ship. "Of course," he says, "we were not, such as to say, intimate."

"*They* were," Mick says. Real tears fill her big old glowing eyes. I can see myself through those eyes—violated, cast aside, a shoddy, surplus woman in body and in spirit. For all her rosaries, my mother worships Chaos, the oldest of the gods.

"What's all about it?" Mr. Conrad says.

"My mother thinks redheaded men are unlucky," Eileen says. "Especially first thing on New Year's Day."

"Our mother thinks men are unlucky," I say, "New Year's and every other day."

"My daughter Kitty has been handed round like snuff at a wake," says Mick. "She'd have you to believe she's a pure young girl, but not a bit of it."

"She *is* a pure young girl, though," Eileen, who is clearing the table, says. "She's just one of your more seasoned pure young girls."

I love Eileen, she is trying to save me, and she's looking less than splendid, which I know she hates. Though the top of her still looks grand enough, the bottom half is wearing a pair of shorts Mick made for her when she was a rather-less-opulent sixteen. Every garment Mick has ever made for us is interred somewhere in this house, but none of them quite fits us. We revere them, though, they are totems.

"Sit you down and hold your tongue," Mick says to Eileen. "Look at you in your little tiny pants. One of your asses is laughing at the other." My mother thinks this is funny. Actually, I think it's funny too. Eileen doesn't think it's funny; it's not a bit funny to our Eileen. She sits down hard, all splotched with flush. Eileen is hell with a cold sore or a stye. Once poor Gordon, right after they were married, said "Eye, I like that dress, it does wonders for your hips," and she picked up a dinner fork and pronged it through his thumb.

"I think you look adorable," I say to Eileen.

"Oh, shut up, Kitty," Eileen says. I perform a public service, the way some people pick on me—it relaxes them, like painting watercolors or doing needlepoint. All the same, I'm a little ticked. I'm sitting there, an afghan mummy bundle. I'm trying to be a sport about it, I'm trying to hold my end up. There's my sister, sulking and snarling because her buttocks have a beautiful swell and nobody's ready with a round of applause. There's Mr. Conrad, who's practically my ward, my child, in his ducky pullover and his shirt with the teddy bears holding onto the balloons. There's my mother in a cardigan she made out of wool left over from dozens of sweaters, all colors, all kinds, she knitted for Eileen and me. This cardigan is cheerful really, in a folk-artsy way, if the woman wearing it doesn't happen to be your mother.

"Why Kitty can't be nice?" Mr. Conrad says, thus introducing a diverting topic of general and vociferous interest.

There's quite a bit of discourse; I don't listen. I'm ticked, as I told you.

When after a while I come to again, they're conducting a testimonial for Rambeau over the devil's food cake.

My ma says that as God is her judge he has his good points as well as his bad ones. Once he tripped over her doorsill and he swept off his hat and saluted it. He taught her to play slapjack which she quite enjoys. And after all, our Kitty is a trial, and still and all, he is some mother's son.

Mr. Conrad says he's hell of nice guy.

Eileen says that Kitty perhaps can't do much better. She doesn't enlarge on this.

Mick says that Rambeau, for a man with two handfuls of hair on the head of him, and it red, for a man who was probably a roué and a rummy and a rounder and a tinhorn and a feather merchant, for a man who frequented taprooms and pool halls and gambling dens and gin mills and roadhouses and houses of ill fame, for a man of this kind, he had a light hand with pastry and made a decent sponge cake. She cannot tell a lie on him, she says.

Eileen says kindly that Gordon has told her that Rambeau provided him with a really quite challenging game of chess. (I forbear to tell her that Gordon knows even less about chess than he does about making babies.)

Mick says that Kitty put years on the poor soul, so she did.

Mr. Conrad points out that he is occasionally driven to speculate on just why Kitty can't be nice.

Mick says Kitty's tongue goes like a hand bell.

Eileen says Kitty is her own worst enemy.

Mick says Kitty was ever a wee rip and a wee tory and had better get wise to herself and catch herself on before she finds herself on her hunkers.

Eileen says that Kitty drove poor Rambeau out because she was afraid he'd leave her. She says that Kitty fears commitment. Kitty can only be described as self-destructive. Eileen's therapist will confirm these views if pressed.

Mr. Conrad declares for Kitty! Kitty, after all, *is* nice and if any of us were even moderately eloquent in the languages of various paprika principalities he would delineate Kitty's virtues and make this lunatic position more defensible.

My ma says you couldn't dislike our Kitty.

Eileen says you *could*, or *she* could. Though, naturally, she doesn't.

Mr. Conrad says Kitty is rare as a mountain flower, wild as a mountain sheep.

My tongue is black and swelling and saliva trickles slowly from the corner of my mouth. My mother is feeding the dog—which is purring, or near to it—devil's food cake. The goddam dog is sitting on her lap. My mother can do anything with animals. I've seen it over and over again. I've seen her capture goldfish in her two cupped hands; I've seen a hummingbird try to feed from the flower on her dress; I've seen a squirrel clasp her toe and love it like a walnut. The goddam dog eats its cake and smiles and sighs and thrusts its snoot into her armpit and subsides into a big happy dog lump. My mother is smoothing its ratty hide and its coat begins to shine beneath her palms.

"What made our Kitty ever think she could get that man to marry her?" my mother wants to know.

It was then that my blood turned to wax.

Kitty

◆

I have dinner with Gordon and Eileen, at their table:

"*Try these rolls, darling. Aren't these delightful rolls?*"

"These ARE GOOD ROLLS, DARLING. WHERE DID YOU PICK UP THESE ROLLS?"

"*I think these rolls are every bit as good as my rolls, don't you?*"

"THEY'RE EXCELLENT, DARLING. AND THE MEAT IS GOOD."

"*The meat is excellent. You don't think it's underdone?*"

"IT'S EXCELLENT."

"*I think, next time, a minute or two more. I thought I'd brought it to room temperature before I slipped it into the broiler, but perhaps I moved just a little too fast.*"

"I WOULDN'T WORRY, DARLING, IT'S EXCELLENT. ISN'T IT, KITTEN?"

"Excellent," I say.

"THIS IS A NICE LITTLE RED, KITTEN, I THINK IT WILL AMUSE YOU."

"*Oh, don't darling.*"

"THAT'S PRETENTIOUS? THAT'S OBJECTIONABLE? I'VE MADE MYSELF ODIOUS TO YOU?"

"*No, no, I just. No, I don't know.*"

"Try this red, Kitten. Dago red wrung out of a shitty rag."

"*Well, if you're going to pour her some wine, pour her some wine, that wouldn't fill a thimble.*"

"This *is* an amusing red, this red would make a cat laugh."

"*Oh, shut up, Kitty. Fill her glass for godsake.*"

"Tomorrow is a working day."

"Not for me, I'm going to spend it in a gutter, soused."

"*Just eat, Kitty. Eat the meat, don't fill up on rolls. You never get a decent meal, that's why you look so awful.*"

"Who says the Kitten looks awful?"

"*I say she looks awful. And if she's a kitten, I'm a crow.*"

"Yes."

"*Yes, what do you mean, yes. Did you mean that, yes?*"

"No, no, you should try these carrots, Kitten, Eye does them with cream and brown sugar. And a little butter."

"*And a little garlic, you like garlic.*"

"Garlic, I like," I say. "Carrots, I don't like."

"These are excellent. Allow me. These don't taste a bit like carrots, do they, Eye?"

"Our mother always got us to eat stuff by telling us it tasted like other stuff," I say.

"*Mostly white meat of chicken.*"

"I hate white meat, as you know, I hate white meat, don't I, Eye?"

"This wasn't real white meat, this was mystical white meat of the body of chicken. Wasn't it, Eileen?"

"James Beard detested white meat. He discarded white meat. Dark meat is far more flavorful. I never eat white meat, do I, Eye?"

"*I hope there's another bottle of this wine.*"

"Are these sprouts Julia's? Or Craig's? I'll bet Craig's."

"*Craig's.*"

"What makes them Craig's? How did Craig put his stamp on this perfectly ordinary brussels sprout?" I say.

"*The chestnuts. The chestnuts keep the sprouts from being ordinary. They raise the sprouts above the ordinary.*"

"They make them soar," I say. "I like chestnuts."

"*I know you like chestnuts, that's why I made chestnuts and sprouts, eat some sprouts.*"

"I don't like sprouts, I like chestnuts."

"*You can't just sit there eating all the chestnuts and leaving all the sprouts. It's childish and it's rude. And with your fingers.*"

"What do you care? I'm your sister, not your kid. You're not raising me. You don't have to take me out in company."

"*You never eat anything green, it's bad for you. You need vegetables, green and yellow leafy vegetables.*"

"Let's discuss the four major food groups," I say.

"*It's bad for you. Isn't it bad for her, Gordon?*"

"I DON'T KNOW, HOW DO I KNOW WHAT'S BAD FOR HER?"

"*You went to medical school, for Christ sake, don't you know anything useful?*"

"I'll eat them, I'll eat them."

"*Give some sprouts to Gordon.*"

"I HATE SPROUTS."

"*You hate sprouts. Since when do you hate brussels sprouts? You love brussels sprouts.*"

"OH, PARDON ME, MY MISTAKE. I THOUGHT I HATED THEM, I MUST HAVE BEEN MISTAKEN."

"*It's news to me, you hated them, that's a new one on me.*"

"Gordon is a man of mystery."

"*You stay out of this, Kitty.*"

"LET HER ALONE, CAN'T YOU, YOU NEVER STOP PICKING ON THE KID FOR A MINUTE."

"*The kid, the kid, she's ten months younger than I am, I never hear you call me a kid.*"

"THERE'S A LOT OF THINGS YOU'LL NEVER HEAR ME CALL YOU IF YOU'RE LUCKY."

"*Look at her, just look at her, look at how unwell she looks.*"

"IF SHE WANTS ME TO EXAMINE HER, SHE'LL HAVE TO TAKE HER CLOTHES OFF."

"*Don't do it Kitty, it's far more trouble than it's worth.*"

"OH, I DON'T KNOW, EYE."

"*I do.*"

"OH, YOU BIG DUMB IRISH BITCH, YOU LOOK LIKE SUCH A BREEDER, LOOK AT THE TITS ON YOU, LOOK AT THAT PELVIS."

"*I don't know what's the matter with you. What is the matter with you. What is it you want from me.*"

"I'LL TELL YOU, I'LL TELL YOU, I'D REALLY LIKE TO TELL YOU."

"You open up your mouth to her, I'll kill you," I say.

Then Gordon puts his hand across his face and starts to cry. Then she cries, then I cry. Then, after a while, we eat the dessert.

Dreams and Secrets

♦

Rambeau dreams. His dreams are rapt and vivid. Rambeau flies. He spreads his arms, he pushes off, he catapults aloft. He soars. His power and control excite him. Prone and supine, he rolls upon and rides the waves of lucent air.

Kitty dreams in simple, saturated color. She sits in a bath; the tub is stony, high-sided, white and scintillating. The water is a rich and plummy blue. This tub, she knows, is a dogs' small drinking trough, it exists outside a New York shop. She appears, nonetheless, to have plenty of room. The water is chill; there is dog spit in it; her situation is not comfortable. With a crusty lump of brilliant coral, she scrubs at a pair of unfamiliar feet. These feet are nasty, calloused, bleeding, they are an occasion of shame. When she has worn them down to something wonderful, she will slide between smooth sheets with her lover, sweet Rambeau. It is uphill work. Poor Kitty shivers. She is irritated. Even in her dream she knows this dream will make a dopey poem.

In his dream, Rambeau, flying, extends his hand and
closes it upon the wrist of Kitty, now beside him. His
thumb rests on her pulse point, her life ticks there beneath
his fingers. He is her magic, without him she will fall. She
wears his old blue pleated evening shirt. It flutters sweetly
about her warm bare thighs. Her white hair streams, it
whips across her mouth. She is frightened; she is smiling.

Mick dreams of babies, babies, snuggled in fleecy bunt-
ings, nappy blankets; powdery, milky, chuckling babies,
swaddled and swathed in pastel icing-sugar colors. She
dreams of the sweet weight of babies, their tender skulls,
the secret mirths and sorrows of their small, closed faces.

Her own voice, bitterly disgusted, says to her in her
dream, "Sure, that's not the way of it at all." And, "What
do *you* know of what any child is thinking?"

Mick's dream doubles back and revises itself. She dreams
of the weight of babies, those small arms locked forever
about her aching neck; those skirls and snorts and sighs
and jabbers, welcomed and dreaded, forever in her aching
ears.

Mick dreams of babies, how smelly they are, incessant,
real, sucking and smacking at her old, dry breasts until they
draw her blood.

Eileen dreams of the convent where she spent a lugubri-
ous and exalted year. She dreams of herself on her knees.
She is not praying. She is scrubbing the convent's checkered floors. She has volunteered for this task, never having
scrubbed a floor and not at all looking forward to scrubbing
this one. But the postulants, forbidden newspapers, are
made to spread newspapers over the wet clean floors. Eileen, not incurious but cautious, has cared little "in the
world," as they phrase it in the convent, for the drift and
lurch of incident. Greedy now, she crawls about on hands
and knees, snuffling up events from crisp old newsprint.
The story she longs for and fears does not appear.

Gordon dreams. Usually of things that have recently happened or soon will. Gordon enters a patient's room in Mexico City. Two aides stand gossiping, they are talking about anchovy pizza. The patient in the bed is dead. "Your patient has expired," Gordon says. The women look at him. "Your patient has expired," Gordon says. The women look at him. Gordon is displeased, he feels he must speak sharply. "This man is dead," he shouts. Shameful tears, uncalled for, slide down his shaven doctor cheeks. The women look at him. He sees that the corpse is himself. A fearful surge of grief now shakes him. He sees that the corpse is Eileen. His grief recedes, returns. He wakes. Eileen's knee is rammed into his kidney. They are terrible bedmates, all arms and legs and angles, not what he had wanted—unconsidered fleshly comfort. Her knee is cold. He wonders if she's dead.

"Get your knee out of my kidney," he says.

"Oh, sorry," she says, "do what?" She shifts.

He rolls on top of her. "I love you," he says, "I do love you."

"Oh, good," she says, "I had a ghastly dream."

He fills her mouth with his tongue; she pulls away, politely. "About my father."

"Not *now*," he says, "move your leg—not *that* leg. Put your hand here, no, no, no, not *there*, *here*."

"Gordon," she says, "let me tell you this dream."

"Eileen," he says, "let's fuck."

"Well, of course," she says. "Sweetheart. I'm almost certain it's a dry run, but. Have I ever refused you? I've never refused you. Go right ahead."

At once he is unmanned. He is angry and ashamed.

"We know how to deal with *that*, don't we?" Eileen says, assuming a hostessy manner. "We know how to handle *that*." They have had sexual counseling. "In the meantime, let me tell you this dream."

"People describe their bowel movements to me. People

tell me the color of their phlegm. But I don't have to listen to their dreams."

"I killed my father," Eileen says. "That's a confession I think might interest you."

"It doesn't interest me in the least," Gordon says. "You are a castrating nonorgasmic woman, of course you killed your father. Naturally. What else."

She withdraws from him, goes rigid, folds in two. Like an ironing board, he thinks, like some patent appliance. "Eye," he says, "let's get on with this. Tomorrow is a working day." She is sniffling. He loves her when she cries, fastidious Eileen all wet and weepy. "Talk to your therapist," he says kindly, twiddling the hair on the back of her neck, "he's the dream man. I'm the blood man. Dreams give me the pip." She sweats when she cries, he wonders why; he likes it.

"I have, I have," she sobs. "He thinks I have a screw loose."

"Well, of course," he says, doctorlike, gently reassuring, "I think all my patients are anemic." This is nonsense, but he wants to get laid. "Mommy," he says, nuzzling her, "mommy, mommy. Mommy?"

"Baby," she says, but she doesn't turn. "Nonorgasmic," she says. "Castrating."

"Eileen," he says, "I have to get up very early in the morning."

"*Right*," she says, flopping over. "I'm at your disposal. Do you want me to wear that nurse's hat?"

"Eye, you have no sense of the moment."

"Well how do I know? We have that drawer full of gadgets and sex toys and pornographic videodisks and we never even look at them. You're such a mass of brittle defenses," she says, in the voice of his enemy, her therapist.

"Go to sleep," he says.

"Remember the butterscotch topping? What a fiasco."

"Go to sleep," he says.

"Gordon," Eileen says, "let's adopt."

Mick is old, she is wakeful. Each of her joints aches separately and all of them ache together. She lies in her bed washed in moonlight; she watches the headlamps of passing cars spend more light on her ceiling. "Be happy while you're living, you're a long time dead," she says. Although alone, she speaks aloud, she has always done so. She testifies; for a long time now she has been on trial in a vast, impossible courtroom. "I'm not sorry, indeed I'm not, I like your bloody cheek," she says. "If I had it to do over —I'm telling an untruth," she says. "Of course I'm sorry. If I had it to do over. But I don't. I don't know what to do, to do the right thing. Oh sorry, is it? Divil the bit."

To lie abed awake affronts her wonderful frugality. She rises, puts her nightdress off, puts her housedress on, her cardigan, toils down the stairs. Unobserved, she is not spry or chirpy.

She makes herself a drink of tea, says a decade of the rosary, thinks of the poker that was her only doll, a heavy, sooty poker, wrapped in a bit of rag. It seems to her remarkable, the way she loved the poker, the same way exactly as the way she loves her daughters, exactly the same, in kind if not in quantity. And how, when told to, she used to take the poker and strip off its bit of raggedy dress and stir, with neither scruple nor remorse, the scrap of dying fire. "Sometimes I think I'm round the bend," she says.

The house is drafty, cold currents drifting through it. She checks all the locks on her windows and her doors, switches on her lamps and turns them off again, inspects her pilot light with deep misgiving. Shades and curtains are a problem; she can neither bear them drawn nor bear them open and so must infinitely alter allotments of light and of shadow.

She soaks her feet in a basin of water. Her corns need

paring, she'll have to get the girls to do it, the necessary postures are beyond her; she can no more do them than "swing on a trapeze," she says. Her toenails are painted, she hates that, a whimsey of her daughters'; she fears that age has made her their pet and their plaything.

She reads, with scandalized, rich interest, a news account of a little girl who has tried to feed her brother to a trash masher. "Did you ever hear the like of that?" Her heavy hair slides out of its pins, she strokes it like an animal. Her hair is never neat now, her shoulder joints are frozen, she cannot raise her arms enough to properly do up her hair. "Me hinges have give out," she says, "me hinges and me hinches. My body just won't let me."

She dries her feet, she dozes. She dreams of flittering knives and firing guns, of barking dogs and wounds and labored breathing. "God will punish me," she says, on waking. "Sure, I was ever less afraid of God than of my mother. There was always that possibility, that God would listen to reason." She laughs. She makes herself a drink of apple cider vinegar and honey. She tears from the newspaper an ad from Macy's Housewares Department. The ad is for a long pole with a suction cup on the end of it; useful, so the advertisement claims, for inaccessible light bulbs. She folds the ad and puts it underneath her breadbox where she hides her private papers.

She climbs the stairs; she does this very slowly. She puts off her cardigan, her housedress, puts on her nightdress, puts herself back into bed.

Mr. Conrad snoozes at his drawing board. His clasped hands rest upon his knee, his whiskered cheek reposes on a freshly finished drawing, slightly smudging its colored inks.

Mr. Conrad is a miniaturist who, when he draws, wears spectacles rigged with an extra set of magnifying lenses that jut on wire stalks. This apparatus has been forced awry by the position of his head, and now, in his sleep, assaults his nose. His pose is awkward; he is lightly dressed; his room is cold; he is hungry. But Mr. Conrad courts discomfort.

The drawing he has finished is filthy, funny, curious and curiously romantic. His characters are dogs. They rejoice in dogness, they display an absolute exuberance of dogness. They are also, mysteriously, human. Indeed, he has drawn a tiny, skinny white mutt, a bit too long in the legs, that looks like Kitty, and a tiny, thin-napped rosy hound that certainly resembles Rambeau. Mr. Conrad is afraid of dogs; they can make him pant and tremble.

He dreams that his mother is twisting his nose. It is on her account that he makes and sells these drawings which so delight and puzzle him. He needs the money they earn for him, to visit, every other year, his faraway, high-handed, cruel-mouthed mother. And the drawings earn far less than once they did, when he peddled them clandestinely, with sighs and frowns, leers and winks and nudges. Now they hang quite openly, in a gallery of erotic art in SoHo.

He dreams of his mother as a winter squash, polished, tan, hard, flecked with velvet moles like spots of mildew. He dreams of his mother as a creature somewhere between toad and cat. Her cold skin, dense and creamy, smooth as cheese and flossed with little hairs. Her tilted glinting eyes and wide mouth packed with tongue. He dreams of her voice. Moist and husky once, now it is parched.

Mr. Conrad wearies of his mother, whom he loves. Surely, one day she will die. He has been his mother's lover for nearly forty years. It is not steady work, but it is tiring.

"Betrayed," she has written him on thin airmail paper in her scornful letters of magical command. "Discarded. And Disdained." She is crazy, of course. Misguided at the very least.

Still, summoned, Mr. Conrad yearns for and deplores his importunate old mother's bed.

Each evening, on his biennial visits, Mr. Conrad and his mother dine exquisitely. Afterwards they gamble, then they copulate. This often seems to him unbelievable. What it seems to her, he cannot know. Surely, forty years ago, he was obsessed with her. But he was just fifteen; hot, pretty, small and rather stupid. She was newly widowed, vindictive, histrionic. Perhaps one of them seduced the other; each of them has claimed the blame.

It is the central event of their histories. It is the only significant thing either of them has ever done, or else it is a fearful bit of silliness. Perhaps they were no more than bored and itchy.

Mr. Conrad can remember the occasion of debauch but he cannot altogether reconstruct the circumstances. Sometimes he is washed by guilt and horror. He is a chaste, abstemious man. He is timid, he fears dogs, he is tiny and tidy, he writes poetry, he paints, he is not of a nature to corrupt his own mother. Nonetheless, he has done so.

Or perhaps not; perhaps it is she who has ruined him. But is he ruined? He would prefer to feel ruined, but often feels instead merely foolish. It is not dignified for a man of his age to be screwing his mother; he knows this. It is not American, either. It is foreign, and considered in this country rather rustic. Americans annoy him with their childish moral imperatives, their stumbling. And he has discerned about him pats and wrigglings, pouts, caresses, turns of sentimental phrase, that lead him to suspect, now and again, that every man in America is humping his old mother and simply keeping still about it. Mr. Conrad, incapable of keeping altogether still about it, tries to dig meaning from his life in his poems.

Once a lawyer, trained in another system of law, no more nor less lucid than this one, he works now as a law clerk and sometimes as a kind of private investigator, although he is not licensed. He is bullied and patronized by the people who employ him. He works also as a waiter in a private club. And he draws his doggy pictures.

He dreams of his mother who is Kitty and not-Kitty. She is younger, this Kitty, smaller, more succulent, silent. Silent, and very nice.

Kitty wakes in anger. She has bitten the inside of her mouth. She is cold. The dog has taken all the blankets. The dog is making twittery, tweety, birdsong dreaming noises. "Wake up, dog," Kitty says. The dog paws scrabble against her arm. Its pads are coarse, she can feel its black, doggy toenails. It is pumping and pushing against her arm, thrusting its paws most desperately, like paddles or like wings.

"Are you sick?" she says. "Are you horny?" She is touched and repelled by the feel of its feet; these are not the terms of their agreement. The dog wakes angry. There is drool on the dog's hairy chin. The dog turns three times, each time eyeing her; she makes no attempt to reclaim her blankets. The dog lies down with its rump at her cheek; the whole hind end of it is on her pillow.

"Listen to reason, dog," she says. The dog backpedals, its infuriated ass tilts up her chin. She thinks of a thing her mother says to her. "Kitty lie over, you're next to the wall."

Rambeau flies. His left arm ends in a saxophone; his right arm ends in Kitty. They climb and climb. Their heads bump the glass-roofed top of the world, they can fly no higher. From the ground, the sound of joyful barking. Rambeau looks at Kitty.

He finds Dorinda, walloping black hair and thrusting foxy face and angry grin. He tries to shake her off, to knock her to some distant doom, he wakes. He observes at once the evidence of an erotic dream. But it had not seemed to him to be that kind of dream at all. Dorinda grips his hand with both of hers. She barks in her sleep, she snores. Worn out, he supposes, from sloshing him with scented oils and slobbering on his toes.

Dorinda's father has turned her over like the keys to a

summer cottage. Now, four weeks after he met Dorinda, Rambeau has met her parents: her father dressed as a waterfowler, her mother dressed as a duck. They are grave and plucky. They make asides and pun a lot. They treat Dorinda, or treat of Dorinda, as a jokey crucifixion. Whoever she has run with, a balding, aging saxophone player who lives in a furnished room would seem to be trading up.

Awful Dorinda, gravid, dreamless, sleeps.

Rambeau

◆

Rambeau calls his mother every month. He calls her on a pay phone from a bar; for preference, a noisy bar. No drinker, he doses himself with whiskey for these calls, one bourbon and water, one double bourbon on the rocks. He changes bills into silver at the bar and takes the second drink with him to the phone.

Now that he is saddled with Dorinda, he finds it hard to enter the kind of bar he needs to call his mother. He takes Dorinda everywhere. He means to keep her out of trouble. What kind of trouble he can keep her out of that she hasn't already been in, he fears to contemplate.

Dorinda is installed at a gummy table, behind a glass bucket of big dill pickles. These are a staple of her diet. In front of her are spread packets of potato chips and pretzels and old-fashioned glasses full of olives and pickled onions. Rambeau has provided this fare. He watches with awe as she puts catsup on an olive and eats it.

He has plaited her hair in one long braid that she hauls on and fiddles with all the time. Her skin is clear and pearly, very white. She has painted up her face in patriotic colors, her lips and cheeks are cherry red, there's cobalt

55

over and under her eyes. She is wearing a headband, fringes and beadwork and a prairie-flower skirt with a flounce. Over all this she wears a shawl. She is pregnant. She is fat. She looks like something let loose from a pageant.

Rambeau calls Cherokee; there is no answer.

Rambeau stacks his coins, disarranges the stacks, begins to restack them in date order, pulls himself together and calls his mother.

Zeke, his mother's consort, answers.

"It's me," Rambeau says.

"It's *you* is it?" Zeke has a booming bronchial voice and the manner, just the manner, of a card. He is short and very dapper, he looks doll-like. He walks on the balls of his feet and displays his deep voice. He too is a red-haired man. He is older than Rambeau, and younger than Rambeau's mother.

"Is she there?" Rambeau says.

"Is she *here*?" Zeke says, in the way of a wit getting off a good one, "is she *here*? Where would she *be* if she wasn't *here*?"

"Don't know," Rambeau says. "Out picking up sailors?"

"I don't appreciate that one little bit," Zeke says. "I believe that was entirely uncalled for."

"Didn't mean anything by it," Rambeau says. "Is she there?"

"Is she *here*? Is she *here* . . ."

Rambeau holds the receiver at arm's length for a moment. When he returns it to his ear, his mother is saying:

"*Beau*, Beau! *Jacky*, Jacky! *Beau, Jacky*, don't hang up!"

"When did I ever hang up on you?" Rambeau says. "I never have hung up on you."

"Of course you haven't," his mother says. "You're my boy. You're my sweetheart. Aren't you?"

Rambeau says nothing. Salt sweat drips from his eyebrows into his eyes.

"Aren't you, lover?" his mother says.

"How've you been?" Rambeau says. He looks at his watch.

"How do I sound?" his mother says, and how she sounds is canny.

"Well, there's the usual tremolo of self-pity," Rambeau says and is surprised to have said such a thing. It reminds him of Kitty. Could Kitty have said such a thing? Surely not, since Kitty has never heard of his mother.

"Why, certainly," his mother says, more pleased than not. "That's what Dr. Freud says. He says, 'Mary, self-pity is your worst enemy.' "

"Dr. Freud? Mary? How do you spell Mary?"

"Same way our Blessed Mother spells it."

Rambeau has known his mother, whose name is Julia Mary, as Juliet and Mimi, as Juli and Miki, and as some other things but he's never known her to own up to unadorned Mary. On the other hand, she's become both a therapy junkie and pious. "His name is really Dr. Freud?"

"Oh, don't be silly, Beau," she says, laughing, flirting. "That's our joke." She goes on laughing.

Rambeau laughs too. "You sound really good," he says. "It's nice to hear you laugh."

She stops. She can stop on a dime. She begins to sob with a pause and a lurch, like a vehicle going into reverse.

"I'm not laughing," she says. "What have I got to laugh about?"

"No, no," Rambeau says. "That's perfectly all right."

"I abandoned you when you needed me most," his mother says. "I ran off with another man. I had my needs, I admit that, but the fact remains. I ran off with another man."

"Well, it was only Zeke," Rambeau says. "And it was thirty years ago."

"Thirty-four."

"Thirty-four in May," Rambeau says.

"And you can't find it in your heart to forgive me," Rambeau's mother says. She is triumphant.

Rambeau sucks an ice cube. He looks into his heart. There is an eight-year-old in there. Personally, Rambeau would be glad to forgive her, but the eight-year-old has different sentiments.

"You have oedipal problems, Beau," his mother says confidingly.

"No such thing."

"You've been living with a white-haired woman, a woman older than your mother, Beau."

Then he knows she has had a detective on him; she has done this sort of thing before.

"Goddam Zeke and his money," Rambeau says.

"Don't you take the name of the Lord."

"Goddam Zeke and his money," Rambeau says.

"Zeke is good enough to come with me to the meetings of a wonderful organization for the parents of gays," his mother says.

"Goddam Zeke is not my parent," Rambeau says, "and I am not goddam gay."

"How do you know who your parent is?" Rambeau's mother says. "I know who your parent is. Nobody else knows. I know."

"I know my own father," Rambeau says. "I was with him when he lived and with him when he died, which is more than you were. You never set eyes on Zeke till I was seven or eight years old."

"Nobody knows," his mother sobs, "but me."

Rambeau thinks of his feckless, dark-haired father, a man who never told the truth if a lie would lead to trouble; he thinks of Zeke, the rich and redheaded horn-voiced dwarf. He makes a fist and raps his knuckles on his forehead, hard. He thinks of the girl called Cherokee, who is redheaded too and just Dorinda's age. He thinks of his mother in her youth and his, a good-hearted girl but a tease. He thinks of his sisters, who look like their father in a way he never has.

Zeke's voice is in his ear. "I don't appreciate it, Boy, when you aggravate your mother," Zeke says. Zeke has always called him Boy. Perhaps it's as close as he cares to come to Beau, or perhaps he uses it in the, to Rambeau, too-familiar sense of "Well, he took the girls, but of course he couldn't see his way clear to taking The Boy." Or perhaps, awful possibility, he knows that Rambeau is his boy.

"Zeke, are you my father?" Rambeau says.

"Sugar," Zeke says. "Sugar. Oh sugar, sugar, *sugar!*" Zeke hangs up.

Rambeau stands chagrined. At first he thinks that Zeke, indeed his father, is voicing an endearment. Then he realizes that *sugar* is a stand-in word, the word Zeke uses because he's not allowed the word he wants.

Rambeau stops at the bar and brings another double bourbon to Dorinda's table.

"What are you doing," Dorinda says to his glass, "what are you putting in your body?" She is sitting with a man who wears a dirty chef's apron and toque, and is further fitted out in a startling brocade of purple rash. He represents, to Rambeau, present evil. Dorinda does her head loll and reel for this man; he is silently attentive to her breasts.

"Go," Rambeau says to him. The man smirks at him and leaves. Rambeau has a clear, bad feeling that some deal was going down. "Who was your chum?" he says to Dorinda, who twitches her braid and lolls again. "I won't have you messing with dope," he says. "No buying, no selling, no nothing. Do you understand what I'm saying?"

"Don't try to jack me around," Dorinda says. "I don't have to take that kind of stuff."

"Yes, you do. You have to take that kind of stuff." He is angry partly because her attitude toward the aproned stranger was neither closer nor more distant than her attitude toward him. On the other hand, there is comfort in this.

"I've just been on the phone with my mother," Rambeau says. He has never so much as mentioned his mother to Kitty but Dorinda is different. Dorinda doesn't care.

"You're too old to have a mother," Dorinda says.

"This is true."

"Nobody should ever call up their mother," Dorinda says. "Calling up their mother has ruined a whole lot of people's lives."

Rambeau likes the celebrational smell of bourbon, but now it seems to be making him sick. He covers his glass with the waxed chip bag.

"Why don't they just die already," Dorinda says. "They already had their life, who needs them?"

"Speaking of motherhood," Rambeau says, "I made an appointment with a doctor. You go tomorrow. And I go with you, God help me. Also Lamaze. I talked to a person there. You can't do that until about your seventh month. I'll go there with you too."

"Unreal," Dorinda says. "You are one weird wombat."

"You can't have this baby on the floor of the room."

"I could," Dorinda says. She is threatening him.

"You could, but you're not going to."

"What do you care?"

"I don't know," Rambeau says. "I care, that's all. Dorinda, did I ever tell you about the time my mother abandoned me—when I was a little boy?"

"Big, big deal," Dorinda says, scowling. "Do me a favor. Gimme a break. You really knock my lights out."

'Dear Kitty,' Rambeau writes in his mind, 'since you left me I have taken to drink. Since you left me I've not drawn a sober breath nor known a tranquil hour.' This is not true, but he has had several hangovers and he resents them, they are Kitty's fault.

'Dear Kitty,' he writes, 'I never told you this, but when I

was a very small boy—when I was just a little boy—my mother, who I loved, ran out on me.' Though a silent man, he has told bits of this story to women all across the country; not a one of them but her eyes swam with tears and her legs flew open. But he never told it to Kitty.

'Dear Kitty,' he writes, 'I miss you like I missed my mother when I was eight years old.' This is true, but seems unmanly.

"Want to hear something weird?" Dorinda is suddenly cheerful. "Know what that guy in the apron wanted? He wanted to buy this baby."

Rambeau plucks the chip bag off his drink and swallows the bourbon, all of it.

'Dear Kitty,' he writes, 'I used to love you, save me. I'm just going to tell you this story. Don't interrupt.'

Rambeau's Letter to Kitty

◆

There are things about me, Kitty, you don't know. Before I met you I had hard luck with women and before I left you I knew my luck had not much changed. But in between time I had a winning streak with you that nearly drove me crazy. I like to win but winning drives me crazy. I've seen me throw down a hand just to get the winning over. This is not a wholesome trait in a gambler.

When we were together, before you took it in your head to drive me out, I used to lie beside you in the bed with my hand laid on your throat to feel it purring. I would hear the sound of your voice but not the words and I don't think I ever had a better time. The bed was like a little boat, and we would bob along in it and the sound of your voice was like natural sounds, rivers and wind in trees. And you would be so warm. When I first knew you, I used to think you must be running a fever.

I would lie there and I would be thinking of these things I'd tell you someday. But I never told you. Maybe I thought it would be throwing down my hand.

I have a mother living, she's a doozy. She gave birth to me in New Orleans, the third child of three. She was originally from Saratoga Springs. I took you to Saratoga once for the Travers. I hit on a quinella and we ate clam chowder out of plastic cups. I never let on I knew the town, I banked on nobody spotting me. I don't know why I did that, since I lived in Saratoga for years.

Where my father was from I'm not sure. He was a tale spinner. He couldn't tell the truth if a lie was handy. The first thing I remember of my father is his gun belt slung on a standing lamp. That was in New Orleans in the forties. I think now that he was some kind of a security guard in a war plant. I thought then that he was an admiral in the Navy.

My father was a handsome man. He had shining eyes, bright eyes, and his mouth turned up, though he was sulky in his disposition. He liked whiskey and cards and fooling around with women. I can't fault him on any of those tastes, but he didn't like his children. My mother was crazy about him.

My mother was a looker and a dresser—I heard my father use those very words. She prided herself on being peppy and taking a positive outlook. She had a chattering laugh I liked to hear.

My clearest memory of my mother in New Orleans is from the time I took to running away. I was a small kid, five or six. I would let myself out of the house in the middle of the night, so she started sleeping on a quilt on the floor to block the door. She worked as a nurse, seven to three, and some nights she slept like a stone. On those nights I could step right on over her. One night I was halfway out the door when her hand closed on my ankle. She was lying there, laughing and smiling. She wagged my foot. I could see she liked my style.

My father got into a scrape in New Orleans and we moved to Saratoga Springs, back to my mother's hometown. My mother and my sisters, Lucie and Veronica, went to live in an apartment that was part of the second floor of a big dark brown house that had scaffolding around it.

I didn't go to live there with them. My father and I moved in with my mother's parents. The theory was that he would help them with their house, but it wasn't much of a theory if you knew my father.

My grandmother was a sweet-faced, quiet-living woman with a natural appetite for rascals. My grandfather had been one, a gambler and a rake who'd owned trotters and been a golf pro. He'd come down in the world and been a greenskeeper and then his mind went back on him and all he could do was hang around the house and look at pictures in magazines and wonder if he'd looked at them before.

My grandmother took to my father right away. She didn't take to me right away, partly because she couldn't stand my red hair, which was a shade she said she had never seen before, certainly not in anyone belonging to her. But my father was bad to me and she took my part against him often and pretty soon she and I got to be friends.

I was pining for my mother. Maybe my grandmother felt sorry for me, although she never acted like it. But she kept wanting to give me things and she didn't really have what to give me, so she started out to teach me everything she knew.

She showed me how to make a white sauce. She showed me how to bone a fish. She was a fine cook and had worked in some of the biggest houses in Saratoga in her younger days. I had never seen anybody do anything really well before and that's what held my interest. We would clean a chicken together. We would have the encyclopedia open and we would try to figure out where the chicken's kidneys were, or its lungs. We worried about the same things, like do chickens pee. She made a little money sewing and she would show me about sewing too, and knitting and so on.

I would embroider, I would iron. Every time she showed me something she would say, "Do you understand that now? Now you have that by you." It was her capital and she was passing it along to me.

My father wasn't any too happy, watching his only son crochet, but I didn't care, I was interested. She had told me about men being chefs and sailors having to know how to knit and sew and iron. My father wasn't around much anyway. When he was around she was trying to make his life lovely for him. She cooked him things he liked to eat, baby food—creamy, sweet stuff—and she did up his gabardine shirts just so, weak starch, touch more in the cuffs and collars. She loaned him money for the horses, borrowing it from the roomer, Mr. Moon.

I hadn't been given a room in my grandmother's house, although there was a room available. This was partly out of a convention that my family would all get together again in what my grandmother called "the foreseeable future." And partly because my grandmother didn't want to be a patsy, taking on my mother's spare kid.

Sometimes I slept in my father's room, but mostly I was grabbed up like a puppy and taken to bed by anyone in the market for good will and body heat. My grandfather, my grandmother, Mr. Moon, they all used to quarrel for my company. My father too, though my father couldn't see the point of children. He couldn't believe what they got away with and how messy their personal habits were.

It was a fine time in my life, because everywhere I went somebody was glad to see me. The red hair that was supposed to spoil my looks made me popular in school. My mother and sisters fussed over me. My grandmother always had something new to show me. Even Mr. Moon gave me nickels.

I had fallen in love with my mother in Saratoga. I couldn't get over her, how amazing she seemed, how strange and special. Afternoons and sometimes after supper I went over to my mother's apartment. My sisters were twelve and fourteen, great big juicy girls, full of mischief and popping out of their skins with sex. My mother was popping out of her skin too. I loved that apartment, it was a female place, noisy and jammed full of terrible furniture. Bedroom furniture, streamlined and sleazy, that my mother had bought in New Orleans. An awful lot of pieces of it, white and gold lacquer, took up the floor space that should have gone to me. (We had been taught to treat it as if it had human feelings, but I used to kick the furniture.)

I loved that apartment. The girls would be all over me. I was a boy and practice material. I was harmless. I loved them. I loved all the radios playing and the gold threads in the new. turquoise couch and their small dog barking. Lucie and Veronica would be fighting with my mother over the bathroom and the telephone. The place was always hot and it always smelled of different kinds of perfume.

I used to help my mother dress. I used to shave her legs for her and rub them with pink lotion. I enjoyed doing this and then it made me so uncomfortable that I wouldn't do it anymore and the three of them laughed and teased me.

My mother was always getting ready to go some place, always fixing up. I thought she was meeting my father, but I don't know why I thought that, I never once remember him being there when I was. I thought he was the person she talked to on the phone. And it may be that he was.

My sisters were fixing up too and I was in big demand. I was the back man and the toe man. I washed and powdered and dabbed. I was half nuts with usefulness. I poked the wires of my mother's earrings through the holes in her ears. I colored her eyelashes with mascara and a little brush and spit. I plucked the stray hairs from between her eyebrows.

I would be zipping and tieing and doing up the clasp on my mother's necklace and fastening hooks and snapping snaps and painting on the nail polish very carefully. The girls would hold me down and she would kiss me. The dog would bark and the radios were playing and the goldfish were swimming in the bowls. Even her name was beautiful to me. Julia Mary. I used to roll it on my tongue.

My mother was working as a private duty nurse at the hospital. When it rained, I used to carry an umbrella to the hospital. I never opened it until I saw her face. She had a lunch box with the '39 World's Fair trylon and perisphere on it. Every night she brought me home some scrap of her lunch in it, a piece of cake or a piece of fruit that tasted fine to me because it had aged in her lunch box. Whenever she saw me, her face lit up.

I thought of nurses as angels and martyrs. My mother's back and feet would hurt her after a day at the hospital and this would worry me very much. My grandfather had a medicine show apparatus called a violet ray—an electric handle with various glass pipes and blobs and tubes that fitted onto it. A kind of purple neon sizzled and buzzed in the glass parts when you plugged it in, and a strong smell of ozone came out. I would run this thing over my mother's bare back and legs while she lay on the bed and coached me. The room would fill with leaping purple light and smell just like a thunderstorm.

My grandmother wouldn't let the violet ray out overnight, so I brought it to my mother when she wanted it and took it back when we were through. One afternoon after school I got the violet ray in its fitted case out of my grandfather's closet and took it to my mother's place. I was thinking on the way of my mother's imitations of her patients. She imitated all her patients for us, especially the ones who died. These imitations made me laugh and shiver, but mostly laugh.

When I got to my mother's place, nobody was there. The door was unlocked and the place was emptied out. There were some magazines and some cartons full of buttonless blouses and odd socks. In the middle of the floor stood the new turquoise couch with the gold threads. On the windowsill in the living room were some eggshells I had painted and planted bean seeds in.

I knew right off that my mother and my sisters were gone. The logistics rocked me. I had been there the night before, when had they packed up their stuff?

I got crazy, yelling and stamping and banging around. The woman from downstairs came up and tried to comfort me. Or pump me, I don't know which. I was yelling my mother's name, "Julia Mary," I was yelling, "Julia Mary." I had never called my mother Julia Mary, not even for a joke.

For a week I went back every day. After that I went back only sometimes. I would sit on the couch. Then the couch was gone, then the lock was changed, then I didn't go back anymore. I never said a word to my grandmother and she never said a word to me. My father had taken a job as a deckhand on some high roller's yacht. He was in Florida.

My mother went off with her last private patient. He was a rich man, made his pile on a gauge they used in the oil fields. Got struck down with bleeding ulcers as he placed his bets on a nice day at the track. My mother could have gone to him with nothing but the rags on her back. But she took every stick of that lousy bedroom furniture that I had kicked hell out of. She took the girls and the goldfish and the little dog and the pots and the mirror that hung on the wall. She didn't take the turquoise couch she seemed so proud of. And, may she roast in hell for it, she didn't take me.

Kitty

◆

Poor Kitty does not thrive, she does not prosper. She cannot move her story forward. Limp with fatigue, she huddles on half the bed once shared with Rambeau; she does not sleep. Or sometimes she does sleep; sleep, sleep, long sweaty sleeps that obscure the days' ends and beginnings. She does not eat at all, or, sickened and hungry, she stirs together greasy sweet messes, gobbles them, repents. Her body thickens but her cheekbones jut. Her complexion has a gray translucent pallor and an unbecoming sheen. When she looks at it, she hears her mother's voice saying, "Now there's a nice bit of sole."

She does not dress but trollops about in derelict nightgowns; jivey little numbers splashed with bleach or yellowing white lawn full of draggled lace and great unmendable rents. Over these she wears a glamorous and expensive cashmere sweater, a man's sweater, stone green. She stole it from a set, her single theft, ever, on the ground that it matches Rambeau's eyes. On the same ground, he declined to wear it for anything much above radiator painting. The sweater is smeared and shadowed with silver-colored paint.

69

Kitty is repellent. She is unwashed. For mysterious reasons, she fears to strip naked and step alone into a tub of water. Similarly, she is afraid to stick her dirty head beneath a tap. Something appalling will happen, she cannot say what, she chooses not to speculate. "I am dying of a broken heart," Kitty says. She knows this is absurd. Women do not die of breaking hearts. "A broken heart is a metaphor," Kitty says. She says this to the dog, which skulks about the house, fasting, gorging, shitting in the closets or on the few decent rugs, surly and wise-looking, visibly wasting. Dogs, she knows, do die of broken hearts, and indeed are congratulated for it.

She is swollen, engorged with self-pity, tumid, flooded by it, so filled up that it spills out all her orifices nastily. Her bladder burns; her entrails are molten; her big eyes slosh out scalding tears; her ears are wet and muck drips from her nose. Once in a while she bleeds a little very dark blood. This does not seem to her to constitute a menstrual period; she has not had a period so far as she can tell, though of course she has lost her calendar. She considers, briefly, that she might be pregnant. But since she thinks she would like to be pregnant, pregnancy, on the whole, is unlikely.

Two possible events inform her day: Rambeau may telephone; there may be a letter from Rambeau. She does not believe that Rambeau himself will appear. If she did she should perhaps take pains with her appearance. On the other hand, perhaps she wishes him to see how he has brought her low. She has an answering device connected to her telephone. As a free-lance stylist she must have this. She has recorded for it, in a false, skipping voice, a statement that says Kitty is still knocking around Paris but is expected to return any day. Because she is so frightened of missing Rambeau's call, she lifts the phone each time it rings, and her mother and her sister and the few friends who call hear repeatedly her true and muddy voice blatting over the cheery, lying one.

Her mother has no time for her. Mick says Kitty is making a show of herself and should have more pride. Mick says there are bigger fish in the ocean and prettier pebbles on the beach and that life is a scourge and a treachery entirely. She sends Kitty a column by Ann Landers and an article from a magazine which serve to reinforce these points.

Eileen says that Kitty is dramatizing; that she is heading for something dire; that soon she will have a humongous ass and then no man will want her; that she is willfully squandering her capital: her slender body, skin and eyes and hair.

Eileen wants to talk about her own problems. So, of course, does Kitty's mother. Each of them wants to cheer Kitty by telling her something that exceeds in terribleness anything that has yet happened to Kitty.

Kitty is ruthless, she will not listen. She wants to talk about Rambeau. She wants to talk of their lovemaking; to tell someone how, when they made love, he slipped his hand between her shoulder blades and raised her tenderly toward him. But there is, she knows, no audience for this.

Eileen, it is true, has sent her a book about falling out of love. This book suggests that Kitty must undergo denial, awareness, depression, fear, anger, ambivalence, acceptance, and some other things.

Kitty has already undergone all these things, over and over, sometimes in the course of an afternoon, and to no profit. She has no intention of falling out of love.

Mr. Conrad has brought her another book. This other book says that the emotional and social support of friends is necessary to help the cast-off lover cope with alternating feelings and changing needs. Mr. Conrad quotes this passage, it is his ticket of admission. He is forever turning up on her doorstep.

Mr. Conrad brings her poems too, since she is unable to appear at their poetry workshops. Sometimes he brings an elegant small bag of sexy groceries—artichokes, figs, tiny oysters. He wants not to eat these things himself, but to watch her eat them. She is quite unable to eat them. She would like to hear from Mr. Conrad what Pushkin or Goethe or Rilke had to say about her predicament, but Mr. Conrad is absorbed in the book he has brought her.

He quotes "human development specialists." These, according to Mr. Conrad, are all for Kitty's taking up with another man. Soon. Someone she already knows, perhaps —"informal unstructured meeting." Or someone she has met at, say, night school—"more structured resource."

Mr. Conrad, ducking and bobbing, points out more than once again that Kitty is rare as a mountain flower and wild as a mountain sheep.

Kitty is quite a bit outraged. She knows, of course, that the degree of outrage is indirectly proportional to the degree of attractiveness of the outrager. But Mr. Conrad, really. With his baby clothes and baby talk and dainty manners. It seems to her duplicitous that in there all the time he has been harboring ordinary gonadal male ambitions. But she is glad of his fealty even as his presence taxes.

Sometimes he walks her to the mailbox. There is no one else she would let do that. She thinks it will be years before she can confront a mailbox without her guts shriveling.

On these walks, Mr. Conrad deals with the dog—insofar as anyone can be said to deal with it. Largely, he makes didactic remarks, of possible dog-interest, having to do with trees and shrubs, clouds, stones, birds and squirrels. His tone is placating as well as instructive. She is aware now that Mr. Conrad fears the dog; she doesn't care. It makes the dog a more efficient chaperone. The dog's attitude to Mr. Conrad is quite striking and she means to think about it at some future time when she is, unlikely as it now seems, up to it.

The dog's golden glances are deliberate and assessing. Perhaps the dog wants to make a friend of Mr. Conrad. Or perhaps the dog wants to kill and eat him.

When Mr. Conrad and Kitty share some awful thing she's cooked—never involving oysters, artichokes or figs—the dog is there between them like a sword. They drink no wine; she's afraid of getting pally. Afterwards, she plows out to the gate with Mr. Conrad, towing the disapproving dog, wearing, as she has since mailbox time, Rambeau's smelly, huge rubber boots; inside them her feet shift damply.

Each night as she lies on the same glum sheets, she is glad that the day is over. This is her only moment of honest gladness. One day down, another day coming, a day on which Rambeau may write, may call. She must hear from him, she must talk with him; she has something important to tell him.

The demented dog roams the house, it will not have its chain removed. The chain trails after it, noisy. Noisy as the chains of the family ghost.

Kitty and Eileen

◆

Kitty gets Eileen on the telephone.

"What's new, don't keep me, I have to remove my mask."

"Egg white or avocado?"

"Both, I have two kinds of skin."

"Don't tell me now, I think I know why Rambeau left me."

"Rambeau left you because you fear commitment. He left you because *he* fears commitment. Also you made his life a misery, you never shut your mouth. Or else you wouldn't talk to him at all. And maybe he met someone else."

"I think he left me because of what happened to our father. It's God's way of fixing my wagon."

"Another possibility. I must go rinse my face, my pores are screaming."

"Deny it, will you? Why do you think I called?"

"I think it's a distinct possibility."

"Of course it's not. God wouldn't do that."

"Why wouldn't God?"

"God is too nice of a person."

"How well do you really know God?"

"I see our father everywhere, Eileen. Rambeau's *dog* looks like our father."

"Rambeau's dog looks like a pork roast. I must go."

Kitty

◆

Luckily, Kitty has run out of money and so must take a job. She replaces the tape on her answering machine with one that says she is available. In a few days she is booked by a photographer named Darq. She knows him and has shot with him before. He is not exactly a hot photographer, but he is semi-hot.

Darq has made a curious and probably temporary name for himself by taking a series of pictures of naked children for editorial fashion spreads. The pictures are dim, shot by the smudgy light that filters through Darq's oversized studio windows, and the solemn jewel-laden children, further obscured by studio junk—paper flowers, feathers, shells, fans—are not doing much of anything. However, the photographs have excited an unusual amount of comment and critical squabble. Some viewers find them disturbing and, in never clearly articulated ways, profound. Some others find them vapid. Some find them haunting and beautiful and some dismiss them hotly as detestable. Moreover, there is no agreement on whether the photographs are "serious." Are they art? Are they dirty? Are they dirty art?

As a result of these photographs—the Jaybird Series,

Darq calls them—or of the publicity they've brought him, he has been retained to take the advertising pictures for a manufacturer of children's clothing. The advertising agency that effected this arrangement now lives in terror of it. Darq is enjoined to flood his photographs for the Mummy and Me campaign with artificial light and to see that his overdressed child models grin. Kitty has already styled two of these shoots. Not easy, for Darq is an irascible man. She is engaged to style the third.

"It's a hustle," Darq says. "It's a hassle, Baby Girl. Rush job, Beauty. Just the rest of today to shop. Tomorrow for fittings. Thursday to fix up your awful errors. And Friday we shoot. The client adores you. The client *asked* for you. Don't let me down."

Kitty suspects from all this that Darq had hired another stylist, who has canceled. She needs the job too much to care.

She hauls the dog into her bathroom and secures it to a silver-painted radiator. She bathes in scalding water, scouring herself with palmfuls of shampoo, for she has omitted to buy, or lost interest in buying, soap. She cannot bring herself to close the bathroom door, which admits an icy seasonless draft. There are books of poetry beside her on the bathroom floor; she keeps them there for company, although she seems to have forgotten how to read.

"This is crazy," she repeats as she washes. "This is crazy." She shampoos her hair, wringing it roughly. Once her eyes are closed, the dog lets go a cannonade, bitterly fouling the air. When she shakes the water out of her eyes and looks at it, the dog runs its tongue across its lips. She throws a washcloth at the dog; she misses.

There is too much body in the tub, she fills it too full, she is pudgy, protuberant, awkward with flesh. If Rambeau came back now, he wouldn't like her. But of course he would like her, he will always like her, some dreadful mistake has been made.

She considers cutting off her long wet curly hair, so wild, so absurdly white. But if she cuts it off, will Rambeau know her? She towels it a little, then rolls it up wet. She will be neat. She unrolls it, rolls it up again, now it looks a little wacky, but deliberately so, as though she were onto some trend; she is getting into her tack. However none of her clothing fits her; none of her buttons will do up properly; somehow, in her misery, she has lost her waist, has sprouted breasts. She improvises, after all it is her trade. She paints her face, dislikes it. She has lost herself.

At the agency, Kitty talks to the art director and looks at the layout for the new ad in the Mummy and Me campaign. The ordinary hazards of her job seem impossible to negotiate. The layout, an all-right layout, not a hat-smasher, shows a woman and a boy of about four. The woman and the boy are looking at each other and a borzoi is looking at them. All faces register rapturous approval. The little boy is wearing a fussy, tricked-up sailor suit, which is the product and so is painstakingly drawn. The woman is wearing a droopy floor-length garment of remarkable vagueness. Securing this garment is one of Kitty's chief responsibilities. It must be "perfect." It must be beautiful, to indicate refinement of taste. It must be unobtrusive, so as not to "overpower" the sailor suit. Everyone must admire the mother's dress but the client must not get phone calls asking him where to buy the mother's dress because phone calls of that type madden the client whose interest is in selling sailor suits. No one is sure what color this dress should be or if it should be a dress. Kitty is offered the conflicting opinions of the writer, the art director, the photographer, and the client's wife. The client has no opinion except that it had damn well better be perfect because he is beginning to think the agency wants to put him out of business.

Kitty writes "better be perfect" underneath the models' sizes in her notebook. She walks to the elevator with the art director. She has done this sort of thing a thousand times, she tells herself. A thousand times. The trouble is, she doesn't want to do it again, not even one more time. However. She sighs.

"Are you throwing up a lot?" the art director says. "I threw up a lot with my kid, but with my kid, who wouldn't?" The art director's troubles with her daughter are a nervous, running gag.

Kitty, who disapproves of this kind of joking, displays a businesslike, all-purpose semi-smile. She steps into an elevator. She has descended several floors before she realizes that the art director thinks she is pregnant.

She finds herself on the sidewalk in front of the building, holding her notebook in her hand. She is groggy. Perhaps she *is* pregnant. She waits to feel something. She feels nothing but faraway prevailing hopelessness.

If she is pregnant, perhaps she should somehow tell Rambeau. Perhaps it is the honorable thing. No pressure, of course. Exchange of information. Do you love me? You don't? I'm pregnant. Ah so. This does not sound like Rambeau, but she cannot capture him, his voice, his face, his hands upon her body; she is losing him.

Then she remembers him lying across her, head down, strapping Band-Aids on her blistered toes. She remembers him naked, the coarse, curly red-gold hair that covers him, a corruscating pelt of light that dances just above his flesh.

The area from her waist to her knees declines to have anything to do with her. She totters into a phone booth on the street and tears the receiver from its mooring. "Rambeau, come back," she says into it, loud, "come back."

Her tone is imperious, she tries to amend it. "Rambeau," she says, as before, "come back. Write to me, oh, write to me. Call me, call me, I have something to tell you. Rambeau, Rambeau, please listen to me. I think I can *explain*."

She is weeping, she is raging, she is altogether without shame. "I love you," she says into the telephone, which does not connect her to anyone, "I love you, I won't hurt you, let me try to *explain.*"

The morning of the shoot, she rises in cold darkness. She has been told to arrive at Darq's studio at "oh-dark-hundred." She suspects he says this often—"This is Darq, darling, I'll want you at the studio Friday at oh-dark-hundred." Clunk; down goes his phone.

Darq called poor Kitty names at the fitting, but he did make four picks. The client has not seen the picks; he will see them today. The picks are pressed and cloaked in plastic with several identical sailor suits and all these clothes hang on a rod in Rambeau's car in the driveway.

Kitty has backed Rambeau's car from the garage and set it idling in the driveway because she believes this to be good for it, salubrious, a kind of limbering exercise. The old car, because he loves it, she thinks of almost as a dear domestic animal, one she is minding and must maintain in vigorous condition.

The dog is an animal of a very different kind. Rambeau saved the dog from death on the West Side Highway, where someone had shoved it out of a car, the mark of a collar still on its fur. He saw the dog ahead of him, bounding and dodging, trapped in the traffic. Cars swerved and honked, but the animal was doomed. Rambeau managed to stop his car and catch the maddened dog; he threw it in his window and drove away with it; he told her that some drivers cheered. If the dog hadn't been in shock, he said, it would have killed them both. Later he cut from its infected, stinking jaws the rubber bands that muzzled it. The dog was starving, perishing of thirst.

Rambeau loves the dog; it has been so wickedly punished that it is for him infinitely innocent. Kitty's feelings for the dog are more ambivalent, since it hectors and accuses her. Sometimes she wonders, secretly and guiltily, what the dog may have done to earn itself such justice. For the most part she considers that, although it is no fun, it is a sacred dog and it is Rambeau's.

It is Kitty's policy to treat the dog at least as well as she treats herself. Lately, this is not perhaps so very well at all. But this morning she can offer it superior dog food as well as the leavings of her breakfast.

She has tried to feed herself up for the Darq ordeal, but she feels a bit sick in the mornings. This is not the same, she tells herself, as morning sickness.

She is cheerful in her dark neglected kitchen. Not because she feels at all cheerful but because she owes it to the dog.

The dog scuttles in, unusually alert and responsive.

"Oh, dog," Kitty says, bending to its plate, "have I got a bitch of a day."

Without a sound, the dog springs for her face. Its teeth knock hard against the bone above her eye. Pierced, her flesh drains blood. She's blinded, screaming. Blood splashes down her face as she drops to her hands and knees. Her heart is hammering, her ears ring with metallic noise.

The dog attacks again, its body thuds against her. Its teeth seem to lock in the scanty flesh beneath her eye; she feels the meeting of its teeth and their tug at her; she smells the dog's evil breath. She hears the dog panting, and then the dog releases her. Blood runs down her face like rain, like a spray of salt seawater. She is drenched with it, sodden. She has not seen it, blood like this, since the night she killed her father.

The dog has backed away. It is belly down. It is frisking. Frolicking and grinning, it flirts its stumpy tail. Kitty picks up an iron skillet. Kitty picks up a cleaver, a knife. She puts them down.

She presses a dish towel against her running wounds. Such a lot of blood. Oh, messy, Kitty thinks. Oh, head wounds.

She unrolls a quantity of paper towels and shoves the wad around with her foot, trying to dry the floor. She watches the dog. The dog is not contrite, the dog is simpering.

Kitty is not afraid of the dog. She fears the loss of her eye, but distantly; she is exhilarated, exalted. Really, she fears nothing. A message has been sent her.

The pain in her eyes is not dreadful; she is alternately frightened and not at all alarmed. She has a mad sense of destiny; her life has been moving toward this moment. Not this moment, not this inferior moment, but the moment after this one.

Kitty gathers her courage and eases the bloody towel from her eye. There is a short laceration, a zigzag tear above her right eye; an uglier wound below it, near the cheekbone. Her eyelid and lashes are disfigured by congealing blood; when she looks into the mirror her bloody eye looks back at her in a way that is horrible to see.

Kitty is so muddled and distressed that she cannot tell if she is blinded. Surely she is not. Perhaps she is. She feels light and gay with awfulness, with crisis. "I knew you all the time," she says to the demon dog. "You didn't fool me for a minute."

The dog now cowers and whines. Kitty cries.

Later, but not much later, she pads her eye with tampons rolled in a handkerchief and sticks the awkward dressing down with masking tape. Her wounds are hard to bandage, she is clumsy and hurried. She washes the blood from her breasts and neck, she cannot seem to get it from underneath her fingernails. She feels indelibly damp, ammoniac, bloody.

In the kitchen, the dog, as content, she thinks, as she has seen it, crouches on the floor, one paw steadying the half-empty can of dog food she let fall. It licks at the food in the can; it ignores the food she has put upon its plate.

Oddly, she is glad to see the dog eat with appetite.

Kitty

◆

Before my sister married Gordon, she told me she was doing it because, if she didn't do it, pretty soon she was going to wake up next to someone she had never seen before in her life.

I was sick when my sister told me that. But to tell you the entire truth, some secret part of me exulted. Because it would not happen to me, to Kitty. I hadn't met Rambeau yet, but I knew Rambeau was coming. He was coming, coming. He would keep me safe from harm.

I don't know exactly what happened at Darq's shoot, or afterward. By the time I had driven to the studio, I felt very awkward, very strange. My eye was hurting me a lot.

The shoot was probably no worse than other shoots I'd been on; no session with children and animals is likely to be smooth. But that day was the ugliest working experience I had ever had.

All the ordinary things went wrong. Nobody had checked the little boys to see if they loved dogs the way their mothers said they did; they didn't. Nobody had checked the dogs to see if the strobe would spook them; it did. The clothes I had carefully fitted and pressed wouldn't hang right. The model cast as the mother in the ad looked awful. Pregnant or hung over or coming down with something, she could hardly hold her head up. She hated the dress, the dog, the backup dog, and little sailor suit boy, the backup boy, Darq, me. The client and the agency clucked around, phoning their offices and complaining and eating up the food.

This was not the really bad part. The really bad part was that Darq made a dirty joke of me and the whole crowd played along.

I had told a stupid lie about my eye. I couldn't bring myself to blame the dog. I said I had splashed hot water on my face and burned my eyelid.

"See your hands!" Darq said like a flash. My hands were not burned. Darq was off and running then; he didn't like people to have secrets. He pretended to think that a lover had beaten me, beaten me because I liked that. His crew, the boys who worked there and the ones who just hung out, joined right in. The boys were not mean so much as saving their own skins, deflecting Darq's temper from them.

Darq's nasty joke was like a horrid schoolyard torment and I was like a child. Inside my head there was a picture of the dog, flat sharky head, red ears laid back, those fangs with the taste of me on them like meat. My head felt dry and empty like a gourd. Then it would fill and turn fleshy, surplus, like a tumor. Bright pain coursed to the roots of my teeth. Meanwhile people teased me about whips and chains.

The sailor suit boy was obstreperous; looking at the camera, sticking out his tongue, shying from the dog, he ruined every shot. Darq called the mother in and gave her his brand of ambiguous instruction. As always, Darq sent out cues that contradicted the sense of his words; that way, he was never wrong, he was more knowing than anyone.

"Reason with your child," he said to this nervous woman. He said it in a sly sort of way. "*Reason* with him."

She took the little boy by the wrist and hit him hard across the face. You could hear the crack when her hand connected. She had an obedient look about her. The child began to howl and so did I. The place was in an uproar.

The next thing I knew I was in the dressing room with one of Darq's boys, a good-looking boy who'd worked me over plenty in the whips-and-chains department. He had a big red capsule on the palm of his hand. I was crying.

"Care to split a tomato surprise?" he said.

I said I didn't want it.

"Little children suck on these at recess," he said. He was being nice to me. "Take it," he said. "You'll feel better."

I took it. He gave me a drink of water with it. He brought into the dressing room a potted orchid in a brown paper shopping bag and had me look at it. He even tried to fix up my eye. I don't know why I took the pill, perhaps because he spoke to me so kindly.

We broke for lunch. I had a drink at lunch. The little boy and his mother had gone, more children were being sent over. Darq was just hitting his stride. He said various awful things to me. They bothered me and then again they didn't. I felt distanced. Capable and wild and dreamy. When one of the other boys gave me another kind of pill, I smiled politely. I was greedy for the thing, I gulped it down. The whole long shimmering horrible day passed. I was eating food with some people, drinking. I was trying on hats. Then I was nowhere. Then I was in hell.

I thought I was sitting on the stairs with Eileen and our parents were pounding up and down the stairs between us, screaming.

Then I came to myself a little and realized I was hearing the metallic rush and screeching of a moving subway car. I was standing, swaying, in the aisle, holding on to a pole.

Across from me, holding on to the opposite side of the pole, was a man who looked like Mephistopheles. I was flooded with hopelessness and doom.

I had lost my scarf and my bandage. When I shifted my grip on the pole to raise my hand to my mutilated eye, my head swam. My eye was blind; crusted and pouchy. Darkness was beside me. To see at all I had to tilt and duck and bob my head around to aim my other eye.

The subway car was nearly deserted; just a few desolate-looking heaps that were people. It was foul, covered everywhere with excremental smears of graffiti.

The train would stop with a hissing *pssst, pssst* sound and the doors would open and then close. Nobody got on or off. I tried to make out the stations but all I could take in was broken bits of words and numbers. I saw HOSPITAL and COLLEGE. The numbers I took to represent years. I had the frightening idea that I was racing backwards in time to my childhood in Queens.

"Wake up, Kitty," Mephistopheles said. It was Darq. I recognized his leather pants first. Then I saw it was Darq, greasy and stubbly with beard. But Darq would never ride the subway. Darq ordered stretch limos and drove a Maserati. Still, he looked right underground.

I got distracted by my clothes. My shirt and skirt were damp and wrinkled but the coat I wore was dry. The coat disgusted me. It was a man's sport coat, very flash, with a garish stain, like a prop bloodstain, and dog hairs on it.

I had no memory of what had happened to me but I felt some terrible line had been crossed. I felt as I had the night my father died.

"Let me go," I said. I just wanted to be someplace he wasn't.

"Let you go? What do I want with you?"

The train was pulling into a station. He swatted me on the backside and disappeared through the doors.

When the train started I put my hand in the pocket of

the coat, which I didn't want to do. There were some coins there and some keys. I took the coins. I shucked off the coat and folded it and put it on a seat. I sat beside it for a minute. A derelict old man began to shout at me. I got off the train and up to the street. I blundered around until I finally found a phone that worked. I was somewhere near Fourteenth Street. I didn't know who I wanted to call until my fingers pushed the buttons. It was Gordon.

Kitty and Gordon

◆

"Is this a police matter?" Gordon asks as he somberly swabs clean Kitty's wound. "In my view this may be a police matter." He is rough and deft. He is rigid with distaste. He has examined her. Kitty has never felt his hands on her before.

"No, no," Kitty says weepily. "Don't be this way, Gordon. Be cozy. Be nice." At Gordon's command, she wears only a thin paper smock. It does not properly cover her. She fiddles with it, plucking and tugging and adjusting to no purpose. She is fat and messy and sniffling. Penniless, she is shamed.

Gordon is Olympian. He is taller, leaner, cleaner, calmer than she has ever seen him. To her painful, skewed vision, he is brilliant, new-minted. His thin fair hair is most severely combed; he is closely shaven and his breath is keen with cinnamon. Over his shirt and trousers he wears a stiff white coat. On its pocket is embroidered his name with DR in front of it.

This office, where Kitty has never been before, is full of serious-looking equipment. Even the examining table she sits upon feels important, untrifling. Sick people

87

come here, he is a doctor; he saves them or he lets them die.

"I'm sorry to take you away from your work," Kitty says respectfully. "On the other hand, this is your work, isn't it?"

"No," Gordon says. "It is not."

Kitty now wants her injuries to be serious enough to merit his attention, though not, of course, serious enough to be serious.

"I can't see, you know," Kitty says. "I mean I can sort of see out of one eye, but not out of the other." She longs to drop against his starchy bosom, his sober, unfamiliar tie. "I imagine you know which is which. I mean I realize you really are a doctor. Not that there was any responsible doubt."

"Oh, shut up, Kitty," Gordon says. "If you didn't wreck that car, where did you leave it?"

"Don't know," Kitty says. "Photo district, must have. In the twenties, near Darq's. Near a photographer's where I was working." She has told Gordon nothing, she intends to tell him nothing. He has assumed she has wrecked Rambeau's car.

"If anyone else has been hurt, Kitty," Gordon says, he is conspicuously delicate, "if anyone else has been hurt, this is certainly a police matter and things will go better for you, Kitty, if you report it right away. Do you understand me?"

"Sure," Kitty says.

"Do you take my meaning?" Gordon says. His mouth is prim.

"You want to know have the verges of the highways been strewn with bloody corpses," Kitty says. "Not by me they haven't."

Gordon sighs. He presses together the torn and smoldering edges of her flesh and fastens them down with butterfly-shaped dressings. He is hurting her in an impersonal but deliberate and vengeful way.

He has told her she needs sutures, he has told her she will scar, but Kitty has carried on, sobbing and sulking, refusing to go to the Emergency Room to be sewn up properly. She cannot believe he doesn't know her wounds are the bites of a dog; surely, a man allowed this table, these cabinets, all this white-enameled metal and mean shiny steel, knows everything. But perhaps a hematologist encounters few dog bites; or perhaps her dog bites are peculiar. At any rate, they're old dog bites now, and not at all improved by that. She is surprised that her instincts sent her to Gordon and, just for a flickering moment, quite pleased with both of them.

"Tetanus," Gordon says gloomily, and gives her an injection. "Penicillin," he says, and gives her another.

"Gordy," Kitty says, "I'm glad that Eileen married you."

"Kitty," Gordon says, "you're a dirty little whore."

Kitty is astonished. "Of course I'm not," she says.

Gordon washes his hands at the foot-pedal sink. "Some one of your lovers beat you up," he says, "knocked you around, beat your stupid face in. Some pinky ring wearer. I knew it the minute I looked at those lacerations. No dashboard did that."

"I need my clothes and some money," Kitty says.

He looks at her over his shoulder. "I'll give you your clothes and some money when I've shared my thoughts with you," he says. He walks out of the examining room into his adjoining office. "Come in here," he says, "I have something more to say to you."

Kitty sits on the table. She swings her feet. When Eileen and Gordon were courting, Eileen told her that Gordon had become a hematologist because of his feeling for children. All those dying children, he had said, bleeding children nobody could stand to watch die. Somebody, he had said, had to treat the dying children. She and Eileen had been very much taken with this idea of Gordon and the dying children.

Then at the wedding Gordon told her he had become a hematologist because diseased blood cells, under magnification, were beautiful. They looked, he said, like Kandinskys.

Kitty supposes there is no real contradiction, no paradox in this. Is there a poem in it? Probably not. Kitty is cold in her shredding paper wrapper. Why does she assume she is in custody, a prisoner deprived of clothes?

"Kitty," Gordon summons her.

He sits behind his large desk, in a noticeable, expensive, designed-looking swivel chair. His legs are spread out. He plays with a paperweight, a drug company giveaway which represents a greatly oversized pill. Kitty recognizes the pill, it is an antidepressant much favored by her colleagues. This pretend pill is bigger than a golf ball, flattened like a space ship. He passes it from hand to hand and frowns at his knees.

Kitty sits on the slippery lap of the leather patients' chair. She is unable to get up and go away.

She considers telling Gordon that Rambeau's dog has bitten her. It seems to her an adequate explanation for almost any horror. But perhaps that would make her injury a police matter. She certainly cannot have him tampering with the goddam dog.

"I need my clothes and some money, Gordon," Kitty says. He has paid the cab that brought her there, but she herself talked the cab driver into risking it.

"Shut up, Kitty," Gordon says, "I'm collecting my thoughts."

"I'm extraordinarily tired of being told to shut up," Kitty says. She attempts to collect her own thoughts, but it is very hard to do. However, the atmosphere of a doctor's office, even in this unfortunate instance where Gordon is the doctor, has a sniff of sanctuary.

A picture of Eileen is set on Gordon's desk. Moodily lighted, heavily retouched, Eileen's head appears to float in blackness, unsecured, unmoored. Not at all like her rounded pink and gold self.

When Kitty called the hospital and had Gordon paged, she pretended to be Eileen. Hectic as she was, she had done that. She thought it would make him take the call, and it had, and even when he spoke with her he had thought her his wife, their voices being so alike, and what he had said, his own voice like ice, was, "Now what?"

"Why were you so mean to me?" Kitty says. "On the phone before, when you thought I was Eileen, why were you so mean?"

"Habit," Gordon says. "Don't distract me. There are things I want to say. I want to say that it's no surprise to me that Jack Rambeau walked out on you. And you lost a good man there. A bit of a diamond in the rough, but a good chap, Jack Rambeau."

Kitty is less offended by rough diamond than by chap. "Rambeau is the best man I ever knew in my life," Kitty says.

Gordon looks miffed. "Be that as it may," he says. "You have disrupted my day, my working day," Gordon says. "You have interrupted my rounds. You have taken me away from sick patients. You have come here intoxicated and you have come here drugged."

"I came here bleeding from a crack in the face," Kitty says. "You patched me up. You're more or less my brother, or at least that's what I thought. Now lend me twenty dollars and give me back my clothes."

"Your life has glamour," Gordon says, "I don't deny that."

She sees that he believes her life has glamour, although she has never entertained this thought.

"Drugs," Gordon says. "Beautiful people. Tokes and toots. Alcohol. Sex." His longing is clear and silly. He is priggish and lascivious.

"Oh Gordon," Kitty says. "Not really. I had a bad cut,

my eye hurt. I was styling a print shoot, a regular mess. One of the boys gave me a painkiller, I don't know what it was. I wouldn't have taken it ordinarily, but I was hurting, my head hurt. And I was upset. And then another of the boys gave me another. And then some of us had drinks somewhere, somebody's studio, somebody's loft. I mean I'm lovelorn, Gordon, my heart is broken, it was just, you know, dinner and some drinks, I think."

Gordon casts up his eyes.

"Get Jack Rambeau back," Gordon says. "And marry him."

"I tried," Kitty says. "I tried at the shoot, after the pills, I called Local 802. I said I needed to trace a saxophone player named Jacques Rambeau. Or Beau Jacks."

"Beau Jacks," Gordon says, "is who, exactly?"

"Well, you know musicians," Kitty says. "I think he used that name. Sometimes. And I think he used another name too, Bo Jackson. You know, maybe he owed a few people money, or whatever."

Gordon groans. "I don't want this in the family," Gordon says. "Do you understand me?"

"No," Kitty says, "I must say I don't. Local 802 told me to hire a detective."

"Grand," Gordon says. He presses the paperweight to his forehead.

"Then I think I called the FBI," Kitty says. "I thought there was a whole thing about fingerprints and cabaret licenses, like you remember Billie Holiday? There isn't, not anymore. The FBI was barely civil, I was sore. After all."

"I met Eileen at a focus group," Gordon says. "They were researching attitudes toward OTC hemorrhoid ointments. They wanted proctologists. I was there by error. They paid me a hundred dollars. I didn't need a hundred dollars. I don't know why I gave up an evening to that but I did give up an evening to that and there was your sister, moderating. A lovely girl. I thought I'd like to have children that looked like that lovely girl. I took her out for meals. I took her to the ballet. She loves the ballet."

"That's all you know," Kitty says.

"She loves the ballet," Gordon says. "Concerts. Plays. Conversation. We were two rational people, interrelating in a rational way. Together we learned to decompensate. *Controlled* decompensation."

"Oh, shut up, Gordon," Kitty says. "That's not the way it was at all."

"The zoo," Gordon says.

"Stick it in your ear, Gordon," Kitty says. "That's not the way it was at all."

"I have no more time to waste," Gordon says. "Soon I have appointments. I have missed my rounds; there are sick people, dying people over there in the hospital and I am here, frittering away my time with you."

"Well, I'm dying," Kitty says, to console him, "you're dying."

"True," Gordon says. "But not as rapidly." He sits back and puts down his paperweight. "If you don't straighten out your life, Kitty, I am going to tell your mother."

He punches a button on a futuristic control panel that attaches to his phone. Kitty's voice fills the room—it is not Kitty's voice, it is Eileen's.

The voice, which says it calls from Bettendorf, Iowa, where it is staying at the Jumel Palace, threatens suicide.

Gordon slaps at buttons on the flat mysterious machine. Another voice, a younger, coarser one, says it is Drindy from Steamboat Springs and it is definitely, definitely pregnant. It says that Gore had better send money, it says his ass is in a sling, it recites an address in Atlantic City, it mentions a sexual trick that Gore enjoys.

Gordon slaps and punches at the answer box. Another voice is heard, a shaky woman's voice, it says her baby's mouth is full of ulcers, it says her baby's bleeding from the mouth and nose and ears.

Gordon hammers the flat of his hand hard against the box. The voices mix and babble, then they stop. Gordon is trembling. Kitty watches him; it seems to her he looks thrilled. He takes his wallet from his pocket and gives her twenty dollars.

He opens the sliding door of a closet. In it, on hangers, next to the official-looking white clean sweater of Gordon's office nurse, are Kitty's clothes, forlorn.

Kitty

◆

"Sweetie, where are you?" Eileen says, worn and competent, far away in Iowa. "Is Mick all right? Is Gordon all right?"

"Are you all right?" Kitty says. She is hanging on to a public telephone in a short row of stalls on a street near Gordon's hospital. All of these stalls, mounted on posts and looking somewhat like feeding devices, are occupied by distrait shouting women.

"I'm on my way out the door," Eileen says. At once Kitty sees her, silk-shirted, pearled; gilt hair, after thirty minutes' ardent attention, artless and perfect. (If you can't spend half an hour on your *hair* every morning, what sort of woman *are* you?" Eileen once said to Kitty in a fight. "Exactly," Gordon said. "Exactly.")

"Talk to me," Kitty says. "I went through a whole third-party billing thing here with this phone company, don't make it all for naught."

"But sweetie," Eileen says, "the facility is miles from the hotel and I can't be late."

"Talk to me," Kitty says. She thinks she hears the desperate Eileen of Gordon's phone call inside this cool one, but she is in a trance of exhaustion.

"I have a disposable diaper group in forty minutes," Eileen says. "We're getting such rich verbatims, Kitty, really these respondents are a pleasure." Her voice is warming, coming to. Eileen enjoys her job in market research. She believes it to be useful and interesting.

"They all have diaper-age children," Eileen says. "And they really love their little babies, you should hear them."

"Most people speak well of their little babies," Kitty says. "Try not to get carried away." Eileen's voice disturbs her, so sappy and zealous and rapturous and miserable.

"You've got to help me," Eileen says, talking very fast. "The clinic wants me to have intercourse first thing in the morning and go directly there the minute they open so they can check the motility of Gordon's sperm in my vaginal tract. Maybe I provide a hostile environment for Gordon's sperm. Of course Gordon won't cooperate, you know Gordon. I've begged and I've pleaded and I've yelled and even thrown things and he won't do it, he simply will not do it. I can't look those people at the clinic in the face. It's not very much to ask, I do plenty for him. I left him with gallons of chicken à la king, I left him with a big bowl of tuna fish salad. That's the kind of food he really likes. He's white bread and grape jelly, he's mayonnaise out of a jar. Don't let that raspberry vinegar and walnut oil fool you. I should have used wiles."

"Come and live with me."

"This is an issue we never addressed in that human sexuality forum. Naturally, something practical comes up and you find they haven't touched it, all they do is blather about lights and music and lotion. We have to discuss seductive techniques, Kitty. You must know more about sex than I do, you're single."

"Do you think it's because of our father?" Kitty says. "All this trouble we're having?"

"What trouble?" Eileen says, quickly cautious. "You have no sense of proportion, Kitty. This is not trouble we're having, this is just life we're having."

"I sincerely hope you are mistaken," Kitty says.

"I wouldn't run around saying the sort of thing you just said, Kitty. People might misunderstand."

"I think I should confess," Kitty says.

"Oh my God," Eileen says. "Are you crazy? You *are* crazy. No one will believe you but you'll make a whole lot of trouble. Why are you doing this to me when I'm in Iowa? I have trouble enough with sleepy ovaries."

"I may be pregnant," Kitty says, "by the way." When Gordon examined her, he remarked disparagingly upon her bulk, but he certainly did not suggest that she was pregnant. "I consider it a possibility."

"You are *not* pregnant," Eileen says. "Because you know that if you *were* pregnant, I would never forgive you."

"The family logic," Kitty says.

"It's just Rambeau," says Eileen. "He's making you crazy, Kitty, it's just love garbage. But you'll get over him, I promise."

"I have no intention," Kitty says, "of getting over him." She has said this before, but now it hits her with the force, the velocity of truth.

"Hang up, Kitty," Eileen says.

And Kitty does so. The telephone clanks and trills, then tidily excretes some coins, not hers, into the little hopper. Kitty has a sudden sense of luck. She drops the coins back into the telephone's slots; she calls her mother.

The ringing goes on and on. Kitty reviews in terror her catalog of catastrophe. Her mother has fallen, has fainted, has taken a fit, has had a stroke, an attack, a seizure, has been robbed and beaten; her mother is not dead, but wounded, helpless, frightened, hurting and alone.

Kitty knows she must go there, pregnant though she may be, one-eyed though she is, tired out and raggedy and looking like no mother's daughter.

Just as she, despairing, reaches out to put the phone back on its hook, her mother's voice darts from it.

"Hold your horses, can't you?" her mother says quite

amiably, "I was downstairs with the curtains at the washing machine. It's you, Kitty, isn't it, I knew it was you."

"Yes," Kitty says, pleased, "how did you know it was me?"

"The phone has a different ring to it, I'd know it anywhere, it's like the banshee's lonely wail."

"That's impossible," Kitty says. She is no longer pleased.

"I don't see that atall," Mick says. "Why is that, why do you say it's impossible?"

"Because it is, that's all, it's impossible, just take my word for something once."

"The trouble with you, Kitty, you're a smart aleck."

"I'm not going to listen to anything that comes after 'the trouble with you, Kitty.' "

"The trouble with you, Kitty, you're a know-all."

"Would you like to take down this number? Because I'm in a phone booth and I haven't any change and any minute now they'll cut us off."

"They'll no such a thing," her mother says firmly. "Why are you out at this hour of the morning and no money in your pocket and you in a dirty telephone booth that some dirty man passed his water in? And you with a perfectly good telephone at your own home with nothing at the end of it but a nasty, rude answering machine?".

"No dirty man passed anything in this phone booth, it's far too breezy."

"Why do you contradict each word I say?"

"I don't."

"You see there you did it again. Give me that number, do, though God knows I can't see a thing without my specs. And I haven't a pencil, I'll write it with my nail."

"Oh dear," Kitty says, squinting and straining, "I can't quite see it either. I forgot to tell you I did something to my eye."

"Your *eye*," Kitty's mother says, as Kitty knew she would. "How could you be so careless?"

"Maybe I should just call you later."

"Do then," her mother says. "For I haven't had sight or light of you for this long time and I'm worried. And I have a little tidbit I think will interest you."

"Okay, then," Kitty says; she feels no faintest interest, only deep fatigue. "Call you later."

"Jock Rambeau was here," says Mick.

The receiver slips from Kitty's hand and swings at the end of its cord, banging and thudding. Kitty rescues it. All her joints have gone liquid, great shudders travel up the backs of her legs and down the backs of her arms. She presses her head against the coin slots and closes one eye. She shouts the number at her mother, who shouts it back, incorrectly. They do this another time while Gordon's twenty-dollar bill, crushed in Kitty's palm, grows wetter. When Mick at last has the number right, they wait. Nothing happens.

Then Kitty says, "Thank God."

"I gave him a meal and a place to put his head," Mick says. "And I gave him no news and he gave me no news. I hope I did the right thing, Kitty."

"Where is he? He was with you last night? He slept there last night?"

"He slept in your bed in your room. He showed up on my doorstep with a stewing hen and he asked me to make him a chicken fricasee and I did and the two of us sat down and ate it. And he mended the float in the toilet tank that's been broken this long while. Then this morning he pulled down the curtains for me and he took his leave just as the telephone was ringing. And I said, 'That will be Kitty, I know her by the telephone's ring. It's like the banshee's lonely wail,' I said. 'It is,' he said. 'I'll be off, then,' he said. And off he went."

"Where did he go? What's his address? Where can I get hold of him?"

"He never said and I never asked."

"I suppose you warned him off me. I suppose you told him what a mess I am."

"He said, 'How is Kitty keeping?' I said, 'Much as usual.' "

"Oh my God," Kitty says.

"He says, 'How is the dog keeping, I hope it's not too much for her.' 'Not atall,' I says, 'it's a nice wee article and Kitty's very fond of it.' "

"Did he give you any message for me?"

"He said to get a lube job."

"Oh dear, oh dear, oh dear," says Kitty. "Whatever shall I do?"

And Kitty's mother, to Kitty's vast surprise, says, "Cheer up, why don't you, you sulky little chit? Show a little patience, show a little spunk. I'm ashamed to have you for my daughter."

Kitty is angry. "I showed a little spunk," she says. "I think it's been the ruin of my life. And much thanks I got for it."

"You did just what a child would do."

"I killed my father," Kitty whispers. "To save you from him." She has never before so spoken to her mother.

"It was me killed him," her mother says, panting. "To save you."

"No!" Kitty says.

"You don't like that," her mother says. "You heart scald, you. But that's the truth of it."

"No!"

"There's no saving of you, is there? You have my eyes sore looking at you, with your grizzling and your greeting and your carrying on."

"I killed my father," Kitty whispers.

"Oh so what about it. Many a one has done the same I'm sure."

"I am a murderess."

"Poo."

"Goodbye, mother."

"Just a moment there. Did you get his letter, Rambeau's letter? He wrote you a letter some time back."

"I never got a letter." Kitty's heart closes tight like a fist and springs open painfully. "A letter, are you sure?"

"Goodbye, Kitty," her mother says. The phone goes dead. Kitty puts the receiver up; the telephone does its digestive jangle, but no coins spill from it now.

When Kitty reaches at last the driveway of her little gate-house, Rambeau's car is parked there. Mr. Conrad, soundly sleeping, snores alertly at the wheel.

Quietly, Kitty slips into the car beside him. It is nice in there, leathery and calm, the curve of the seat an undemanding embrace.

Mr. Conrad's porkpie hat sits firm upon his sleeping head, blue and yellow feather brave and bonny. His speckled hand, brown and smooth as an egg, rests upon a small, old, open book. It is called *Colloquial Malay*. Mr. Conrad has been learning to say:

"Baby's frock was much smeared yesterday. Why don't you tie on his bib when he feeds?"

"My word! He is a fine baby."

"This evening you must take baby out in his mail-cart."

"Many babies get fever with teething and also thrush."

Mr. Conrad's enterprise seems sensible and pleasing to Kitty, and the contemplation of it fills her with peace. Perhaps the swelling of her wounds has diminished, for she seems to see quite clearly through the car's clean windows.

She sees that the dog is secured to the apple tree with a filament of kitchen string. The dog is snoozing poochily, one paw raised to mask its eyes. Something about those baleful eyes has always put Kitty in mind of her father. The set of the dog's thick shoulders has done so too. But many things put Kitty in mind of her father. The dog rests now beneath the apple tree and blown blossoms litter the ground all around it and lie like confetti upon its coat.

The trees have flowered and the blossoms blown and Kitty has not seen them.

She closes Mr. Conrad's book and puts it near his sleeping hand. She slides from the car and goes into the house.

Her blood has been cleaned from the kitchen floor. The floor has been washed and glistens with fresh wax. But she sees that blood, so hard to clean away, still freckles the white kitchen wall. She grew up in a small house dappled with blood stains. Her mother lives in it still.

In the living room, Mr. Conrad has made a bed for Kitty on the couch. He has removed from her linen closet for this purpose new flowered sheets.

The prospect of a bed on the couch in the daytime makes her feel like a convalescent child. She enjoys this. She knows too that her bed must be made on the couch, for Mr. Conrad, who makes free with her house keys, her car keys and her linen closet, who snoops and spies and trails her, would not step uninvited into her bedroom, even if her bedroom were empty.

On the couch is a white nightgown, virginal and new; she has never seen it. It lies there as though it covered a slender, invisible girl. Its waist is made small with pinched-in pleats, its skirt is spread prettily, and its sleeves, for it has sleeves, are so placed that the ghost-girl's hands might be folded on her breasts. Folded, Kitty, sees, on two envelopes.

The smaller contains a note in Mr. Conrad's steepled script. She reads no more than "Kitty dear, forgive me, but I am getting so in love with you." There is more, and the note is signed with Mr. Conrad's name, his real name, inscrutable and elegantly penned.

She knows at once that the other envelope contains the letter from Rambeau. She holds the envelope in both her hands and rubs it. It is gray and downy with wear. One of the corners has a little hole in it. There is nothing on the envelope, no address, no name. It is blank and unsealed.

Inside it is another envelope, this one addressed to her in Rambeau's handwriting. At the sight of Rambeau's writing, her heart quickens. This envelope is as soiled and worn as the other. She has a clear, wringing vision of its perils and its present safety.

She studies the envelope, a white, plain envelope. It seems to her extraordinary; singular and handsome. She presses it to her cheeks and to the cruel dog bites that burn near her eye. She opens her blouse and strokes the envelope over her neck and chest and breasts. She examines it. There is a stamp but neither postmark nor return address. She touches her tongue to the stamp's uncanceled face.

The envelope bulges, burgeons, with some sort of message from Rambeau. What he has to say may not please her, but his having anything at all to say must please her very much.

Kitty's breath comes easy, her mouth is moist with hope. Clear bright morning light sifts through her old lace curtains; it is dulcet, clean.

She feels the loosening, the giving way of the meshes and snares of old anguish. Perhaps her griefs and guilts are, after all, voluntary and ignoble, personal and implausible. Perhaps she has more courage than she knows.

She must, she thinks, be quiet. She must get the lay of this new land. She must be patient, be waiting. Like milk in a dish, like flour in a bowl. "I will be silent," Kitty thinks.

She holds Rambeau's letter in her teeth and strips off her clothes. She steps into Mr. Conrad's bridal nightdress and tucks Rambeau's letter into its demure and dainty bodice. She moves very carefully; she is a stranger to tranquility and fears to startle it away.

Kitty listens. She hears grace hovering above her flowery couch. She hears the aches fly out of her bones, the diligent blood run humming through her veins, the faint creak, the rustle, of the possibly quite ordinary letter at her living heart.

She prays to be done with wretchedness and desolation, subjugation and defeat.

She practices silence; she practices keeping her mouth shut.

Gordon and Dorinda

◆

"Have you been true to me, my child?" Gordon says to Dorinda. He is lying naked, drunk, on top of the spread of an enormous bed, one of two enormous beds in a motel room on Route 1 in New Jersey. The room is Spanish in intention, like the public rooms of several nursing homes he's seen. Its colors are a chalky cocoa pink and a ferocious grotto blue. He finds these colors seedy and sexy.

Gordon's long flanks shine with sweat. The month is June. He has been drinking from a pint bottle of gin. He hates gin and warm gin right from the bottle, a pint bottle, feeds his sense of depravity.

Just in case his mood changes, he has arranged on the night table a plastic bucket of ice from the machine in the hall and two glass tumblers still in sanitary wrappers. He has also brought along another bottle of gin, a small bottle of vermouth, a jar of pickled onions, a loaf of French bread, a round of cheese, a crock of pâté, a checkered tablecloth and napkins—but on second thought left all this stuff in the car. Dorinda likes butterscotch Krimpets and root beer. She sucks on a can of root beer now.

Gordon sorts through his feelings. Is he bored? Is he

having a good time? Surely he should know, one way or the other?

He has had a bad week. Four of his patients have died. One he had not expected to die and one he had not expected to die so soon. Patient deaths affront him. He avoids his patients once it is clear he can do no more to save them; neglects them, in a sense, though not in a sense he recognizes. He is brusque and tony with the next of kin.

The father of a little girl who died has called him a snot and a quack and a Jewish fairy and socked him. It wasn't much of a blow, but it caught Gordon off guard and sent him sprawling in the hospital corridor. He has bruised his coccyx and a blue stain smears his handsome temple. His behind hurts but the stain on his temple is becoming to him.

When the assault took place, it is his distinct impression that no one tried to subdue his attacker, that in fact a loose ring of nurses formed, silently egging the aggressor on. Gordon has a secret, shameful passion for nurses, their hideous crackling synthetic uniforms, their squeaking shoes. This passion is so secret and so shameful that he is barely civil to any nurse. He does not blame the man who hit him. He does not condone his action either. Violence, Gordon often says, settles nothing.

"Have you been true to me, my child?" Gordon says to Dorinda.

"You got some unit on you, you know that?" Dorinda says.

Gordon conquers his impulse to cover himself. He is delighted. He would like to hear more of this sort of talk. Specifically, he would like to hear it from Eileen. Eileen has said, however, that she finds it fatuous. That she considers it no more relevant—relevant—than praising the size and shape of his thumbs. Gordon has beautiful hands and no one has ever praised them. Gordon would like to hear his thumbs praised.

"Oh really?" he says to Dorinda. He is hoping to elicit further comment along the same lines.

"Yeah, really," Dorinda says.

Dorinda has had her heavy hair cut. It stands up, spiky, punky, black and dangerous, all over her head, except in front where bangs like a Shetland pony's hang down to her nose. There are feathers threaded through the lobes of her ears and small metal studs in curious shapes stuck through the cartilage. She is naked, Buddha-bellied, globular and pearly, juicy with hormones. She is scowling. She is Drindy, the mother of his child.

"Talk to me some more," Gordon says, he waves his gin bottle. He is drunk but playing drunker, smug with sexual achievement. He believes Dorinda is in thrall to him, his toy, he means to be very kind to her. "Praise my accoutrements, my equipment, my endowment."

"I'm having my nose pierced," Dorinda says. "You can get these weird, like you know, earrings that go in your nose. Like nose rings. Only not rings. You know? Weird? I love it."

"Drindy, sweetness," Gordon says, repulsed and delighted. "Is that wise? Is that prudent? A hole in your nose? Suppose you tire of it? Who's going to do the procedure? It sounds like a simple procedure but any number of things can go wrong. Your whole sweet little nosey might be eaten away by infection. I'm afraid I can't allow that, Drindy. Your father would agree."

Dorinda does her head loll and swoon. She protrudes her tongue and makes farting noises.

"Dorinda, don't misunderstand me, don't misinterpret what I'm going to say," Gordon says. "Have you been tested for neurological deficit?"

Dorinda bulges her eyes and crosses them. "I didn't know you were Jewish," she says in a deep cartoon voice.

Gordon realizes he has told Dorinda something of what happened at the hospital—the father knocking him down.

He hopes he has been careful to put himself in a good light.

"I'm not actually Jewish anymore," he says. "I had to be baptized to marry my wife. I didn't like being Jewish," Gordon is into a party piece now, an old one. "It was too vivid," he says, "too strenuous, too demanding. I had to put up with all those Jewish doctor jokes and Jewish mother jokes and chicken soup jokes. Unfortunately, Roman Catholicism is a bit lurid, a bit déclassé. But that's the only model she came in. My wife, I mean."

Dorinda is not listening, she is plucking at her painted toenails. Each nail is painted a different color, all of the colors equally ugly, and each nail is decorated with a paste-on motif, also ugly. Her belly is so round that he cannot imagine how she paints her own toenails, but perhaps her roommate, BoBo, known as "this person I stay with," does it for her. He has an image of BoBo, red-haired and bunny-eyed, the kind of plain, hopeless girl who needs an object of devotion. She looks after Dorinda, gets her to the OB/GYN that Gordon recommended, keeps her off, or mostly off, pills and weed and junk food.

"You don't want to hear about my conversion," Gordon says. "Well, too bad." He sighs, he is teary. "The interesting thing about my conversion," Gordon says, "is that my family thought it was a great idea and my wife's family was dead set against it."

He looks at Dorinda who frowns at her toes.

"Not interesting. Well, too bad. My parents think I'm a prig," he says.

He looks at Dorinda, who has told him he is the most sensual man she has ever seen. "Me. A prig. Prissy. My mother is dolled up and moisturized within an inch of her life. I hate that. I love a classic simplicity in women."

A classic simplicity and heavy white oxfords with red rubber soles, he thinks; is Dorinda ready for that yet, maybe not.

Dorinda yawns. "Is this the end of the action or what?"

she says. "Because if it is, I got to catch a bus to Atlantic City, don't forget."

"Drindy," he says, "I am telling you things." He is really quite drunk. He doesn't want her to leave. Neither does he want to touch her. He feels that he has touched her to the limit of possibility and after all the poor thing is pregnant.

"My little broody hen," he says. "My hatchery. My little incubator. Let's take a nap."

"I don't wanna take a nap," Dorinda whines. She wipes icing off the top of a cupcake and packs it carefully into his navel.

Gordon drinks some gin. "Broody," he says. "Bawdy. Booty. Beauty. Batty. Baddy. Body. Brought-e." He is pleased with the sounds he has made. "What do you do with the money I send you?"

"Spend it," Dorinda says, looking up at him in a way he finds threatening.

"Have you told your father yet?"

"Never mind about him," Dorinda says, busy with her tongue.

"Tell him not to worry," Gordon says. "Tell him I'll do the right thing."

Dorinda's father introduced them, in the hospitality suite of a pharmaceutical company, at a medical convention in Steamboat Springs. Gordon knows Dorinda's father slightly, and is impressed by his professional reputation.

That night, in Steamboat Springs, Dorinda, unbidden, came to Gordon's room. He had never before had a girl do that; in fact he was astonished as well as titillated and dismayed. He was sorry she was so fat, and worried because of her father; flattered, but flustered. She had memorized his name from his convention badge because he was the most sensual man she had ever seen. Gordon feels that his sex therapist has hinted at something along this line: his extravagant sensuality; there, perfectly apparent, but veiled, subtly hidden. He was distressed when Dorinda asked him for Quaaludes.

"Couple 'ludes to get off on and somebody to get off with," is what she says she wants. He gives Dorinda a good talking to. Dorinda rubs her body against him and he feels her big round bubs and her bum. He takes her to a Chinese restaurant. He has an enormous erection, stiff and curving like a tusk; it is painful, conspicuous, he cannot walk upright.

They eat soup. A large green leaf, seaweed, spinach, lodges itself in the fine white teeth he is so proud of. While he is working it loose, she tells him that what he is doing is the most sensual thing she has ever seen. He is enraptured. He feels that he has been, for the first time, *perceived*, made *visible*. They return to the hotel. Gordon has never before left a restaurant with his meal uneaten.

There follows such a night as he has only imagined. Even his earliest love with Eileen was faltering and impatient. The very thing that excited him, Eileen's politeness, her reserve, had made him indistinct in bed. This girl, the first he's bedded since his marriage, has come to him, sought him, drawn blindly by the power of his sexual allure. It is absurd, it is ridiculous, but it is true. This young, instinctual girl, the daughter, moreover, of a distinguished father, has scented him, like a plains animal scenting water. His virility delights and fulfills her; her joyous, sated shrieks tear through the night. He has had to say to her, on more than one occasion, "Must you make those horrible noises?" Her very coarseness is refreshing. He thinks it is refreshing, sometimes it annoys him.

She is healthy; she will free him, strip away Eileen-imposed inhibitions. She is outspoken, natural. Or she is a dirty little whore who knows the score. No, he declines to believe that. He knows human nature; he is a doctor.

Of course he knows she is sexually experienced, sexually active, as one says these days, but sexually awakened, well, he rather thinks not. When he discovers that he has impregnated her, he is not startled. Well, he is startled, but not deeply startled.

He feels fated, elemental; invincible necessity is taking shape. He *knows* he has made her pregnant, as he knows he has provoked her ardor, knows he has made her wail and flail and beg him to continue. He is so pleased with himself that he can hardly forbear to share it with Eileen.

"Let's *do* something," Dorinda whines, "now, let's do something different."

"There aren't that many different things to do," says Gordon kindly. He has absolutely no intention of doing one thing more, he feels she has had her quota. Really, she is cute, like a mongrel puppy. Like the mongrel puppy Eileen and he bought in the first week of their marriage. It was sick, sneezing, sticky-eyed, in a pet shop. They took it home and spent a fortune on it and fought about it constantly and finally gave it, cured, away.

Dorinda is a bargain, Gordon thinks, as mongrel puppies go, because half of her is purebred; after all, there's her father. The mother, well, he hasn't met the mother, but the woman—this is unscientific, but he holds to it, it is experience, observation—the mother doesn't count for much.

He has thoughts of cleaning Dorinda up, straightening her out, settling her down. Perhaps he will ditch Eileen, who abundantly deserves it, who bloody well deserves to lose him. Perhaps he will send Dorinda to nursing school and make of her a colleague and a helpmate and a lover who will appreciate, who will abet his rich investigation of his deeply carnal nature.

He looks at the rows of holes punched out along Dorinda's ear rims and wonders if plastic repair is feasible. Dear God, Dorinda, perhaps it will be simpler if she dies in childbirth. Dorinda is a tiresome puppy. Not *affectionate*, somehow. Restless and whimpery once through her tricks.

"Amniocentesis would be nice," Gordon says. "We'd know the gender."

"You dork," Dorinda says. "Pond scum. Retardo. Gimme a break. No way."

He does not press it yet. Amniocentesis. He would like to know the gender. "Ultrasound," he says merrily. "Noninvasive. Perfectly comfortable. When you're a little further on."

"No way," Dorinda says.

"We need to buy little clothes," Gordon says. "A layette, it's called. I saw them in Saks. They're gender-indicative. Pink, blue. You don't want our baby dressed in green and yellow, do you? I don't care for green and yellow."

"Gross," Dorinda says.

"Exactly."

"I'm just doing this for the experience," Dorinda says. "I'm not doing it for the kid. I'm selling the kid. You get good money for them."

Gordon sits up. "What the hell are you talking about? This is a child you're talking about, not a gerbil, not a litter of pups, this is my child."

"Make me an offer."

"*You cannot sell a baby.*"

"Yes I can."

Yes she can. Babies are sold every day; he knows this.

"I already had a lot of offers."

Gordon pulls on his shirt and trousers and goes out to the car for the other bottle of gin. He brings in the cheese and the pâté, the bread, the vermouth, the pickled onions and the checkered tablecloth as well. When he sees what he has done, he flings them around in a fit of temper.

For an hour he drinks gin and fights with Dorinda, often yelling at her. Once he tries to strike her, but she ducks. When he passes out, Dorinda eats a piece of cheese and makes a phone call.

"Hey, Irv," she says. It is Irving the drummer. "Hey, Irv," she says. "It's Drindy, Drindy from Atlantic City. You know what we talked about? You know what I'm saying? I just wondered if you're ready to deal?"

From Kitty's Confession

---◆---

My father died on my eleventh birthday. I was responsible for his death. I don't mean I left a roller skate where he could trip on it or breathed germs on him so he caught a fatal cold. I actually pushed him down a flight of stairs and killed him. I didn't push him, exactly, I hauled on his pants leg and he fell. (Sometimes it seems to have happened a few minutes ago and sometimes it seems not to have happened yet, or at all.) I don't know if I meant to kill him. (I couldn't have meant to do him any favor.) I think he had it coming, but of course opinions differ. (I'm not *sure* he had it coming, or anyway from me.)

Eileen had nothing to do with it and neither did my mother. Eileen's hand flashed out but I don't think she touched him. She may have tried to break his fall. We share a make-believe complicity. This is so as not to leave me all alone. And also, I suspect, because guilt, alas, is a little alluring. My mother is also innocent. If she is not entirely innocent, that is only because she sought to protect me.

I am not sure anything I have written on this page is true, entirely, exclusively true. Perhaps the bit about the pants leg.

Rambeau

◆

Rambeau takes Cherokee dancing. She snuggles up to him or caroms off him in ways that make him edgy, tense and silent, though he smiles. When they sit at the table, she holds his hands or places her palm on his thigh. Sometimes she licks his ear. On the whole, he would rather be dancing.

She calls him Pappy; he calls her Baby. Over and over again, she inquires if he loves her. Rambeau nods and grunts in reply.

In the checkroom, Rambeau has left paper bags containing a rolling pin, lollypops, fresh lemons and electric switches. The first three items he has purchased for Dorinda. They are part of a natural childbirth kit he has read about. Dorinda's confinement is months away but ever in his mind. The switches have to do with a repair job he is undertaking for his landlady, who now dithers her lashes at him and addresses him in fragments of French.

Under all these concerns, as he fends off Cherokee and nods and smiles, is a ground bass of worry about what Kitty has made of his letter. He had not meant to write any letter, certainly not that letter, the letter of an abandoned child, though also a declaration of a kind.

"Do you love me, Pappy?" Cherry says, mooching up to him, flinging her arms about his quailing neck, colliding with his wary hipbones.

"I love you, Baby," Rambeau says. He is tired, but he smiles.

From Kitty's Confession

◆

The night my father died, Eileen and I were on the stairs. We always hunched on the stairs when there was trouble. We were twelve and eleven, young, but we were tall girls, as tall as we would get to be, and we pressed against the sides of the stairs, Eileen against the wall, me against the spindles of the banister, trying to make ourselves smaller, keep ourselves out of the way; useless, as our parents ran up and down, up and down, close between us, screaming. My father had a terrible tool in his hand, a thing we called the chopper, an ax. All of us were barefoot. She, my mother, was trying to get away from him. There was nowhere she could go that he couldn't follow in that house where no door locked. The house shook, the staircase shifted with the weight of them and their running. Eileen and I pulled back, swayed back as they ran between us. We were almost courteous, the way we did it. Sometimes one of them grabbed at our heads or shoulders to help them in their climb or their descent. It was not at all like a comic strip or a sitcom, if that's what you're thinking. Their voices were hoarse with screaming. To see my mother scream like that was a closing down of the spirit, a glimpse of the end of the world. I shut my ears with my fingers, shut my eyes. My mother said something to me, shouted something at me, but I didn't see or hear her. She pulled down my hand as she passed me. She was angry. She wanted me to hear them, screaming.

Kitty

◆

Kitty sits in a window nook of her little house. She is watching Mr. Conrad negotiate with a roofer.

Mr. Conrad's July wardrobe is immoderately cheerful. He is wearing a Smurf tee shirt, a Pac-Man cap, little yellow running shorts and punked-out lavender shades. He owns a pair of pretty sandals, but he is not wearing those. On his feet are black polished dress shoes with very pointy toes, laced up over solemn socks with clocks. Kitty thinks this footgear is meant to convey to the roofer that Mr. Conrad is a rooted, serious person, conversant with gutters and downspouts.

Kitty herself wears a bright ruffled dress, a thrift shop dress chosen to please Mr. Conrad, who likes to see her in low necks, full skirts, small waists, and ruffles. Her ruffles are damp, since her house has become a dewy grotto with a spring erupting from one of its stone walls. (The dog drinks from the spring with pleasure.) Kitty has skidded on a mushroom, an actual mushroom, grown up between the chinks in her floor.

The roofer, a handsome man with appraising eyes and hair combed up in rills and terraces, has explained the

118

phenomenon. Heavy summer rains sheet off the steeply pointed roof, overshoot the gutters meant to carry them away, soak into the earth around the foundations and through them into the house itself.

"This place," the roofer said, disparaging the house, "it's only got up to the eye."

Kitty is annoyed with him. She is vain of her little house, its playfulness and oddity. She admits that it doesn't work very well as a house. Its closets, for example, are all in eaves, so they come to stingy points. Its bubbly window glass is pretty, but declines the light. Nevertheless, it is a charming house, the more so since its grounds have grown neglected. When Rambeau lived in it, he kept its gardens tidy, and Kitty teased him about suburban pride. Now sprawls of ivy grow across the crazy paving path and so do wands of blackberry. Though Kitty has taken up Rambeau's clippers once or twice, she cannot bear to clear the path. But she likes to feel her hand where Rambeau's hand has been, so sometimes she sits on the steps with blackberry suckers tangled in her hair, opening and closing his secateurs and thinking wryly of battlements of branches, moats of ivy and of thorns.

Now, in the window nook, she thinks of Rambeau's letter; it is some sort of declaration, but is it an earnest of love? She thinks of her mother, who has denied the central drama of their lives. She thinks of her father—but she cannot truly think of her father, her mind flares away from him. She sings to herself a little Irish song Rambeau used to sing to her in bed:

> Kitty me love will you marry me?
> Kitty me love will you so?
> Kitty me love will you marry me?
> Either say yes or say no!

She used to sing the answers, but she has forgotten them now.

Mr. Conrad has established himself as the man of the house, so far as the roofer is concerned. It is true that Mr. Conrad almost lives with Kitty, although he never sleeps in her house. Where he sleeps she is not certain; she suspects he is squatting at the empty mansion. Since he is not sure she would approve of this, and neither is she sure herself, they do not speak of it.

In any case, Mr. Conrad is a busy man, forever hurrying off on stern mysterious tasks. He has several jobs, but he is inexplicit; one of them has something to do with dogs, arranging buyers for exotic breeds, something like that. Very odd, because he fears Rambeau's dog. However he insists upon feeding it himself; he is protecting Kitty from another attack.

The dog is snarly but withdrawn; it has a deep cough, its breath creaks and rumbles. The dog will not be touched, it is impossible to catch it or to treat it. As Kitty grows quieter, the dog seems to make more noise. Mr. Conrad tries to lose the dog, leaving doors ajar, but the dog just mopes in the garden, pissing on the vegetables. When it gapes and yawns, its teeth shine in its blue wet jaws. Mr. Conrad feeds the dog by slowly lowering himself with its dishes, his aspect bland and unaccusing. A garbage can lid is held in front of him, gripped by its handle like a gladiator's shield.

"What you need," the roofer is saying to Mr. Conrad, "what you need is your K, what we call in this country your K gutters. Also new flashings. Also a new roof, I wouldn't lie to you. Also put on the new roof, gotta pull off the old roof, gotta cart it away, savvy? You are in for big bucks, amigo."

"Nonsense," Mr. Conrad says. "Twaddle," Mr. Conrad says. "Is not nice."

"Your funeral, amigo," the roofer says. He is stroking and weighing Kitty with his eyes; shepherdess flounces and white hair drying in geriatric ringlets. The wounds the dog has dealt her are healing now, pink and puckered around her eye. They look deliberate, like tribal scars.

"You wanna see me walk on that roof?" the roofer says seductively to Kitty, who wishes she had stayed indoors.

"No," Kitty says. His ladder rests against the house. The roof is very steep. The roofer has been up to peer and poke at it, but his feet have never left the ladder's rungs.

"You cannot walk on such a roof," Mr. Conrad says. "Those shoes you have been wearing are insupportable and you will fall."

The roofer is wearing white patent leather loafers. Surely roofers should wear roofer shoes with rubbery tentacle soles.

"I can walk on any roof in any shoes," the roofer says.

Mr. Conrad turns his flashing purple spectacles upon the roofer, so big and muscular underneath his decorated head. "You will fall," says Mr. Conrad.

"Hold the ladder steady, sweetheart," the roofer says to Kitty. No one has held the ladder before. As Kitty moves to hold it, the roofer leans close. "Tell me something, Snowy," the roofer says (he breathes on her, his sweet breath smells of spices), "what have you done with the other six dwarves?"

Kitty steps back from the ladder. The roofer shoots up the ladder, shoots up the shining slated slope, capers on the ridge.

"He will fall," says Mr. Conrad.

"*Fall!*" Kitty commands though not aloud.

The roofer at once does fall. His feet fly from beneath him, his legs stretch in the splits, his arms flail, *splat* he falls astride the roof ridge. His legs straddle, arms straddle, desperately his hands and feet scrabble for purchase along the shingled precipice.

"Very painful in the balls of the testicle," Mr. Conrad observes without passion. "Go into the house, so," he says to frightened Kitty. "And write in your little book."

Kitty watches Mr. Conrad. He coaxes, as he would a cat,

the roofer from the ridge of the roof. Together the men—
the roofer limping—load the ladder on the roofer's truck.
Then Mr. Conrad leaps lightly into the truck beside the
roofer and together they tootle off.

Kitty drops to the lawn because her legs will not support
her. Perspiration stands on her body. "Fall!" she hears in
her mind's voice. *"Fall!"*

When she can, she goes into the house and finds a notebook with a marbled cover. She has worked on some verses
in this notebook and she tears these pages out. She sits at
the dining room table with the notebook and a pen. She is
determined to write a plain account of her father's death.
The pen will not move on the paper. Her mind feels sore.
She feels exposed; alone and deeply self-conscious. The
events and emotions of her father's death, rehearsed and
avoided for so many years, entirely elude her now. She
writes:

> I would bid them live
> As roses might, in magic amber laid,
> Red overwrought with orange and all made
> One substance and one color
> Braving time.

Pound's lines offer a mysterious precept and comfort,
but she cannot connect them to her father's death. She
tears this page from the notebook, quickly tears it to small
pieces and then reproaches herself for the touch of stagi-
ness in such an act.

I AM DOING THIS FOR YOU, she writes on a clean page in
the notebook. She looks at the words for a long time. They
seem to mean something, but she can't decipher them.
WHAT WILL HAPPEN TO ME NOW? Kitty writes. She is unbear-
ably sleepy. She puts her head on the notebook. "What will
happen to me?" Kitty says. "What will happen to me now?"

When last she slept in this room she wore Mr. Conrad's bridal nightgown. When she woke, she found it delicately stained with watered blood; a stain like a blossom or a butterfly.

She began that day to bleed in earnest, a bleeding that wrapped her in an aromatic fog so that she hid herself, taboo. She read and reread Rambeau's letter. Her wounds were still raw. She had to read it with one eye. She bled and fasted for a week. Her phantom pregnancy bled right away from her. She wept for it, but not a lot.

Kitty is sleepy. She has worked hard all summer, dashing around at silly and demanding jobs. She hurries home to cook for Mr. Conrad; they speak with animation of, as Mr. Conrad puts it, "the rushing hour and whatever is."

When Kitty was a little girl, her mother put her down for naps, lying, as Kitty remembers it, almost always next to her, and saying in a soft lulling way, "Go you, now, put your head down and sleep."

Kitty rests her head on the notebook. "I am doing this for myself," she says, and is greatly relieved, and sleeps.

Dreams and Secrets

◆

Kitty dreams she's died and left two corpses. These ladies lie exhibited among her garden's roses and its squash. Near them, there behind the garage, is one hole. Near the hole is one box.

A crowd of handsome people, none of them known to her, mill and throng through her verdant garden, complaining of her. Outrage and the thrill of crisis animate these cheerful mourners. They stamp and shout. Kitty, who mingles with them, sees their point. It is awkward and showy to die in superfluity. Nevertheless she is irritated that no one seems to mind her double death.

She looks for her sister but cannot find her.

She looks for her mother but cannot find her.

Frantic, she looks for Mr. Conrad and for Gordon.

Frantic, she hunts for the dog.

She does not look for Rambeau but he is there beside her. He presses a shovel into her hands. He does not speak. She tries to give the shovel back to him. He will not take it.

Kitty buries the dead Kittys. It is hard but satisfying work. She is alone now. Before she is finished, the shovel bleeds her palms.

When she wakes the dream is so real to her that she looks inadvertently at her hands. Of course they are unmarked. She takes the rubber band off her poetry notebook and writes in it OVERKILL. She will write a poem about this dream.

She will take the poem to Mr. Conrad's summer workshop, which is held in the tiny apartment of a particularly impoverished and randy poet who likes Kitty.

Kitty will read her poem and the poet will kindly tell Kitty to bag it.

Mr. Conrad will read a poem, something from his *Mango Cycle*. Mr. Conrad's poem will be full of *eres*, *o'ers*, *ofts*, *yons*, *whiloms* and *I weens* and Mr. Conrad will be vibrating with pride and apprehension.

The poet will weakly compare Mr. Conrad's poem to the works of John Ashbery, Tennyson, the prophets of the Old Testament and Gary Trudeau. Mr. Conrad will glow and fumble and clutch his shoulder.

On the way home, on the subway to Grand Central Station, Kitty and Mr. Conrad will talk about line breaks. Neither of them has a good grip on the line break.

Eileen lies alone in a great big hotel bed in North Carolina. She has moderated a focus group on feminine hygiene deodorant sprays with contraceptive possibilities. She is pleased with her work and bone tired.

She has eaten a bad, elaborate, expense-account dinner with the agency and the client. Five people, three men, two women, have remarked upon her beauty and her grace and more than that number have praised her tact, her quickness and her concentrated skill.

She dreams of crinoline, bare sleek shoulders, flowers, columns, veneration. Gone, done with, riffled through, this dream is rapid, dumb, obligatory.

She dreams of her First Communion. The day, the dress, the veil, her father.

Her father, who looked in life like a Roman emperor, in her dream resembles Scott Fitzgerald. He admires her in her dress and veil. He holds a camera.

The dress is simple, elegant, it suits her. Her mother made it and to this very day, Eileen has never worn a dress she likes so well. The veil is frumpy. A mandatory, legislated veil, since impious competition has disfigured these occasions in the past. Eileen's mother has a tiny scarf of lace—"real" lace—she planned to sacrifice for Eileen's veil. (Wreath-and-veil, her mother calls it.) But Eileen wears instead the stiff net scrim, the elasticized mobcap trimmed with paper flowers. Pulled down to her eyes, it makes her squint and musses her self-cut, disobedient, becoming bangs.

The lace wreath-and-veil had made her look like a bride. She cannot envision anything to match in splendor the glorious, satiny refulgence of a bride. Eileen resents her mobcap veil. Eileen is seven years old.

Eileen's father, in her dream, smiles upon her, proud, approving. Eileen poses for him, blinded. (As in all her childhood snapshots, she is faced into the sun.)

Slowly, a look of horror takes possession of her father's smiling face. She is puzzled.

And then she feels it. Inching up, the hem of her skirt is inexorably rising. She stands revealed in new, white, lace-trimmed panties (not, of course, "real" lace).

Worse, she sees on her childish thigh a red silk garter with a woman's face. From it bobble ornaments like walnuts. These objects are shrunken heads. The numerous shrunken heads of laughing men.

Eileen wakes with a cry.

"Oh God," she says aloud, "did I cream my face?"

Of course she has creamed her face. She turns on the hideous lamp beside the bed. She takes up the hotel notepad and begins to make notes on the dream. Really, what's the point? She is embarrassed by her dreams, almost ashamed to relate them. Dr. Carp is numbed by her dreams.

"Mummuh," he will say, "this material isn't too difficult."

"Why do I go to all the trouble of having a dream if it's going to be in the public domain?"

"Mummuh," Dr. Carp will say. " 'Treasure the dream, whatever the terror.' Gilgamesh."

"I wasn't terrified," Eileen will say. "But why are my dreams the kind of dreams that any fool can unravel?"

Dr. Carp will send out beams of wounded vanity. She will think she hears him suppressing a yawn. He will stand up. "Mummuh," he will say. "This isn't new material."

Eileen does leg lifts. She does sit-ups, cheating, on the bed. She thinks of calling Kitty. One wonderful thing about Kitty, you can call her up in the middle of the night. Eileen gets out of bed and finds her purse and in it her fertility pills. She puts one in her mouth and spits it out again into her palm. Worse than never, never having even one baby would be, she thinks, throwing a litter of babies—six of them, or seven. The papers have been full of just such cases. She drops the pill bottle into the wastebasket. The spat-out pill adheres to her palm. She looks at it awhile, then lifts it with her tongue and swallows it. She takes the pill bottle out of the wastebasket and gets back into bed.

If Gordon were here she would tell him her dream but she would edit it. She would tell him that each of the wizened little heads was his fine handsome priestly blond one. He would incline toward her, all absolution, delighted to disrupt her life with sexual remorse. Gordon! Eileen! How happy each could be without the other. Possibly. Possibly not.

Eileen gets out of bed and kneels beside it. She prays for her baby. She feels that this baby exists somewhere. It is a particular baby, a specific baby, and she is trying to get pregnant with it. She is impatient with this baby, angry

with this baby. She prays until she feels on better terms
with it. Finally, she subsides into sleep.

Gordon dreams he is crowned Miss Mexico. He wears a
gown of cloth of gold. He is not a woman; he is himself. He
is conscious of how well he looks. His hair is fuller, shimmering and fair. His profile is eloquent. His eyes are beautiful. Gray, metallic, judging, strange, these eyes have
caused him shame and pleasure. His eyes, Gordon knows
in his dream, are the color of tears and he has won a prize
for them.

He receives his crown. The hall is hushed. He will say
something important. He will announce his cure for a malady the name and nature of which escape him. He raises
his arm. His arms are beautiful, thatched with fine hair.
His shoulders slope touchingly. His gown is cut low to show
the cove between his speckled, faintly lavender pectorals.
He is the Pope of Mexico.

Tiny children, almost recognized, cluster all about him.
Suddenly they stamp their tiny feet and mud spatters soil
him. Mud drizzles down, spoiling his pretty dress.

He sees a professional journal in his dream.

Blood it is called. He has published many papers in this
journal. His photograph is on the cover. He is wearing high
combs in his golden hair, he is wearing his soiled golden
gown.

Gordon stirs. He wakes weeping. "Mexico," he says.

On Gordon's first trip to Mexico, seven years ago, he was
eaten by trouble. He had met Eileen and was obsessed by
her. He heard her voice in other voices. She was lovely.
She was tasteful. She had either no opinions or ones he
could support. She was devout, but not, he thought, in an
unwieldy way. Her family appalled him, but he clouded
that, even in his mind, with references to ambience and
color. She was impressed by him, he knew; she shared with
him the view that he was a superior marital catch. But she

declined to catch him. She would not sleep with him nor
marry him nor even let him touch her very much. Sometimes she seemed repelled by him. And yet he represented,
she admitted, everything she wanted in a husband.

He decided that her scruples were religious and neurotic.
He knew that she had been a nun and the idea of her
nunnishness entranced him even as it caused a dull alarm.
He thought she would marry him if he became a Catholic,
although she denied that this was true. It was a pointless
debate, since he found Catholics smug and sacerdotal and
had no intention at all of ever becoming a Catholic.

He was in a sort of religious crisis of his own, sprung
from his practice of medicine; a practice he then thought
to leave. Medicine was driving him mad. He was an excellent doctor, he was sure of that, he was careful to do all
that could be done. And yet his patients suffered, some of
them deplorably, and died. This suffering and death was
an affront to him. Filled with a deeply personal rage, ran-
corous, he bent above the beds of the dying. Sometimes he
detested them, their sick and squandered cells, their disin-
clination to oblige him by surviving, the lie they gave voice
to that his was the power, that he was in command.

He quarrelled with his parents on the ground that they
had never had him bar mitzvahed. This complaint astonished his parents, second-generation Ethical Culturists, as
much as it astonished him. Dressed, as a child, in the Gordon tartan, he regards all Jews as odd and oriental and
regards himself as an approximate Scot. Nevertheless, he
demanded an accounting. His father urged him to get married; his mother spoke up glowingly on behalf of shiatsu
massage.

Gordon began to read the religious ads in the *New York
Times*. He attended lectures at Carnegie Hall, read tracts,
took notes, bought tapes of sermons and played them in
his car. None of these undertakings helped him. He became abrupt and tetchy with his patients and his col-

leagues. His reputation as a good clinician soared. He began to tithe. He took a tenth of his earnings and sent this off to radio ministries, crank television healers, failed suicides whose photographs were published in the *Post*. He neither hid these acts nor showed them off; they did not ease his mind at all.

He began to suffer a second torment: sexual fantasy of the crudest and most brutal sort assailed him. He saw sexual symbols everywhere and no speech to him was free of sexual allusion. His nightmares were garish. He ran miles every morning and miles every night. In the middle of the day he locked himself in empty offices and dialed the numbers of telephone hookers: Fone Sex, 24 Hrs., Major Credit Cards. He lost weight. His priestly air intensified. He could hardly bear to be in Eileen's company. They met at restaurants, since her mother had forbidden him the house. He was grateful when his beeper let him flee from her. Eileen, of course, commenced to fall in love with him.

Gordon weeps. He wants his wife. "Eileen, Eileen," he says into his pillow, "why have you forsaken me?" He has offered Dorinda seven thousand dollars for his baby. Dorinda is taking sealed bids. It occurs to him that the child Dorinda carries may not, in fact, be his. Nevertheless, hot tears wet his cheeks and he wipes them away with his palms.

Rambeau dreams of Dorinda. He dreams he is blowing into a nozzle, like a mouthpiece or a reed, a rimmed and august opening in the crown of awful Dorinda's head. Blow. Blow. Blow against resistance, as into an oboe or a needled egg.

Finally extruded is an infant, fully clothed. He cannot see its face or know its sex; but it is present, safe, entire, his.

Rambeau wakes because his pinkie hurts him. In a fit of temper, Cherokee has bitten him at the base of a nail. He

regrets not having walloped Cherokee. He reflects on op-
portunities missed for walloping Cherokee. He turns his
head to study Dorinda, sprawled beside him in the moonlight. Dorinda has bitten him too, on the shoulder. She has
also clawed his back. A corn is leaping on his toe. The
unmarked petal whiteness, petal thickness, of Dorinda's
skin, the gleaming blackness of her ruffled feathers hair,
the exceptional redness of her mouth and intimate parts,
convey to him a sense of accidental lewdness more powerful and disturbing than anything Dorinda could do or say.
Her breasts are majestic. They seem to swell as he looks at
them, each of them nearly the size of his head, chocolate-
colored nipples cocked like thumbs. He rises on his elbows;
hovers over Dorinda. In a moment, he lies down. Dorinda
does not snore, exactly, but chuffs and chunters in her
sleep. It is the only specifically childlike thing about her.
He thinks of easing out of the bed and working awhile on a
letter he is writing to Kitty. He thinks he would perhaps
like to write her a "love" letter, but he does not know quite
how to go about it. He is pining for Kitty, but her absence
is a positive relief to him. This predicament of feeling does
not boil down to a love letter so far as he can see. He is
afraid to leave the bed; to do so may rouse Dorinda.

Mick dreams of an item she read in the *New York Daily
News*.
A woman, a foreigner of course, has thrust her youngest
in a plastic bag and thrown it down an airshaft. And her
oldest girls, two of them, she's hidden in a closet back
behind the garment bags, all amongst, half-stifled from, the
crystals of poison that snuff out moths and silverfish. And
she did it, she says, because of the demon, the demon
being after them. The demon is wanting to eat them, *eat*
them, who could believe such a thing? And when they are
rescued, the poor dear children, frightened right out of
their wits to be sure—when they are rescued, poor dear

children, they are covered with the bites of their mother's
mouth. The bites of their mad mother's mouth. Deranged,
she was.

Mick dreams of her daughters covered with bites, the
bites of her bitter mouth. These bites take the form of
vulgar kisses, lipstick kisses such as Mick has seen only
once and years ago on the wall of a ladies' toilet in R. H.
Macy's department store. Her last outing, when the world
seemed to fall away from her and leave her alone with her
juddering heart. She has never again chanced a journey
out into that chaos. And she has let no one know she is
housebound.

Mick writes a letter on coarse ruled paper. This paper
helps her lines stay straight. She writes to the Maryknoll
missioners. She says she would like to work in Peru. Take
up her bed and follow them, follow them to Peru. Get shot
for her trouble in Peru, where the women wear the derbies.

She encloses money, it's not her money, as she takes
some trouble to explain; it's her daughters' money, who
would be better served to spend their money on dancing
dresses, the like of which she could never have obtained
for them, beg, borrow, or steal; or furthering, if such a
thing is possible, furthering their already greatly furthered
educations. Much luck it brought them.

Mick writes these letters, worries about the grammar and
the spelling, looks up every other word in the dictionary,
the numerous dictionaries, her girls have brought her,
looks over all her self-help books with pleasure and for
inspiration.

Kitty taught her long division, how to write a check,
Greek myths. They are both of them good girls, though
heart scalds, Eileen and Kitty, and the way she treated
them they could never claim she showed them one hand
longer than the other. Eileen is better-looking but Kitty is
her favorite, Lord have mercy on us. I'll not tell you an
untruth. Kitty, full of trouble as an egg is full of meat, is
her favorite. I'll not tell you the word of a lie.

Mr. Conrad, nestled on a good feather pillow in a cheap thin sleeping bag, dreams in the big, deserted mansion. Votive candles burn about his bed. He has a big and costly flashlamp but he husbands it. Mr. Conrad dreams of Kitty. A plain, sexy dream dense with pleasure.

Then, in his dream, sorrowfully, he notices that he is fully clothed. He inspects himself. He lacks his genital bulge. Yet he pleasures Kitty and she him; they do not touch. Their union glides and soars. He notices that Kitty, nude, cherishes beneath her arm a pretty mole, like a little sugar candy. He teases her. He tells her she's a witch, the mole her supernumerary nipple. The tit, he says, at which she suckles her familiar. She laughs and flings her naked arm about him. His head ducks down, he tickles with his lip her mole, he diddles with his tongue, he sucks, he wakes.

Mr. Conrad yawns. He has an engagement to meet with Dorinda, very early, in a video games arcade in a shopping plaza in New Jersey. It is not their first meeting. Nor yet their last, thinks Mr. Conrad, digging into his tulip-covered suitcase, dabbing himself with Listerine, spritzing his armpits, powdering his crotch, eating a granola bar and drinking sour milk. Nor yet the last.

*F*rom Kitty's Confession

———————◆———————

"I am the master of the home," my father screamed the night he died. The paper parasols on my birthday cake had burst into flames before that. I was two days into my first menstrual period. My sister and my mother and I had spent the afternoon breaking up the concrete path to the house. He had promised her he'd make a crazy paving path instead, I don't know why she wanted one. We had used the wrong tool, the chopper, we had used his sacred ax.

Rambeau

◆

Dorinda disregards her pregnancy. She seems to have lost interest in it. She looks healthy, even blooming, and once in a while she perks up conspicuously, alert to some message from her womb. At these times Rambeau is pleased with her and reminded of a children's story.

"Did you ever read a book called *Horton Hears a Who?*" Rambeau asks her. "When you were a little girl?" The prospect of Dorinda having been a little girl is odd and entertaining.

"Yeah, I think so," she says. "My father read me it."

"I read it to a little girl," Rambeau says. He feels closer to Dorinda because they have read the same book.

"Weird," Dorinda says. "What're you, some kind of pervert? You get off on that?" She tugs on her gilded Fiorucci boots.

"Don't wear those hooker shoes," Rambeau says. "You'll fall and hurt the baby."

"Chill out," Dorinda says. "What're you, on something? I'm not gonna *fall*."

She snubs her pregnancy. She does not fall. She is never the least bit unwell.

Rambeau, on the other hand, is unwell all the time. He has gastric troubles, heartburn, nausea. He is sickened by once-loved kitchen smells. He buys books about pregnancy and these are useful; soda crackers help him. He eats two soda crackers the minute he awakens, before he tries to raise his reeling head. He no longer drinks alcohol. He knows this is, obscurely, because he feels alcohol would be bad for the baby. He is always sleepy. He is touchy, tense. Tears often spring to his eyes.

He thinks of poor skinny, rackety Kitty. He thinks of her all the time. Sometimes he seems to glimpse her in the crowds disgorged by the thronging buses. He almost hears her voice. Once he was sure he saw Mr. Conrad. He tried to follow the brightly dressed small man. He was unsuccessful and unreasonably distressed.

When he can no longer help himself, he dials Kitty's number. Not her number, really, but various combinations of the digits that make up her number. For unknown reasons, this affords him some relief, although his face burns as he begs each answering stranger's pardon.

He does other things with Kitty's numbers: the number of her telephone, the number on her mailbox, the digits that represent her birthdate, his guess at the measure of her waist and hips and breasts. He shuffles and combines these numbers according to various systems and places bets on them at the crap tables and even the roulette wheels. And he wins. He is on a winning streak and deeply mistrusts it. He has been through this before. Luck without elation. He feels that he must watch his step, that dangerous airs rise from the ground before him. Still, he cannot stop it, winning, betting Kitty's numbers.

Dorinda sleeps in the bed with him, but she doesn't sleep much or often. Sometimes she is gone overnight, once gone for three days, once for four. Sometimes she drives off in Kitty's old Rabbit, sometimes she rides the bus. She trundles speedily along behind her great globe of belly, unperturbed. Her breasts jut, heroic. Once in a while she wanders by the lounge where Rambeau plays in the evenings, but he has tried to discourage her from doing this. Her presence distresses Irving, the drummer. Rambeau can see that it might, since Dorinda draws a bead on Irving and sprays him with sexual death rays.

Irving is whey-faced anyhow these days, worried, possibly, about one of his children. He and Rambeau hardly speak—just once he borrowed some Rolaids. Busy with his winning streak, his morning sickness, Kitty, Cherokee, Dorinda, Rambeau isn't much for conversation.

Rambeau does talk a little to his landlady. He tries to talk to her about babies; she tries to talk to him about sex. She has a crush on him. She can't abide Dorinda, but she does abide her, pleasantly. Dorinda is the shell she eats to get the nut, Rambeau.

Sweet Rambeau, he's not the man he once was. A phantom baby dangles in his entrails, head down, heavy, swinging from the trapeze of his guts.

He shows the landlady his list: 3–6 shirts, side-gripper or side-tie; 2–4 kimonos; 4–6 nightgowns; 3–4 sacques; 1 pair of bootees; sweater; bonnet; 4–6 receiving blankets; diapers —cloth or disposable? He tries to engage his landlady in a discussion of diapers. Cloth or disposable? She lays her hand on his red-haired arm. "My husband's been dead seven years."

"Yes," Rambeau says. He wants her to talk of kimonos, to describe a sacque, to debate the merits of side-gripper versus side-tied shirts.

"My daughter thinks I'm a nitwit," his landlady says. "Because I'm interested in dried materials. My daughter the Princeton man. She was a nice little kid, but now she knows it all. High-forceps delivery. Two days of labor. I nearly hollered the place down."

"Yes," Rambeau says, his interest quickens.

She describes her delivery, what she felt. Each blade of the forceps, her pain, the light.

He thinks of Dorinda; no one, he thinks, has told her about pain and light.

Dorinda has been quickly bored by the *bonhomie* of her obstetrician. They go now, when he can make her go, to a birthing center, staffed by midwives. They have seen the birthing chair. It reminds Rambeau of the rude machine used in even darker times to dunk witches. What Dorinda is reminded of he does not know. She rolls her eyes, lolls her head, lets her tongue flop out of her mouth, but seems not greatly moved.

"Are you interested in dried materials?" Rambeau's landlady says to Rambeau. Her house is full of seed pods, empty ones, and sheaves of lacy, crisp dead weeds. She finds some brandy and they drink it. "The marshes around here really excel," she says. "Really excel in dried materials. In autumn of course. When's she due?"

"October," Rambeau says, "Halloween."

"Halloween, pardon me. Halloween. These young ones know it all. They think they know it all." She puts her hand on the back of Rambeau's neck and kisses him drily. "You'd better go now," she says, heavy-lidded like an old-time movie siren, breathing on him nice Christmasy fumes of brandy. Rambeau is greatly taken with her. He puts his arms around her, she pulls back. "I'm a respectable widow," she says.

"I couldn't help myself," Rambeau says. He laughs. He means it. He feels wonderful. It doesn't last. Soon he feels thick and sick again, woebegone and unattractive. His ankles are puffy. He has low back pain. He seems to be short of breath. In bed at night he punches pillows, he just can't seem to get comfortable.

In bed at night—it is not night, really, it is early in the morning—he writes in his head to Kitty. To distract himself. Or for other reasons. The only pregnancy he's had to do with before this one was his wife's. Everything about that pregnancy fills him with remembered horror and when his mind drifts toward it, he wrests his mind away.

'Dear Kitty,' he writes in his mind. 'There's something I want to tell you. Hush now, listen.' He's not sure just what comes after that.

Dorinda, through whose navel he addresses the baby that is his by some deep sense of structure, stronger than biology, disorder or misrule, sits down on the edge of the bed. Her great weight makes the mattress sink and rolls him toward her. Her lap, what's left of it, is full of bills and coins. It is dawn.

"What mess have you been up to?" Rambeau says. He feels like cuffing her.

"Dinging," she says, already bored.

"Dinging?"

"Dinging," she says impatiently and louder. "Like, you know, begging, what an experience." She barks with laughter; she is not amused. She springs to her feet and spills the money from her lap into the wastebasket.

"You can't throw that money away," he says.

"I just did," she says. "You just saw me." She extracts a Nikon camera from her big brash shoulder bag and begins to take it apart.

"You asked for it and strangers gave it to you because they thought you needed it."

"Well I don't need it," Dorinda says, "so that was their mistake." She is trying to break the pieces of the camera with her hands. "Don't talk to me, I'm hostile. When I'm positively orientated toward you, you don't even talk to me and when I'm hostile, you do. You're weird, you know that?" She puts the lens of the camera on the floor and hammers at it with the heel of her boot until it cracks.

"Why?" Rambeau says.

"To see what it feels like," Dorinda says. "Mellow out."

She dismantles and destroys the camera. Her hands are very strong.

"What did it feel like?"

"O *Gawd*," Dorinda says. "I wish I never put the moves on you. It felt like nothing. It's only acting out."

Rambeau thinks about Cherokee, who has quit her waitressing job to become a dance therapist. Cherokee has had, in the past, to be dissuaded from becoming a brain surgeon and a Catholic priest, but perhaps she really will become a dance therapist. On the other hand, probably not. Cherokee is about Dorinda's age. She wants him to take an apartment so they can live together. Cherokee has the goods on him in a way no other woman can.

His life's perplexities and perturbations have exaggerated Rambeau's heartburn. He tells Dorinda to fetch him the soda crackers from under *American Baby*.

When Dorinda is elsewhere, Rambeau gathers up her loot. She has stolen class notes from students at Princeton and Rutgers; she has picked up wallets, keys and cameras, bits of jewelry, some of of it, he thinks, expensive. She has pocketed small toys, not necessarily new ones; swiped candy bars, wands of plum-colored mascara, tins of aspirin, somebody's stash of cocaine, instant noodles. He finds worn watercolor brushes and half-used bottles of Dr. Martin's Dye; a stethoscope; a lock of hair folded in cellophane; what looks to be a baby tooth, or perhaps the tooth of a dog.

Rambeau is constrained to get rid of this stuff. He tries to find a church with a poor box. All of the churches he finds are locked. Atlantic City, beyond the glitz of the casino hotels, is wretched, beaten down and worn out, full of wreckage, full of need. Surely someone wants this magpie trash that he can neither keep nor throw away.

For a day or two he wanders in desolate neighborhoods. He slips a pin seal wallet and a signet ring onto a windowsill;

he walks very rapidly away. A woman in engineer's overalls runs after him and presses the wallet and ring into his hands. She is ferocious. He is scared of her.

He puts some stuff in a paper bag and leaves it on a bench on the boardwalk. He does this when he finishes his work; it is late; he feels furtive and guilty. The next day the bag is still on the bench. The area around the bench feels suspect and avoided.

He leaves a pile of Dorinda's beggar money behind him in a coffee shop. It is not such a lot of money, just a very generous tip. The waitress chases him down the street with the money in her fists. "Your change, sir," she says desperately, "here take it, take this money. It's your change." The money is cold and wet.

He slips some of Dorinda's quarters into a slot machine. The machine pays off, as he knew it would.

Morose, he goes to Mass. He can't seem to follow the drill. He loses his place in the little leaflet and finds the sermon confusing. He awaits the collection. The ushers dodge him; they wave their willow baskets out of reach. It is like no collection he remembers. After Mass he approaches the brass banks of votive candles. He stuffs the coin slots full of Dorinda's beggar money and the money he has won with it. He tries to light a candle, but the candle goes out. He walks in and out of convenience stores dropping money into pickle jars for charities. Finally he has exhausted himself and the cash. He bundles the rest of the junk together and goes off to see Kitty's mother. He will bury the stuff in her yard if she will let him.

Mick and Rambeau have a nice conversation about babies. Why it is nice he cannot say, because Mick is suspicious of babies, which turn out badly, like most things, given half a chance.

She has seen a baby born that walked on all fours from the hour of birth and didn't it bay like a hound?

She has seen a baby that spent thirty years in its carriage in the parlor, never growing, never dwindling, keeping itself to itself, an infant, thirty years, with a little wag of a tail.

She has seen a baby born with two faces, one of them on the back of its head underneath its abundant hair.

She has seen a baby born with a birthmark like the devil's pitchfork and that baby pinched you, pinched you hard and bit its mother's diddy till her blood ran out of her.

Every time Mick passes him, she puts her hand on his head or his shoulder. Women like to touch him and he likes to feel their hands.

"You've failed, Jock," Kitty's mother says. "You were a fine man once. You were the like of my husband. A big man, the full of the door."

Rambeau says he hasn't been feeling well. She says she is not tip-top herself. They talk about their symptoms and both feel better.

He drinks a cup of tea and she reads his tea leaves. She has, they both know it, no gift for this. She usually sees a flying bird, or a flock of flying birds, at last. But first she quarrels with the leaves and says there's neither shape nor make to them and the whole thing is foolish nonsense.

Rambeau often visits Mick, although the trip from Atlantic City to Queens is a long one. She cannot leave her house and yard. He knows this but her daughters don't seem to. She pretends to them that she ventures here and there, nowhere much or far. Actually she never leaves her house except to go into her garden.

Rambeau executes small commissions for her; so does Mr. Conrad. Gordon comes to see her on the sly.

Today there is in Rambeau's cup a dog. Or if you tilt the cup, a devil. No, a dog. No, a flying bird. No, see, a dog. Like poor Kitty's.

"She'll be all right," Rambeau says. He finds it hard to

say Kitty's name. "That dog is no fool. That's why I left the dog, keep an eye on her."

"Our Kitty has gone into a decline," Mick says. "Sits around smiling and not a word out of her. Our Kitty whose tongue would cleave stone. She'd give you the jaundice."

Rambeau puts his shameful bundle on the table. It is foolish to ask this woman if he can bury some stolen property in her yard. On the other hand she's a born conspirator. "Just don't ask me anything," he says. "It's just stuff. It's not anything." His voice and purpose fade.

She tears away the paper and the fugitive objects are bared. She touches each of them. At once they seem to Rambeau commonplace.

"Sure I'll put them in a box for you and the box on the shelf in the closet," she says. "At the back."

"You don't have to keep them in the house," Rambeau says. "I thought I'd just . . ." He is unable to say "bury them in the yard," it is too lunatic.

"They'll do rightly," Mick says. "Don't worry yourself unduly."

When he leaves, though, she examines the objects with interest.

She fetches from the kitchen sink, where she keeps it, a plastic bottle shaped and colored like a statuette of the Blessed Virgin. The crown of this figure unscrews. Quite the ugliest thing Mick has seen, it is a present from her son-in-law, Gordon. It is full of Lourdes water.

She pours some holy water into her palm and dips the fingers of her other hand into it. Her wet fingers spit holy water at the objects on the table. It is just the motion she uses to sprinkle her laundry when she dampens it for ironing. She screws the crown onto the bottle again and puts it back on the sink besides her bottle of dishwashing detergent.

She comes back to the objects and selects from them the stethoscope. It is Gordon's. She knows it is Gordon's because her foolish daughter Eileen has bought it for him and had engraved for it a silver tag which pretends to be Gordon's monogram but is really a swirly GIB. Good in bed. Common and vulgar, not to mention unlikely.

Next, she takes up the watercolor brushes and the bottles of Dr. Martin's Dye. They belong to Mr. Conrad. He has painted her a picture with brushes and dyes just like them. A picture of the dog. It is a speaking likeness, though small and not, according to Mr. Conrad, as interesting as most of his pictures. The other objects, the lock of hair in its cellophane slip, the tooth which might be a child's or dog's, the wallets, keys and trinkets, she can't place.

After a little study, she gathers up the objects, finds a box for them and puts the box, as promised, on a shelf in a closet. Then she takes the box down again and spreads the objects on the table and leaves them there to keep her company.

Rambeau's Second Letter
to Kitty

◆

Hello Sweetheart it is me!

That's how my grandmother started out her letters to me when I went in the Marines. I was sixteen when I went in.

After my mother lit out with Zeke, things didn't go well. My grandmother was rattled for a long time. The old man was upset. My father got word in Florida, where he was working on a boat. He came back to Saratoga, fighting on the way. He lost a tooth in the front of his mouth and when he arrived he had a row with my grandmother over it. The next thing he did was hit me. Didn't make any difference to me, one way or the other.

I was no longer an ornament to the household, perfecting my buttercream icing and practicing my daisy stitch. Nobody wanted to sleep with me now because I wet the bed and also threw myself out of it, dreaming and screaming. Fred Moon, the roomer, was fed up with it. He mentioned something about moving on. My grandmother was frantic.

She put up a cot for me in her sewing room, preserving

my transient status. Every night it turned into a bazooka and launched me. I broke my collarbone. That was all right, prestige resided in a broken collarbone, and it took everybody's mind off the peeing and screaming. Then I broke the other one. This put my reputation in decline at school and didn't do me good around the house. Now I had two arms in plaster, a regular little pharaoh. I couldn't feed myself so I wouldn't eat and I had no sentiments I cared to express so I wouldn't talk. I have no idea what I dreamed about.

My father borrowed a car and put me in it and took me for a ride. We went to Saratoga Lake. He told me he was going to drop me in the lake and drown me. I remember him telling me this, but I don't remember what effect it had on me. He leaned across me and opened the car door and told me to get out but I didn't get out and after a while he got out and walked around the car and slammed the door and got back in again and drove me home. That night when I woke up howling my father pounded up the stairs pulling off his belt. Mr. Moon was behind him, trying to change his mind. My grandmother was behind Mr. Moon. My grandfather was back there somewhere.

My father laid his belt across my hide. Mr. Moon shouted out, "They're coming to get you Black Jack, I have notified the authorities." The minute he got through saying it, a siren sounded right there in the room with us. My father dropped his belt and ran like hell.

It was the funniest thing that had happened since the beginning of time. The siren was really in the center of town and it went off for fires and at ten to nine to warn you you were almost late for school. You could tell by the code the whistle blasted if the fire was on the east or the west side of town. I don't know, but that night the siren was there in the room, I swear it.

After that, I took more notice of Fred Moon. I could see he had his powers.

I began to hang out in his room. He had a pencil-line

mustache, and he did a lot of work on it. He had a statue of St. Joseph and a bottle of Four Roses. He had a watch with the first gold expansion bracelet I had ever seen. He didn't wear the watch, he kept it around the neck of St. Joseph. He had drumsticks and a practice pad and a suitcase record player and some good jazz records, 78s, 33s were new then. The first thing he did for me was to tape a spoon on a drumstick and rig the drumstick to my cast so we could maintain a fiction that I was feeding myself. He had been a trumpet player but he had bad teeth and a dentist messed up a nerve in his lip. He worked as a cashier and bookkeeper in one of the joints in town. He missed the old days, gigging around. He was very courteous, well spoken.

When I could move my arms, Mr. Moon showed me how to hold the drumsticks. He wasn't a first-class drummer, but knew a thing or two. I did paradiddles and rim shots on every surface in that house and drove my grandmother crazy. My grandfather, he loved it though. My favorite surfaces were pot lids, stuck in a venetian blind, which made a hell of a noise, and a big old round leather hassock. The hassock's tone wasn't very good, but it looked a little like a drum.

Somebody gave me a souvenir tom-tom and a bongo and I thumped away on those. I never asked for a drum set, the splendor of such a thing was way beyond my reckoning. But my hands were never still. My wrists got strong. I was tireless, I had purpose. I could practice my patterns in my head and my fill and my cymbal splashes. "Bear down and keeping banging away," Mr. Moon said, "in time it will cater to you." I never had a whole lot to say for myself, but I was never silent. I roamed through the world like the devil does seeking the ruin of souls, but what I was wanting to hear was the sound things make when you strike them.

My grandmother liked Fred Moon but she didn't like jazz. We would bring her in and say, "Here's Teddy Wilson. Here's Art Tatum. This is Coleman Hawkins. This is

Lester Young." But she would shake her head. However, she could see that jazz had spruced me up. Put me back in the kitchen, rolling out the pie dough. I knew I had to play the saxophone. I knew this before I ever held a saxophone in my hands. It nearly knocked me over when who but my father turned up with a horn. (He was jealous of Fred Moon, he called us Fred and Ginger. He used to whistle "Let Me Call You Sweetheart" when he saw us together. Still, Mr. Moon was good for a touch. Fred Moon was our loan society.)

The saxophone my father gave me was an old one, virgin brass with kangaroo hide pads. It was dirty and the D and E keys clanked on the rod. It hadn't been oiled in fifteen years. If you stuck a bulb in it, light leaked out all over. I loved that horn, it was the most terrific article I ever owned, or would.

The first communication I had from my mother, after she left with Zeke, was a box of chocolates and two snapshots of her in a playsuit, ass to the camera in a Betty Grable pinup pose smiling down over her shoulder. My grandmother took the snapshots away from me. She snipped out the little heads. She returned the little heads to me on a saucer. I slit the cellophane on the candy box and slid the heads between the box and the lid. The chocolates sat on the mantelpiece in Saratoga for years, and I mean years. My grandmother lifted the box and dusted under it and dusted the box and put it back. Much later, when I looked for them, the heads were gone. The chocolates were in there. Bleached white, like little ossified turds.

Once my father had a squint at the Tulsa address on the chocolates and a squint at my mother in her playsuit, he went down there to get her back. Zeke ran him off with a gun. She was pregnant but she didn't have the baby. She never did have another baby, though for years she tried.

My father loafed around and hit the bottle. My grandmother gave him money because he told her he was in bad

with loan sharks. My grandmother saw Mafia hit men behind every tree. Sometimes my father worked at the track.
When the season was over he'd disappear. He was a type.
His hair was too long for those days. He liked dark blue or
maroon colored gabardine shirts. He called them twenty-
milers. He wore a big intaglio ring he said some woman
gave him. He claimed he'd won a Congressional Medal of
Honor, when the truth was he'd never been in the service,
asthma and children had kept him out. I never heard him
say a funny thing, but he could make my mother and my
grandmother laugh. I don't know why he gave me the
horn.

When I began to play music, it was like a door opened in
me, to a lighted room. I had a glint of what was possible,
applied to the whole human escapade. That horn was like
a lost limb returned to me. I loved the way it curved into
my body and the way it fit my lip. I sounded terrible at first
—my grandmother put down the windows. But I got over
sounding terrible. I was twelve in 1952 and Elvis Presley
was getting fixed to screw up my future. I looked about
forty. I was tall and worried-looking. I had a Borsalino hat
and a pencil-line mustache and I hung around Jack's and
No Name's with somebody else's ID. I was so good, Kitty,
that they let me sit in sometimes. I didn't actually sit, I
leaned on the piano. That was my style. I was good, but I
imagine they fell out laughing. I was also, at this time, an
altar boy.

Just before I was due to graduate from grade school, I
got in a fracas. Involved were the instrument closet at the
high school, a little bit of reefer, some stolen money and
an older girl who wasn't absolutely the same color I was. It
wasn't anything vicious and it wasn't anything much, but
they took me off the graduation program. This left them
with a cornet rendition of the berceuse from "Jocelyn,"
which suited them about right.

Mr. Moon, who was very straitlaced, made no dark se-

cret of his disappointment. The collapse of my grandmother was pitiful to see. My grandfather had died. Black
Jack, that booze artist, didn't say much, he just reminded
me from time to time how bad my mother would feel when
he wrote her, which he planned to.

Nevertheless and notwithstanding, my grandmother
baked a coconut cake for a graduation party in Fred
Moon's room. She cut the cake and left us. She could
hardly look at me. Fred Moon had gotten sloppy drunk,
the first I'd ever seen him. He took off on jazz, how if I
followed jazz I would always be poor and meet undesirable
people and bum around. I can't tell you how much I
wanted to be poor and meet undesirable people and bum
around. I was in misery—girl, guilt, public disgrace, being
thirteen and ridiculous, crying with a pencil-line mustache.

Pretty soon Mr. Moon was crying too, lamenting how
nobody cared about his chops going bad and him ending
up among strangers in a furnished room. I loved Fred
Moon. I put my hand on his shoulder and tried to tell him
so. He knocked my hand off. He threw St. Joseph across
the room. He said I was always pawing him, always crowding him, always falling all over him. This was news to me.
He told me to get out.

I ran down the stairs and out of the house and all the
way to the grade school. I ran around and around and
around the track in my graduation suit. In my pocket was
a graduation card from one of my sisters. It mentioned a
ten-dollar bill, but there wasn't any money in the card.

After a while I ran back home and shot some baskets by
garage light. I ripped my sleeve off my suit. My father
showed up and shot baskets too. He was pretty good. He
looked different, bobbing and leaping in the holy sort of
light coming down from the bare bulb in the eaves. When
we quit, he put his fingers in his pocket and pulled out a
Cincinnati roll—big bills on the outside, ones in the middle. He peeled off a twenty and handed it to me. Then he

peeled off another and gave me that one too. I was stumped. "I had a good night," he said. "Not me," I said. "Hey," he said, "what can you do? Some nights are like that."

That's the best conversation I had with my father.

Mr. Moon dropped me like a stone. He was never home. I saw him around town and he was never alone, he was with Velvet. Velvet was a hot walker out at the track. The best-looking kid I had ever seen and the blackest. They called him Velvet.

Over the years my father had a few conspicuous romances, one of them with my mother. Letters and phone calls flurried around and they spent a few days in New Orleans together. My grandmother was nervous. I don't know if she hoped they'd make a go of it or hoped to God they wouldn't. They didn't. My mother went back to Tulsa and divorced him and finally she married Zeke. Good duds and a few brilliants and a fur. Also, she likes Zeke.

When my father got back from New Orleans he looked like a certified stewbum. My grandmother cleaned him up and dried him out and got him to join AA. He was peaked and pious for a while. My grandmother got him all togged out, new clothes from his skin. He went to Mass with her on Sunday, he bought her a bunch of flowers, ate vegetables, did yard work. She took on a glow like a girl.

He went out one night, supposed to be to a meeting, didn't turn up for three days. On the third day she tried to get me on my knees, saying a rosary for my father's safe return.

In the middle of the night the doorbell woke us. My father was leaning propped against the door. He was paralyzed with drink. He was wearing his new underpants she'd bought him, his new black gabardine shirt. The taxi he'd come home in was a block off. The taxi driver had found his pockets empty and taken Black Jack's new white linen pants.

Before the week was out, my grandmother took me and

told me that my father couldn't live in her house anymore
and I couldn't live there either. She said she had rented an
apartment for us down the block. She was turning the second floor of her house into an apartment for Mr. Moon
and Velvet.

I said I couldn't live on my own with my father. I knew
this was true. She said she was handing him over to me.
There was something sad in the way she said this. I got
some sense of what she felt for him, different from what
she felt for me. I told her again that I couldn't live with my
father, just the two of us. She said, "You must do as you
wish." I was frightened when she said that.

For two or three weeks I didn't go near them. I went to
school, hung around on Congress Street, slept in cars or at
my friends' or in the park. I finagled my meals, washed pots
for them, and I was always hungry. I had friends, I grabbed
a shower, but I was dirty too. I kept hearing her say, "You
must do as you wish."

I broke into her house on a Sunday morning when she
should have been at Mass. The house was torn up by the
carpenters and my clothes were gone and she wasn't at
Mass, she caught me.

She said it was a hard thing she had asked me to do but
I had done hard things before. She said, "After all, he's
your *father*," as if I had brought that on myself.

We walked down the street to the apartment. My father's
things were there, and mine. She gave me the door key. I
lay down on the cot that had been in the sewing room. I
thought "After all, he's your father" and "You must do as
you wish." I thought those two things over and over until I
fell asleep and when I woke up it was Monday and there I
was.

About nineteen months later I was at a crap game with
my father. Kefauver had closed down Saratoga around '50,
but you couldn't close down the sort of game my father
was into. The crap game was in a garage, big harshly
lighted place with a bloodstain on the floor. Maybe it was a

paint stain, but a bloodstain would have been right at home. I hadn't had much to do with my saxophone for months. This worried me. I didn't know yet that I was already about as good as I'd ever get to be.

For nineteen months of nights—drinking, gambling, whoring—I hung on my father's heels. Every day I reported on him to my grandmother as if he were our ailing child. Sometimes I told her the truth, sometimes I lied. I said what he'd had to eat, how much to drink, how much he'd slept and how his spirits were. After I'd been doing this a little while, it seemed like I'd been doing it forever. It seemed my vocation. Sometimes he tried to shake me, mostly not. I was handy. I was his due. I saw he got home, I waited on him some when he was sick. I called his bosses, lied to keep his jobs. I was sixteen, but we pretended that I had passed my eighteenth birthday.

I had begun to find out how much I like to gamble. When I had dice in my hand, or cards, I wasn't worrying about my father, what shape he was in, how I'd get him out of there, how my grandmother would take it tomorrow.

That night in the garage I couldn't lose. The dice were hot and I just kept on winning. It was thrilling. I felt skilled and privileged. One of the anointed.

My father fixed that. He stopped the game. He said, "You lost." He scooped up the dice and the money. I began to argue with him. He said, "You lost. Say goodnight to the gentlemen."

They wouldn't have let him do it to anyone but his kid, but nobody interfered. I didn't hit him. One of the men in the crowd was a crony of Black Jack's, a broken-down lawyer for a sugar company. He told B. J. to give me my winnings. My father looked at the money in his hand and threw it on the floor. I turned around and walked out. Before I got to the door the lawyer was beside me with some bills that he stuffed in my jacket. I hit the lawyer in the face.

I went back to the apartment. I put the money in an

envelope and sealed it. I thought it would be my case roll, my gambling money. I tried to think of something to write on the envelope, but there was nothing I wanted to write. I put the envelope on my shelf between two books. I got my saxophone and held it in my hands. I knew something was going to happen. I thought what I would do was leave town in the morning.

I could only think of two destinations, New Orleans and Tulsa. I had no reason to go to New Orleans and I didn't want to go to Tulsa, but they seemed like the only places on the map. I got a change of underwear and a clean pair of socks and rolled them in a sweater. I made two peanut butter sandwiches and wrapped them up and rolled them in the sweater too. I broke open the envelope and counted the money again. It was two hundred and eighty-four dollars. That was *money*.

I took a shower, and still wet, I locked the French doors that led to the bedrooms. These were French doors with painted-over panes. I had never locked them before. My father had been setting fires in the apartment. Sometimes a cigarette fell from his fingers onto the mattress or the rug, sometimes he put a coffeepot or skillet on the stove and melted it or heated it red-hot. Twice the kitchen had filled with choking smoke and I had dragged my passed out father out of it. Twice. Another crony, a horse doctor, said I saved my father's life.

This night I had it clear in my mind that I was locking those doors to keep him from setting me on fire before I could leave for Tulsa or New Orleans. But that doesn't make any sense.

However, I put my clothes on and lay down on my cot. I had one hand on my saxophone case and one on my rolled-up sweater. I was trying, simultaneously, to compose a note in my mind that would explain things to my grandmother, and to not think of my grandmother at all. It bothered me that I threw a fist at the broken-down lawyer. I fell asleep.

It would be a lie to say I never heard him, and that's a lie I never told. In the night sometime I heard a sound like a bell tree. That would be the breaking glass. I may have heard his voice.

In the early morning he was dead or I hope so. By that I mean I never saw him, just his arms where he had punched them through the panes in the painted French doors. He had severed some big vessels in his arm. He must have been very drunk.

The disproportion between what I did and what he did on account of it blinded me.

I went out the window onto a porch roof and down a maple tree. I was going to get Fred Moon at my grandmother's house and come back up the front way to the apartment, so we could reach where my father was and help him if he wasn't beyond help. It never even struck me that I should open up the doors from my side.

Before I was out of the tree, I realized that Fred Moon and Velvet were in Lexington, they had sent me a postcard from the horse graveyard there. When my feet touched the ground, I knew I was never going back inside, not even for my saxophone. Not even if my father was still alive.

I called the police from the bus station in Albany. I called my mother too, but first I joined the Marines. I had tried to join the Navy, but the Navy recruitment office was closed. I put two hundred fifty of my two eighty-four in an envelope and mailed it to my grandmother. I waited three days in Albany to get my mother's written consent for the Marine Corps. By the end of the week they handed me a ticket for San Diego. I don't know if he was living or dead when I left him, his arms through the broken panes of the door like a pilgrim in the stocks. I'll never know that.

I wish to God we could be together, Kitty. Together in bed. At rest. In love.

Rambeau

Kitty

Kitty tries to be imperturbable, and feels that she is making progress, though strict serenity eludes her.

Late summer is sultry or steaming or streaming; her roof leaks; fuses blow; her oven is out and so are two burners on top of the stove; water pours from the seams of her washing machine; her dryer chokes on Mr. Conrad's socks. Mildew mists her shoes and salt sweat shimmers on her prickly heat.

Moreover, she is unemployed. No one seems to be shooting; not editorials, not print ads, not commercials.

When she calls other stylists she knows, their answering machines say that Skippy is partying in London, Denise is relaxing in Provence.

Mr. Conrad is no company, although he frequents her vicinity. His little wrinkled face is sallow with enterprise. His fingers are stained with Dr. Martin's Radiant Concentrated Water Colors. April Green, Wild Rose. True Blue.

Bottles of this brilliant inky fluid mark his progress; he leaves them on the breakfast table and in the pockets of his darling shirts. They leak bright targets over his heart. His eyes are inflamed from the fumes of Dr. Martin's dyes, his nose bedews his mustache.

Mr. Conrad has a commission. He is painting dogs. Doggies, probably, sweet soppy creatures with sentimental eyes. Kitty is sorry for him, he has had to put aside his poetry in the interests of commerce. And he had been, she knows, impassioned in his most recent thrust. *The Mango Cycle*. The mango suggests to Mr. Conrad the womb. So, in the past, have a Gladstone bag and a tennis shoe. Kitty feels, on the whole, more sympathetic to the mango image. Although she was extraordinarily fond of a tennis shoe sestina called "?KIDS/KEDS?"

Mr. Conrad is cranky with Kitty. He flings at her exhausted glances and shards of garbled remonstrance.

Now that she is quieter, more reasonable, less gabby, she is even more irritating; she knows this. No one tells her to shut up these days but her kin find her moony and exasperating.

Kitty obliges herself to be calm. She writes in her notebook, adding things, striking them out. She prays that Rambeau will write to her again; she knows that her mother sees him from time to time but in some deeper sense he seems to be out of her country.

Mick and Eileen and Gordon treat her as a widow, a silly one, a giddy little moper who still sets two places at table. "Why are you *smiling?*" Eileen says. "For the love and honor of God," says Mick, "there's a grin on you like the Cheshire cat." "What's so comical?" Gordon wants to know. "You might let us in on the joke." Kitty is certain she shows no mirth; she feels none. But she is watchful, waiting; waiting for a sign.

When it comes, it is absurd. A woman who hardly knows her telephones; a tiny woofy woman who is casting director in an advertising agency.

"Can you do lines, Pussycat?" the woman, Brucie, says.

"Well, I don't think so," Kitty says. "I'm not an actress."

"They don't want an actress, Cupcake," Brucie says, "they want a real person."

"Well, I am a real person," Kitty says, "but what would I have to do?"

"Sell apples," Brucie says. "Nothing hucksterish, nothing crass. Sell the idea of apples, the image of apples, appleness. For Halloween and thenceforward. Don't ask me anything much because I don't know anything much, they keep changing the signals. It's a trade association, apple growers, client of ours. Perfectly sweet people but I've had them up the kazoo. You'd have to travel, Snooks. Shopping centers, trade shows, local TV. Money's good. It's better than a sharp stick, Loveboat."

"Spokesperson," Kitty says.

"Spokesperson. Of course they're crazy. Apple Goddess one minute, Dried Apple Doll the next. Snow White. Eve. Princess. Witch. If an apple drove a car, what kind of car would an apple drive?"

"Poor Brucie."

"You're telling me. They're looking for a quality."

"Which one?"

"Indefinable. Dress youthful."

Kitty washes and starches and carefully irons her thrift shop parsonage dress. She knows the dress may be a mistake, but she can't think quite what to wear. The dress is princessy but repressed. Well, apples. Apples, after all. Apples are wholesome. Are they? Sheep Nose. Rome Beauty. Granny Smith.

She thinks about "The Princess and the Goblins," the withered apple, the shaft of light, the mysterious maiden at the top of the attic stair.

She irons slowly, perspiration slipping down the inside of her arm and sizzling on the iron as she glides it over the thin pretty cloth.

She muses on Rambeau. Rambeau as a peasant boy in green doublet. Kitty as princess in her thrift shop dress.

United at last by a word from a witch in the wood. United at last after many trials.

The smell and heat of ironing make Rambeau present to her senses. Apples. "Dress youthful" echoes in her mind. She smacks the iron down on its stand. But the roof leaks, the stove declines to cook, the washer to wash, the dryer to dry. The money's good, it's better than a sharp stick.

She eats an apple as she dries her hair. The apple's skin is tough and the apple's flesh is mealy. Well, apples have their season, too. Her hair is even whiter, ever whiter. Her skin is pale, silvery. She paints her face a little. How much paint does a princess wear? Is face paint youthful in August? The crimped pink scribble of the scars around her eye looks deliberate. She touches it up with colored pencils. If she is going to do this thing, she will do it.

She puts aside her ingenuous dress, its ruffles crisp and fresh with starch, and finds among her rumbustious rags a tissue-thin short silver evening dress, a gossamer crumple of pleats. An old triumph, it is worn and webby; it may be a Fortuny.

She slicks silver shadow on her eyelids. She is a princess, she is pleased. She looks a marvel. A bit odd, perhaps, for a sodden August afternoon in town. Ah well, she thinks, The Big Apple.

When Kitty arrives at the agency for her audition, the reception area has been occupied by a coven of witches. One of them is wearing regulation witch clothes with conical hat.

"What's new on the block?" this witch says to Kitty.

"Hello, Bryna," Kitty says. The witch is Bryna Beens, an old character actress who works, when she can get work, in commercials and soaps. Bryna is a self-conscious cutup, but at the moment she looks fagged out. She is holding a new broom. "Like the outfit?" Bryna says. "Is it a gas?" The

reception room is frosty after the fetid street. Pale Bryna
has blackened her moles.

None of the other women wears a costume, but one has
an apple in her hand and round red apples printed on her
summer skirt. She has a nutcracker profile. Another of the
women wears a plain shabby dress and a twitchy, disdainful
expression. Kitty has a feeling this woman is a real witch.
All of these women are holding handouts.

Kitty goes to the desk and asks for her handouts. There
is no script, there is a Fact Sheet. There is also a Casting
Sheet with Apple Witch at the top of it, and a list of names
and audition appointments. Kitty follows Bryna on this list.

Bryna has forgotten her glasses and cannot see to read
the Fact Sheet. Kitty reads to Bryna: "Apple. Best-known
and commercially most important fruit of the temperate
zone and its tree *Malus Sylvestris* or *Pyrus malus*, a mem-
ber of the rose family. It lives long, is easy to grow and
thrives in any good soil and at higher altitudes than any
other fruit tree." And so on. The apple in legend and myth.
Apples through the ages. "According to ancient tradition
the forbidden fruit of the Garden of Eden was the apple
(Gen. 3). In religious painting, the apple represents the
fruit of the tree of knowledge of good and evil as do occasionally the pear and the quince."

"Quince," Bryna says.

"The apple was sacred to Aphrodite in classical mythol-
ogy," Kitty reads.

"I thought you did dress shields," Bryna says. "I thought
you did hems."

"The apple is attacked by several diseases," Kitty reads,
"(e.g. canker, rust and scab) and by insect pests."

"Razor blades," Bryna says. "That's what this is all about.
Wackos hid razor blades in the kiddos' apples last Halloween. Put the apple in a very bad light."

When Bryna is called to audition, Kitty folds the Fact
and Casting Sheets. Apple Witch. If Kitty is hired for this
task, it will be because a witch is wanted, not a princess.

Her throat aches with tears, she shivers in her silver dress. She hadn't realized quite how much she wanted to be a princess. She wanted to appear on television where Rambeau, magically, would see her and seek her. She wanted to send her voice out over the audio waves to summon him. She wanted to turn up at school fairs, and shopping centers and spy him in her audience; she wanted to offer him a perfect apple.

However, though apple witching may be a frivolous, humbling job, it is a harmless one and lucrative. Mr. Conrad has borrowed fifty dollars to spend on watercolor paper and Dr. Martin's dyes. He would not borrow money unless desperate. The dog is needing dog food. Mick's bills must be paid. The roof leaks back at the gingerbread cottage. Rambeau's car needs shocks.

Kitty goes into a conference room where a fervent, suited young man describes the upside potential of the Apple Witch. He says it's what the apple growers association needs to move the stick. He says it's more creative than a straightforward delivery of the product positioning. He says it is a product attribute story with a whole new executional jacket. He says it will move the needle. He says it will jiggle the dial. Kitty agrees with him.

Everyone in the room looks done in. She surmises that they have seen every real person who hasn't left town.

The young man says he will give her his time path. He does but she is not listening, she is in a trance of ambition and delusion. What does it matter, princess or witch? Rambeau is still the peasant boy. She will go on television, she will go everywhere, anywhere, she will extend to him a perfect apple.

The art director asks her where she got her dress, the writer where she got her birthmark—or is it a scar—or is it makeup? They agree that dress and scar are sort of cute. The producer suggests that she say a few things about apples. Kitty says something about Cézanne's apples. Then she says something about princesses and witches, fairy tales

and peasant boys. She speaks of Emerson's angel, who offered him the world in the shape of an apple. She mentions
Gregor Samsa's apple, Wallace Stevens' apple, apples
through the ages, peasant boys. She wraps it up with Isaac
Newton, William Tell.

There is a stir in the room; the abyssal waters of boredom
tremble. "Such a gift, it's devastating," says the producer.
Kitty looks modest. She has heard many a producer, many
a director, buttering the talent. "I'm in awe of your gift,"
the producer says. "I've just seen you do such great things.
I'm just going to try to put a little glitch up front. Probably
louse it up, it's so fabulous."

He gives Kitty some unintelligible direction and she gab-
bles on about apples once again. Love Apple. Apple of
Discord. Apple of his eye. Mom's apple pie. Apple pie
order. One bad apple spoils the barrel. Upset the apple
cart. Apple doesn't fall far from the tree. Apple knocker.
God made little green apples. How do you like them apples? Don't give me any of your applesauce.

"Stay away from processed," the account executive says.
"No sauce, no pie slices." Kitty can see the job is hers.

Halloween is coming. The Apple Witch is part of a sales
promotion encouraging householders to offer trick or treat-
ing children apples instead of candy. But Bryna is right.
On other Halloweens, apples concealing pins or bits of
razor blade have been offered. The Apple Witch is supposed at once to encourage the generous giving of apples
to children and the suspicious inspection of apples by children. Without, of course, admitting what she's up to.

Kitty hands over a picture of herself. Not much of Kitty
can be seen, since she's seated at the wheel of Rambeau's
car with Rambeau's dog on her lap. Rambeau took the
picture, one Kitty prizes. The conference room pro-
nounces the picture a hoot, but what is wanted is a head-
sheet or a glossy.

From Kitty's Confession

◆

After my father died, I wouldn't sit close to anybody at church or at school or let anybody borrow my comb. I thought I smelled bad. Not in any usual way. I thought I smelled of my father's cologne. It was a sickening, orange blossomy cologne called Florida Water. I bought it for him, had I any money, on his birthday. He loved scent.

Kitty

◆

I have coffee with Gordon and Eileen at their apartment:

"THERE ISN'T A DECENT NURSERY WALLPAPER IN THE CITY OF NEW YORK."

"Why are you doing this? Are you doing this to torment me? Why is he doing this, Kitty?"

"Hey you guys," I say. "Could we talk about this dog situation?"

"WHAT DOES DIMITY LOOK LIKE, DOES IT MAKE NICE CURTAINS? WOULD DIMITY BE TOO GENDER-INDICATIVE?"

"I'm worried Mr. Conrad won't look after the dog properly while I'm away because he's too busy drawing up pictures of dogs for some client."

"I don't want a nursery, Gordon, I want a baby."

"And Mr. Conrad is terrified of dogs, which is not really all that wonderful for the dog's morale."

"DARLING, DARLING, I'M GOING TO GIVE YOU A BABY. BUT WE HAVE TO HAVE A PLACE FOR THE BABY TO LAY ITS LITTLE HEAD."

"The dog will sleep practically anywhere. And it won't smell or anything because I'll take it to the dog wash place."

"*You're cruel.*"

"You're absurd."

"*I notice we're not turning your study into a nursery, it's my study we're turning into a nursery.*"

"You don't study anything in your study and no apartment needs two studies, it's pretentious. We should have a motif. Circus? Ballooning?"

"Dogs! You can observe the dog while it's here."

"Out of the question."

"Dog people live longer than other people. A dog gets them out in the fresh air. It distracts them from selfishness and vanity and malice and confusion."

"*Why is it out of the question?*"

"Do you want to walk that mongrel dog? Do you want to carry a bag and a scooper?"

"*You're right. It is out of the question.*"

"Babies," I say, "are not notoriously tidy."

"I'm right about most things but you fight me. That has been the dominant mode of our interaction."

"*Don't cry, you fool. Why is she crying?*"

"Don't ask me."

"*Her face looks awful, Gordon. Why don't those marks go away? Shouldn't she sue that cab company? Shouldn't she have a good doctor look at her face?*"

"Babies make doo-doo too."

"A good doctor has looked at her face. I looked at her face. Do you like the cradle? It's a Salem cradle."

"*I can't bear it. An empty cradle. I can't bear it. You're cruel.*"

"It won't be empty long, I assure you."

"*Oh Gordon, oh Gordon—you had the sperm count—did you? You did you did they did something you had something done. Oh Gordon I'm so happy.*"

"You could spread newspaper. You could bribe the doorman. *I'll* bribe the doorman. It's only for a while."

"*Kitty dear I think we'd like to be alone if you don't mind.*"

"Kitty, if it means so much—Eye, I think we should be magnanimous. I think we should mind Kitten's dog."

"No, that's all right," I say. "I've decided I'm leaving the dog with my mother."

Rambeau

◆

"The man just contributes a seed, a germ," Rambeau's mother tells him on the telephone. "But to a woman her child is part of her body. It grows in her body, it's a piece of her own flesh, it's more to her than her own flesh."

"How long have you held these sentiments?" Rambeau says. "Try to tell me without looking at your watch." He is startled to hear these words leap from his mouth. He has never spoken so to his mother. But he is not himself. "I have a big favor to ask you," he says.

"Beau, does that make sense? First you offend a person, then you ask them a big favor. You just don't know how to get on in the world. You never did know how things were done."

"How are they done?" Rambeau says. He takes a mouthful of bourbon and swishes it around like mouthwash. He has given up alcohol except for the occasions of these phone calls, and certain exchanges with Cherokee.

"They're not done the way you're doing them," his mother says. "One minute you're chasing after some white-haired old has-been. One minute after some teenybopper girl. It's just too kinky, Jacky, I know it's all my doing. But it's time you took responsibility for your own destiny. My therapist said so the other day."

"Well if he says so."

"He does say so and don't be smart with me."

"Julia Mary, it's bad enough you hire detectives, but you hire incompetent detectives. And, Mom, tell your therapist I'll meet him in the alley."

Rambeau's mother begins her muted weeping. "Don't call me Mom. Please don't call me Mom. You just do that to upset me."

Rambeau closes his eyes. His breathing is measured. "I want you to look after a baby for me."

His mother stops wuffing and chirring. "How old of a baby?"

"Not very old. That is, it isn't born yet. But it will be. I just want you to keep it for a while, until I can make a permanent arrangement."

"Which'll be what?"

"I haven't the least idea."

"This is your baby we're talking about."

"No. Yes and no. It is and it isn't. I can't explain."

"Chuck you, Farley," she says.

"What?"

"No way, José."

"You're refusing me? You're saying no?"

"Do bears go pee-pee in the woods?"

"But why won't you do it? You've always said you'd do anything for me."

"Well that wasn't true, was it?"

"But you're my mother," Rambeau says helplessly. He is astonished to discover he had counted on her absolutely.

"The last thing I did that I didn't want to do, I dumped you that time in Saratoga. After that, I never did a thing I didn't want to."

"That's impossible."

"Eat your heart out," Rambeau's mother says. "Not that you wouldn't without me telling you."

Rambeau's mother hangs up.

Kitty

◆

"I'm going to ask you a really big favor," Kitty says to Mick. "It's so big a favor that it's dangerous and irresponsible and if you have your wits about you you will certainly refuse and I won't blame you."

"Drink your tea," Mick says. "What is it so?"

"No, forget it, never mind."

"As you wish. Eat some honey."

"Best honey I ever tasted," Kitty says. "Where'd you get this honey?"

It is raspberry honey from an East Side shop. Perfectly ordinary honey transfigured by a pretty jar, a costly, quaint and pretty label. Gordon has brought it. "I disremember," Mick says. "Eat a popover."

"I love popovers."

"Well I know that. Why else would I make them? Has that hound of hell destroyed your eye?"

"Keep this under your hat," Kitty says. "Damn dog bit me."

"It's a blessing the beast didn't leap for your schnoz. You'd have to go wrapped in a veil like a statue in Lent."

"Is it that bad? It feels like it's blazing. Sometimes it hardly shows at all." Kitty helps herself to another popover,

170

spreads it with butter and honey, drinks her tea. She is peculiarly content. "Am I ruined?"

"Aye," Mick says. "Entirely." She pulls Kitty's head down on her breasts and kisses the crown of Kitty's head. Kitty hugs her. Her mother is old but substantial. Mick smooths Kitty's wild hair. Then a slight tension in Mick's frame signals that the interlude is over.

Mick fetches a bottle of Stone's Green Ginger Wine and two fairy thimbles of glasses. Kitty has never known her mother to have alcohol of any kind in her house. Kitty holds the little glass of wine up to the light. "Where'd this come from?" Rambeau has brought the wine.

"I was given six of those as a wedding gift," her mother says. "And your poor dear father shied them at my head soon after. These are the two remaining. Drink your wine."

"Do you think it was funny, that he did that?" Mick's attitudes often puzzle Kitty.

"As well to laugh as to cry," Mick says. She tips the wine from her glass into Kitty's. "This will build your blood," she says, "and strengthen it for the trials that lay ahead."

The wine has the taste of enchantment and a talismanic import; Kitty has never before drunk wine from the hand of her mother.

"I was going to ask you to mind the dog," Kitty says. "While I'm abroad on my broomstick. But that was danger-ous and crazy."

"Not atall," says Mick. "Indeed it's a nice wee article."

"Hell no," Kitty says. "It's not a nice dog; it's vicious. I bought a muzzle for it, but you still have to get the muzzle on and off. Or it could jump on you and knock you down. Break your hip. And you wouldn't want to walk it; it pulls when you walk it. And it would dirty up the yard. Or it might run away. It's an evil dog, it's the kind of dog that maims babies in the *Daily News*."

"God forgive you," Mick says. "The poor wee article. I have a fancy for it. Bring it here."

"Oh thank you, Mommy, thank you," Kitty says. "Could I have a little more wine?"

After Kitty has finished her wine, she goes to Rambeau's car and brings back Rambeau's dog, which looks fuddled. Mick roughs the dog's ears and feeds it popovers and honey and a dish of cream with, Kitty thinks, a drop of tea in it.

Kitty lugs in sacks of dog chow, cans of dog food, frozen blocks of offal. She makes many trips for extra leashes, lengths of chain, water bowls and feeding bowls and plates with saucy French legends on them, bits of rug the dog disdains to sleep on, brushes, combs, flea powder, a rasp for the dog's black toenails.

At last she shows her mother Rambeau's paint-dappled stone green sweater. She is afraid her mother will say something awful. "This is to make the dog feel cozy," Kitty says in apology.

"Quite right," her mother says and takes the sweater from her hands.

Kitty is prepared to spend some time with them, as referee or cicerone; she thinks it only fair. She is also fond of her mother's cooking and fine aromas thrum the air. But her mother shoos her off; she is tired; the dog is tired; they are both of them needing naps; surely Kitty has pressing things to do.

Kitty does: she is to schedule an appointment for a makeover, where they will teach her to hollow her cheeks and draw a white line down her nose and where her scars will be judged "intriguing." She is also to report for coaching in talk show deportment; she is eager for this for she wants to know just how to cross her knees. She is, as well, occupied in designing an Apple Witch costume. She has done five or six of these and all of them have been rejected.

When Kitty's mother is alone with the dog, she sits herself down on a straight-backed chair and regards it.

"Hello Nick," she says. The dog looks up at her out of its gleamy eyes. "Hello Nick," Mick says, in a loud no-doubt-about-it voice. She is bluffing.

The dog trots over to her and rests its jaw upon her knee. "I thought so," she says. She rubs its head with her practical hand. "You were ever the reprobate," she says. "You were ever the basket."

She sleeps a little, sitting upright. When she wakes, the dog is sleeping still, its face in her lap, the dribble from its lip has wet her knee. "Ah, Dominic," Mick says. "Life is strange. Life is full of wonders."

The dog wakes trembling and recollects itself. Its four legs stiffen and it executes a slow, erotic topple; belly up it lies on the rug, vulnerable, submissive. Its sex stands up, it thunders with its tail. It reaches with its front legs and bicycles with its hind ones.

"What's the matter with you," Mick says. "Is it you smell something good in the oven?"

She sets the table for Rambeau's dinner. In another hour, he is there. The dog and Rambeau fall upon each other, noisy with reunion and delight. Rambeau and the dog frisk and rollick, they have neither been so merry for some time.

At last Mick seats Rambeau and feeds him. She sits at the table with him and drinks a little tot of Stone's Green Ginger Wine. Rambeau reasons on and on; she disregards him.

When he has eaten they go to the cellar and find there Kitty's childhood crib, newly scrubbed with soapy water. Rambeau takes it to Kitty's old room. He dismantles Kitty's bed and he and Mick wrestle the bedstead and the mattress and spring to the cellar. A new crib mattress has been delivered from Macy's and hidden in a closet.

Together they set up crib and mattress.

Mick shows Rambeau how to adjust the bumper around the crib; she explains to him the uses and abuses of a bumper. Then Mick unwraps Macy's bounty of baby linens and baby clothes. She has, after lengthy telephone consultation with Macy's Infants Wear, ordered everything in an assortment of colors—two pink, two yellow, two green, two blue—"sortins" she tells him, pleased with her resourcefulness. He takes a lively interest in all she shows him and so, in fact, does the dog.

At intervals, Mick grabs the dog by the collar and urges it into her yard. When she lets it in again, she feeds it. The dog is waddling, dumb with bliss. Twice she and Rambeau stop what they are doing to drink a cup of tea and stroke the dog.

Mick brings out a box of baby clothes she made herself. She is tentative: the clothes were Kitty's and Eileen's, it's thirty years and more since they were new. Rambeau holds them in his hands. He is muddled and exhausted. The baby clothes are plain and exquisite, tucked and smocked and faggotted, elegantly sewn. In the box are two pairs of baby shoes, high-toppers. One little pair is black patent leather; he thinks they belonged to Eileen. The other pair is two-tone, black and brown and rackety. He holds a small shoe on the heart of his hand. Kitty.

"Ah, sure," Mick says behind him. "Shove it in your pocket."

Rambeau shakes his head. He puts the shoe back in the box of baby clothes but later, when she takes the box away, the shoes are gone. She shows Rambeau her precious artifacts: the frock—romantic, long—in which her two daughters were christened; and three photographs. Two are of jolly babies peek-a-booing under hooded blankets; the third is a much older picture, shadowy and brown, the baby is startlingly beautiful, its expression infinitely wise.

"If he had lived, he might have been your father," Mick says, to tired Rambeau, whose body feels clumsy, whose mind is clogged. He thinks she is revealing some mystery; he stares in puzzlement. "My father is dead," he says.

"I mean," she says, "he would have been an age to be your father."

"My father is dead," he says stupidly.

"And so is my son," says Mick. "I wonder do they know each other." He inspects her to see if she's joking, but he is unable to tell.

"Sure that's only one part of the story," Mick says. She shakes out the linen christening robe. "This'll do rightly. There's not a broken bit in it."

Rambeau's vision clouds; the specter of Dorinda bopping around at a baptismal font confounds him. He closes his eyes to banish Dorinda.

"Go you and lie down," Mick says. "We're finished here." The little room now contains one bed, the bed of Eileen's girlhood, and the crib. The white chest of drawers with the ribbons painted on it, Kitty's chest, is full of baby clothes and baby oddments. It is a small and makeshift nursery, but shipshape and accustomed.

Mick makes her way down the stairs. He sees how old she is and pokey. But her spirits are high, she is pink and zesty. Rambeau has hung his jacket from the knob of the bedroom door. He takes it now and from its inside pocket withdraws a bulky envelope. It is his second letter to Kitty. He puts it on the crib's old crocheted coverlet. He feels intense but unspecific trust in Mick.

He is baffled with fatigue. He eats Yorkshire pudding and cold beef and falls asleep with his feet on the rug. Mick lifts his feet and tugs off his boots. He raises his head at her command and she tucks a pillow under it. She spreads an afghan over him and climbs up to her bed.

When she wakes, she knows, he will be gone. She is worn out. Her body throbs with an anguish of age and exhaustion. She thinks she will not live long now. She knows she is incapable of caring for a baby. Anyone's baby. She is too old, she is not able. She will not die, though, not for a while. She wants to see what will happen.

In the morning, Gordon will come. He will take cambric tea with her, puff up a blood pressure cuff around her arm, listen to her heart, feel the pulses in her ankles. He will bully and chide her; she will pat his hair. He will tell her of the nursery Eileen and he are decorating; this nursery, he will say, is going to feature earth tones. It is, he will say, their concept. He will never see the crib that is upstairs. He will hint that he is saving Eileen from a nervous, barren future. He will refer to Mick as a woman of the world.

In the afternoon, Mr. Conrad will come. He will bring an artichoke, six oysters and a bunch of grapes, as well as some circulars from Macy's.

From Kitty's Confession

◆

"You have too much to say," he said. "Nobody wants your opinion. Nobody asked you. It's none of your business, mind your business, nobody wants to hear from you. No man will ever want you. God will punish you."

"I don't need God to punish me," I said. "With you around."

When he fell, he caught his hand in my hair. He fell with his arm around me. We fell, for he pulled me down with him. My hair hurt where he yanked it. Soon after my hair went white on that side. My mother's hair went white in girlhood, so my hair was not so unusual. But she plucked and plucked and plucked, trying to change my hair.

$\mathcal{M}$r. Conrad and Dorinda

◆

Once again, Mr. Conrad must rendezvous with Dorinda at a video games arcade. He hates these places. His faraway mother is ailing with her heart. She is a patient in a cardiac care unit. He has seen her so before, unthinkably old and frail in the merciless light, mortal among the machines and their bleeping. Dorinda's video games, their impersonal electronic exclamations, make him think of his mother among her monitors.

He coaxes Dorinda away from Donkey Kong. They repair to a McDonald's. There he shows her a portfolio of erotic drawings and a legal document. The drawings are artfully done and so, indeed, is the document. Dorinda is amused by all his offerings. Fecklessly she puts her name to the adoption agreement; he knows she thinks she is beyond the law, but he does not think she is correct in her assessment. Although, of course, the law is mad. She takes the drawings; he promises more; they part.

Mr. Conrad has secured a free plastic McDonald's mug with a clever lid. It is designed to facilitate coffee-drinking in a moving vehicle; he will present it to Kitty to take on her travels. Dorinda has invited Mr. Conrad to go with her to a motel but he has briskly declined. Her wombiness powerfully attracts him.

Mr. Conrad, too, has prepared a nursery. In the empty mansion he has found a clothes basket and in it he has placed his feather pillow and a rather shabby folded coat. He has borrowed Kitty's old blue pleated evening shirt and bought a box of Huggies diapers. These preparations, he feels, are adequate. One can make too much fuss.

From Kitty's Confession

———————◆———————

After my father died, I caught my sister wearing his big horn pocketknife on a string around her neck. It was a piece of waxed string from his toolbox. The knife was very heavy and the string had made a red mark on her neck.

Eileen

◆

Eileen is impregnated in a shopping center parking lot. She is in New Jersey. She is conducting a mall intercept. To do this, she approaches visibly pregnant women and asks them a series of questions about, in this instance, support hose. The weather is humid, the respondents are bulbous and blotchy, tented in wilted maternity clothes; resentful toddlers depend like shackles from their wrists. Yet none of them refuses to answer Eileen's questions; they appear to be glad to be asked their opinions about anything at all.

Almost always, the women ask if Eileen, too, has been pregnant. If they ask—she never volunteers the lie—she says she has two children, one of them very young. She says she had wonderful pregnancies, glorious deliveries, handsome children, very bright. Or she says she had troubled pregnancies, difficult births, children who are "handicapped" or "developmentally disabled." Problems she's learning to "handle" or "deal with."

She has told a woman with a hydrocephalic child that she herself has just such a child. They have talked of shunts. She has told a woman with a fingerless baby that

181

her own baby lacks a leg. With a previously infertile mother she has talked at length of temperature charts, coital logs, tubal insufflations, endometrial biopsies, acid vaginal environments, unfriendly mucous plugs, crypts on the cervical interior, hysterosalpingography, culdoscopy, laparoscopy, Clomid, Pergonal, AIH. They cling to each other's hands as they speak of these things, they laugh and cry. Eileen holds the other woman's keening baby.

A tiny bit of this lying, Eileen feels, is permissible, professional. It is all right to say she has had a child. It is all right to say she has regained her figure through sensible diet, judicious exercise. The rest of what she says is all wrong. She cannot help herself; some magic, some mischief has loosed her tongue, the lies fly from her mouth. She is guilty and purposeful; worse, she is excited: her nipples bud, her creamy cheeks and neck and chest flame, some demon lover probes her female vitals.

At the close of each interview, Eileen conducts the respondent to a van where a loop of videotape continuously displays a test commercial for a brand of support hose. As Eileen surrenders each respondent to another researcher, she feels a pang, a loss of this new sister. The women part from her reluctantly; she is lovely, fastidiously groomed and dressed, slim, cool, clean, composed-looking, yet bountiful in her admiration, hot-eyed and confiding. It is true that some of them study her rather closely.

Eileen bids goodbye to the once-barren, now fecund mother, handing over the sorrowing baby. Tears glint on all their faces. She turns to inspect the parking lot for quarry. At once she spies a pregnant girl, very fat, with black, witchy hair and an inappropriate black huge dress, a sort of caftan, spangled with silver zodiacal signs. It is an evening get-up, expensive, eccentric, it has no place in a New Jersey parking lot in late summer. Surely this girl does not fit the demographics, the psychographics, surely one who, vastly pregnant, stumps along in red metallic high-heeled boots, has no opinions on support hose worth recording.

But, even fevered, Eileen is dutiful. She rushes to waylay the inauspicious fat girl. Her attention is diverted by another girl, this one in jeans and a man's voluminous shabby shirt. The girl is transferring a plastic infant's seat, with an infant in it, from her old Honda to a shopping cart. Eileen knows about these infant seats. They are called General Motors Love Seats. The very sight of one in an advertisement has made Eileen ill with longing.

The young mother holds the seat in her arms and bends until her forehead touches the forehead of her child. She sticks out her tongue and makes slobbery mouthfart noises at her baby. The baby replies in kind. The young mother raises her head, her face is transfigured with glee, with pride. She dips her head again, thrusts out her tongue, blows spluttery, fond insults at her baby, raspberries, Bronx cheers. The baby thinks it over, spittily blows them back. They crow with laughter. They are locked in adoring complicity.

Eileen stands very close, ignored among the cars. Eileen, to whom eructive noises are loathsome, shaming, shams them with her lips and tongue. She has never before been witness to so sweet, so full a transaction.

Suddenly she knows that beneath the flapping shirt the girl is pregnant. As clearly, she knows that the girl is herself unaware of this seeding.

Eileen moves as though to tell the girl. Pain stills her. She is ripped; a flashing pain sears into her; she is pierced as by a fearful beak, burned as by a thrust of light. She is pregnant.

The fetus has fled the unknown girl and entered into Eileen's womb. Her womb made a mouth and gobbled it. It seats itself with a suck and a pop, socked into her tissues as a pitched ball socks into a waiting glove.

She pulls her blouse out of her skirt; lets it hang loose on her belly to give the baby shelter, shade and privacy. The girl is of no further interest to her; the girl is an emptied husk. The spluttering tongue play is perhaps a little coarse; she will not do that. Not with her baby.

Eileen looks at her clipboard. A leather clipboard, monogrammed, decorous, costly, gift of Gordon. She sees the notes she has made are garbled. She reads them in a distant, disapproving way. She has somehow bungled this assignment. She is not a woman who bungles things, not a woman who tolerates her own fragilities, but now she is exalted and amused. Pregnant women do such things.

She can think of no way to dispose of the clipboard and disposing of it seems important. She stuffs it, with its notes, into a waste receptacle. She cannot find her car, cannot remember its color. Then she is seated at its wheel, driving back to the city. She will find a store called Reborn Maternity.

She wants to buy maternity clothes, dreary ones, not smart ones. Maternity clothes as they looked in her childhood, smocky, with pussycat bows on the belly and puritan collars and kangaroo skirts. She wants to buy some shoes with Cuban heels.

She doesn't think of Gordon, not at all.

Rambeau

◆

Rambeau's landlady locks her ankles behind his head. She is a windmill in bed. "The thing of it is," she says—she is joyful, she wriggles and bounces, tenderly she claps his ears with the insides of her knees—"the thing of it is, Small Niche is not really my class."

"Dried materials," Rambeau says from the welcome suffocation of her breasts. It is afternoon, she has drawn the shades, the sheets on her bed are the color of paprika. She has won a prize at a shopping mall flower show. He is not sure how they got from that to this.

"I used hardly any dried materials. The asparagus, that was green. The garlic gives a dry effect. The apple, the rose. The beet leaves were a stroke."

"I never would have thought of it," Rambeau says. "I admit that." Dorinda is missing, she has been gone for five days. He has stalked her through the floors of the casinos, especially the Golden Nugget, whose glittery frontier sporting-house style she lately fancies, though the witless parody of Caesar's Palace once pleased her more. Sometimes he thinks he spots her, wearing one of her queer voluminous cassock dresses, following her pod of belly, bearing before her like a votive offering a cardboard bucket full of coins. He has lost her each time on the clattering, jangling, crowded floor. He is so tired that he thinks he sees her everywhere. He thought he saw her at the shopping mall, when he escorted his landlady there to be photographed by the press.

That was just the start of all his visions. He thought he saw Eileen and she was crying. He thought he saw Mr. Conrad. Worst, he thought he saw Kitty, dressed as a fortune-teller, leering and winking and wearing a nasty black wig. Perhaps the shopping centers of New Jersey are thronged with astral projections. Perhaps he is going mad.

He spent the night dancing with Cherokee, a girl who seldom calls him but whose summons is commanding. Cherry makes him timid and tumescent. She is a relentless flirt, grim and clumsy; he is terrified to think she may behave with other men as crudely as she does with him. Cherokee, he thinks. He must do something about Cherokee. "Pappy," she calls him. How he hates it.

His landlady is petting him. "Baby," she says. She has been talking of borax and silica gel, of glycerine and spray paint.

"Baby." He must, he knows, recapture Dorinda. Although she says she is due in October, Dorinda is very big with child. And she no longer goes to the birthing center. God knows when she will deliver the baby. Perhaps Dorinda knows, but Dorinda says she goes by Tarot.

"Baby." His landlady looks up at him. Her eyes are shining. She crosses them and bobs up to nip at the tip of his nose. "The head isn't down," she says. He is used to this; a woman reading his mind. "She hasn't even dropped yet."

"I hope you're right."

When his landlady says "Baby," he sees Cherry in his mind. With Cherry he spends whole evenings, whole, though infrequent, weekends, discussing her terrible childhood. Cherry, once sunny, sulks when he gives her money or, the only presents he can think of since stuffed animals began to seem passé, cashmere sweaters and Liberty scarves. She wants him to court her with gifts that are intimate and significant. But he can't think what those gifts might be. Cherry's IQ is said to be very high but with him it hovers around blood heat. She has told him that she does not want to be a dance therapist; she wants to be a wife.

"I was just about to go back to egg art," his landlady is saying. Indeed the house is full of egg art; big eggs and little ones, ostrich to quail, painted in appalling colors, with little doors sawed and hinged and pasted with sequins and gilded trim opening on rooms or views cut from magazines and greeting cards. Oddly, these delicate constructions, representing hours of painstaking labor, are uniformly ugly and uninteresting.

"I'm not all that partial to egg art," says Rambeau. He is sick of generation and its symbols. He hates particularly an egg in his room which is painted black outside, red inside, and filled with bits of coal. It represents a potbellied stove or a little elliptical hell, or God knows what, and it keeps on falling over.

"You should hear my kid on egg art," Rambeau's landlady says. "Little Frieda Freud."

Later he calls out, "Kitty, Kitty," and is ashamed. His landlady does not mind; she does not hear him; she is calling out a name of her own.

$Kitty$

◆

The account executive on the Apple Witch project calls Kitty to tell her that while he, personally, thinks she's refreshing as hell and intrusive enough to break through clutter, the client has had a few thoughts. He'd like to review the client's thinking with her.

"What's wrong?" Kitty says.

The client has been exposed to her tape and the client feels she may not impact on his target group. Frankly, very honestly, he's leveling now, the client thinks she's so intrusive she's abrasive.

"Oh," Kitty says.

Unless Kitty is prepared to surf on out of the pop stand she has got to swear that she will pull it in a notch, knock off the highs, bland out and Christ sake dye her hair.

"I can't," Kitty says.

"Babe," he says. "You need the work?"

"I'll wear a wig," Kitty says.

Kitty has finally arrived at a costume that is, while satisfactory to no one, mildly acceptable to all. Her ordinary, pretty or funny witch clothes sketches have been rejected. Too downscale. Too leather bar. Too New Wave. Too strident. Too sweet. Too butch. Too traditional. Too upscale. Too chic. Too dumb. In desperation she submits a sort of well-married middle-management look, Eileen's look: silk shirts and finely tailored skirts and jackets. It is approved. Kitty is puzzled but grateful.

She and Mr. Conrad cut moons and stars from Mylar and stick them on an old black poncho of Rambeau's. Mr. Conrad cuts some additional shapes that really do look magical. Kitty does not recognize them and, inspecting them, feels what she has only lately ever felt: an egregious lack of curiosity. The poncho is hot but it is witchy. It covers her head and hangs from her shoulders with the weight of purpose. She holds her basket of gaudy plastic apples (said to look on camera more like apples than apples do) and tiptoes through an imaginary wood while Mr. Conrad, playing wolf, pursues her.

She is told to limber up for the quad cities with a swing through New Jersey—one local television show and loosely scheduled appearances in shopping center malls. She is bad-tempered about being in New Jersey. She does not expect to find Rambeau in New Jersey. She does not expect to find him in Moline, East Moline or Rock Island either, but she feels she can send out powerful rays through the unknown air of those places. New Jersey air is dense with familiarity.

She does rather well on the TV thing and not too badly either in shopping centers, handing out apple recipes near the Piercing Pagoda or the flower show or the video games arcade. Rattling off a little apple lore. She is unexpectedly shy about being the Apple Witch. She hopes she won't run into anyone she knows.

From Kitty's Confession

◆

"You'll bring trouble down on us," my mother used to say. "You're just inviting trouble. Don't start trouble. Don't make trouble. You're far more trouble than you're worth. You'll cause trouble." It was because I talked too much. I talked to divert them. I babbled all the time to distract them. Asked questions, offered observations. I was desperate to stop them fighting. I said the wrong things, I filled in all the silences, talked up, talked back. Eileen was different. She went off inside herself. She was disdainful. I was more horrified. She was more ashamed. "After all," my mother used to say, "he is your father."

Mr. Conrad and Dorinda

◆

Dorinda walks along, playing a game called Merlin. She is blipping out an electronic version of "Row, Row, Row Your Boat." The Merlin game and some other bits and trinkets she has stolen from a store called Kiddy Cornered. Mr. Conrad functioned as her lookout. He did not enjoy this role and is sweating and scowling.

She and Mr. Conrad are in New York City on a sultry Saturday in August. They are approaching Fifty-seventh Street, walking rather fast. Dorinda's sharp elbow is captive in Mr. Conrad's palm.

"Why you can't be nice?" he demands of Dorinda.

Really, he is indifferent to Dorinda's niceness or lack of it except as it pertains to prenatal influence. He has known her for nearly six months. She is now so big, so waddly with pregnancy, so, it seems to him, heroic, monumental, primitive and grand, that he has difficulty gripping her. But grip her he has, all the way from the Port Authority Bus Terminal, round about the city and on to their destination on Fifty-seventh Street; her convoy, her tender, her pilot fish.

For several blocks he carried on his back her large metallic pouch; catching sight of himself in a store window, he realized he looked rather gnomic and with that he gave it back to her.

Mr. Conrad is wearing a Strawberry Shortcake tee shirt and pants of appleblossom pink. On his head is a pink cotton sunhat of the sort sometimes seen on small children in strollers; on his feet are cotton Chinese slippers, bright fuchsia, strapped like Mary Janes. These clothes are not new, since he has now no money to spend on clothing; he watches his pennies; he is saving for the baby. His mother is dying or possibly dead. He has not heard from his brother in weeks; he cannot bring himself to make the costly, dreaded call. Mr. Conrad has secured a strip of black friction tape around the sleeve of his tee shirt to serve as a crepe, a mourning band. It is very hot in New York City; Mr. Conrad is pleased to be suitably dressed, but he is in poor spirits.

When Dorinda sees that he is flagging, she picks up the pace. "This bores my ass," she says. "I'm *bored* of this."

Dorinda has fastened a bangle of spurs about her ankle. On her feet are high-heeled sandals of metallic crimson, fastened over black fishnet stockings. Her black skirt, draped like a sarong, is long but slit to show the length of Dorinda's fat shapely cross-hatched leg. Her upper body is clothed in a huge black tee shirt. On its bosom is the representation of a sneering silver rat, worked in a sort of plastic trapunto. The rat's eyes are glass, its whiskers are free-standing plastic broom straws. Above the rat, across Dorinda's two great lumps of breasts, glittering letters spell out MALL RAT. Below the rat, another legend, this one encased in an arrow, spells out BABY. The point of the arrow does not seem to Mr. Conrad to indicate accurately the whereabouts of the baby. The arrow seems to him to suggest that should anyone wish to put a baby in there, he need only follow the proffered route. The arrow makes him feel embarrassed.

Overall, Dorinda, who does not sweat, wears a Superman cape. Fishhooks and trout flies are threaded through the holes in her ears. Her nose has been pierced and is swollen and inflamed around its golden stud. She humps on her back the pouch Mr. Conrad rejected. Her black hair, tortured into spikes, is sprayed with brilliant punky colors.

Mr. Conrad is taking Dorinda to a doctor. He has begun to believe that the baby is soon due. When he presses his ear to her belly, well above the arrow, it murmurs to him, subaudibly, in all the languages he knows. Sometimes it speaks in the voice of his dying mother. Sometimes it chitters like an attic full of squirrels. The baby is impatient to be born; he knows it. Mr. Conrad is impatient too. He has painted one hundred pictures for Dorinda, one hundred doggy miniatures, erotic and ingenious, some of them the best things he has done. One hundred dirty pictures was the price agreed on for this baby. But Dorinda is restless and greedy. Although she hardly looks at the paintings he has finished, she wants more; she wants cats.

Cats are not Mr. Conrad's métier. He does not wish to paint cats. He cannot, in any case, paint cats in improper postures because cats make him think of Kitty. He too has stolen an object from Kiddy Cornered. He keeps it in the hand he does not use to steer Dorinda. It is a small ceramic bank in the shape of a stylized cat. An awful thing, and yet . . . It is a small girl of a cat. It is white. A red bow is fashioned near its ear. It wears a green jumper with an elephant on the bib. On its base is printed in fat letters HELLO KITTY. He has stolen this bank because it is an omen. Only now does he notice that the plug that should stop up the bottom of the bank is gone, so any coins deposited through the slit in the back of its head will tumble to the ground.

They have reached the doctor's building, an old and rather dingy one on the edge of a fashionable neighborhood. Now, in late afternoon, the lobby is deserted. Mr. Conrad, who knows this building, guides Dorinda to the night elevator. He slips the toy bank into his belt and takes his place at the controls. He has operated many elevators and likes to do so; the levers make him think of submarine commanders in old movies, just as the painstakingly dressed and cared-for women on Fifty-seventh Street make him think of a phantom Europe.

"I don't believe in doctors," says Dorinda, "doctors suck."

"I am telling you many times, this doctor has no license anymore."

"Okay," Dorinda says. "But I'm bored of it."

"I am telling you many times, this doctor who is my friend is very strange, very sinister," Mr. Conrad says. "He is . . ." He cannot find the word. *Crinkly* comes to mind but he knows that's not it. "He will shock you." He does not believe this; it is bait.

"What do I need a doctor *for*," Dorinda says. "It's just a perfectly natural *function*," Dorinda says, "like taking a really big shit."

Mr. Conrad, discountenanced by this disclosure, misses their floor and must jockey and noodle the elevator until he nudges it home. "Kinky," he says. It is the word he has been looking for.

Willie, Mr. Conrad's friend, is an ambiguous figure. He is often described, though not by himself, as a superior, iconoclastic physician stripped of his license through drink, dope, jealousy, high principles or bureaucratic hanky-panky. Sometimes he is said to be a physician so mysteriously skillful that he has never been able to *get* a license in this country.

Mr. Conrad met Willie at a square dancing club, where he noticed first Willie's old, pointed, handmade, ugly, flashy, two-toned shoes. At that time, Willie ran an animal lab in a volunteer hospital. He has also, to Mr. Conrad's knowledge, been a naturopath, a nutritionist, an electrologist, a masseur, the inventor of a contraption for vacuuming impurities from the pores and a faith healer.

Willie works now for a plastic surgeon in this building

full of podiatrists and dental labs. Willie is a nurse and a surgical assistant. If many of the patients mistake him for the doctor, Willie, who never claims to be the doctor, declines to take the blame.

He is a helpful middleman for Mr. Conrad; Willie has sold many of his paintings. Willie himself commissions paintings. These are the sort that Mr. Conrad, with all his experience, blushes to do. Coy, sentimental, cute: poodles in peignoirs, dobermans in bowler hats and monocles. These dogs have no genitals. (Many of the plastic surgeon's patients are transsexuals and this has shattered Willie's nerves. Willie has become antigenital.)

When they enter Willie's office, or the surgeon's office where Willie works, they are greeted by the smells of green peppers, onions, stewing meat. This office is a suite, with a small operating room, a recovery room, and two rooms for patients making one- or two-day stays. Willie is shouting into the telephone in Russian. (Although Mr. Conrad and Willie share several languages, they speak only English to each other.)

Mr. Conrad can see that Dorinda is dazed. It is the smell of cooking meat, the Russian. Willie is telling his wife about the patient in one of the rooms. This patient is having constructed an artificial penis. It is being made from her thigh. So far, Willie says, it looks like a suitcase handle rising from the mutilated flesh of her thigh. If it survives they will detach one end of it to do many many more objectionable things to it and this poor woggling piece of flesh will be described as a penis but will not be a penis in Willie's view. He tells his wife he has looked at his penis carefully and cannot see why anyone should so distress themselves for the lack of one.

Willie's wife evidently compliments his penis and he snubs her. He says he has made a delicious goulash to comfort the suffering creature with the suitcase handle.

Willie's tone changes and he orders his wife to consume some bananas she will find on the sink. She evidently demurs. He demands that she eat the bananas before the bananas turn black and then he hangs up.

Willie wipes his face. "How far apart are the pains?" he says to Dorinda.

"She has no pains," Mr. Conrad says. "She says she is not to give birth before All Hallows' Eve."

"Nonsense," Willie says. "She is ripe as a pumpkin." In fact, Mr. Conrad has thought of Dorinda only as a sacred pumpkin nurturing one valued seed; a magic walnut sheltering one perfect kernel. He has not given thought to pain, to labor. He has expected her to split, to crack neatly; he has expected her to open like a jewel box, the treasure of the child nestled tidily therein, extending its infant arms, ready to be plucked to another life, free of its carapace, its cocoon, its indifferent mother. Of course he knows, he knows this is not true. He, after all, is writing his poems; his *Mango Cycle* is all about wombs and pangs and bitten pillows and bringing forth in pain and sorrow.

"How far apart are the pains, young woman?" Willie says to Dorinda. At once a fearful gripe assaults her. She grips her belly and goes pale, she totters on her fuck-me shoes. Mr. Conrad lets go of her but Willie gently grabs her. "So it begins," Willie says. "Have your waters broken?"

"No, no, no," Mr. Conrad says. "Please no ideas into her head."

Dorinda's waters break at that and cascade down her fishnet stockings, sopping her shoes and splashing Mr. Conrad's slippers.

"What have you done, Willie?" Mr. Conrad cries. "The child will come out dead."

"Nonsense," Willie says. "The child is ready."

Another pain seizes Dorinda.

"I am not ready," Mr. Conrad says. The warm ammoniac smell of Dorinda's birth waters fills the room with a thrilling, deep, essential reek; it mingles with the smell of cooking meat.

"I don't relate to this," Dorinda says loudly.

"Now, now, young woman," Willie says. "Nothing has really started yet."

He takes Dorinda to one of the hospital rooms. He calls to Mr. Conrad to come help undress her, stymied as he is by spurs and fishhooks, but Mr. Conrad, to his shame, has his head between his knees.

Throughout the night, Dorinda yips and bickers; she keeps saying she has changed her mind. Willie and sometimes Mr. Conrad rub her back, pat her temples with alcohol and root for her. Sometimes they read a little Pushkin, sometimes Willie explains about tummy tucks or electrolysis or faith healing or nutrition. They agree that when hard labor starts Dorinda will call for her mother and wonder weakly if Dorinda's mother should somehow be alerted, made available. But Dorinda never calls for her mother, or indeed for anyone else.

Mr. Conrad and Willie eat goulash and drink thick red wine. They play dominoes and cards and give bulletins and sips of apple juice and dabs of goulash to the patient with the artificial penis. This patient has borne three children and offers some useful advice.

Mr. Conrad tries to be sportsmanlike, but really he feels this is not the spot at all for a person of taste, however deep his interests in the mysteries of generation. He is in fear that Dorinda will do or say something that touches his heart, that makes her seem a person, rather than a cargo ship unloading. There is just one moment when this almost happens. Just as the child slithers out, Dorinda seems seized by a force outside herself, an enormous invisible hand that squeezes and shakes her. Her eyes fly open and she gives a cry. It is not a plaintive cry, it is a cry of exultation. Mr. Conrad thinks of his mother. But he has heard too much about the anguish of his birth. It has moved him so much and so early that it cannot now move him at all. His mother has sent him the silk dressing gown stained with the bloody waters of his birth and he has burned it.

Willie is pleased by Dorinda's baby but Mr. Conrad is

not. He has expected something larger, better-looking and more jovial. The baby is covered all over with pale apricot down; lanugo, Willie calls it. There are two teeth in its lower jaw. When Willie presses its little tit, a bead of clear fluid springs out. Witches' milk, says Willie. Willie has heard of this but never seen it. The baby's feet turn up like elf shoes. Mr. Conrad thinks of the one hundred pictures; his enormous investment; his dying mother. He thinks of offering this goblin baby to Kitty, who may spurn it.

But he knows she will not. Women, save Dorinda, are fools about babies. He has forgotten to ascertain the baby's sex and Willie has diapered it in toweling. Willie, when consulted, says it's hard to tell and that this is the case with many babies. Willie says it does not matter. Suppose it is born with a nice little pussy; it will soon be back anyway whining for a suitcase handle. Mr. Conrad peers under the toweling. The baby is a boy.

Willie is willing to keep Dorinda and determined also to keep the baby. Mr. Conrad wants to take it right away.

"She has to give it suck, you fool," says Willie. "She'll never give it up, you fool." He's drunk.

Mr. Conrad arranges to collect Dorinda and the baby in two days. He thinks he will take them to Kitty's house; Kitty is away on her apple tour. Or perhaps he will keep them in the mansion, though the mansion has neither light nor water.

He is sure that Dorinda will soon be, as she says, bored of it. He promises to paint for Willie some sweet and dreadful pictures full of dressed-up dogs with nothing doing underneath their tails.

When he leaves, mid-morning Sunday, the day is overcast. Dorinda sleeps with the baby in her armpit, its toothed mouth fastened to her nipple. Her face has been washed, she is pale as an idol. Willie shouts in German of bananas, black bananas; the suitcase-handle patient eats a bagel and reads the financial pages of the Sunday *Times*.

Gordon

◆

Gordon eats his breakfast, early and alone, on a hotel patio in Mexico City. His feelings are in disarray. He has come to Mexico to deliver a paper at a medical conference, but that part of his trip counts for little. Seven years before this breakfast, Gordon has had, in Mexico City, the only entirely inexplicable experience of his life.

This time he wanted to bring Eileen with him to Mexico. He wanted to tell her here of the baby he has made for her. But Eileen has not come.

Gordon sips his bitter, winey coffee, cracks his crusty, tasteless roll. He has already run, washed himself, put on a white guayabera, cotton trousers, coarse sandals. These clothes chafe and bind him. They are consecrated clothes, seven years old, the oldest clothes he owns. Preserved for their history and worn again in hope, they have so far failed him.

Gordon begged Eileen to come with him. At least he thinks of it as begging. His tongue would not utter his need.

"I just want you to be there for me, Eye."

"I try always to be there for you." It is the barren lingo of their agonized exchanges.

199

"I think you will admit I am a caring, sharing individual," he said. He feels an awful glimmer of disgust. Does he sound like a cartoon in some paper like the Voice? Still, how do people talk, decent striving people? This is how they talk. They talk like this.

"I try to be supportive," Eileen said. "Despite your verbal barbs, which rather irk me."

He had a sense of misadventure. This woman beside him was surely not the woman who so stirred him, years ago, whose light consoling voice and curving cheek delighted and assured him.

"Darling," he said. "Eye, on a personal basis, we discuss very little that's substantive. Our interactions are not of the best. Our communication has faltered."

Eileen took his hand and moved it on her body. "I get so damp in hot countries," she said. "I wilt. My hair goes funny. I spend all my time with a blow dryer and a curling wand. I might get prickly heat. I might get the green apples."

"The green apples," he said. "Diarrhea, diarrhea, say it." He used his hand in a way that hurt her. "Too inhibited to vomit, too fastidious to shit," he said. "What do you want from a bride of Christ?"

Viciously, she pinched the insides of his thighs. He fell on her, aroused, and as they thrashed and pummeled he told her that she would do just as he said, do anything he asked of her, anything.

"Anything," she gasped in wild agreement. "Anything."

In the event, she was offered and accepted what sounds to him a particularly pointless and possibly upsetting assignment that has to do with interviewing pregnant women. He is philosophically opposed to minding that she's done this, but, practically, he does mind.

Gordon fiddles with a newspaper, scanning it, squinting at it. Muertes, he reads. It is the only word he recognizes.

Nevertheless, he affects an interest in the news. His only audience is the hotel cat. When Gordon realizes what he is up to, irritation heats him like a blush.

He puts down the newspaper and picks up a jeweler's box. In it, on funereal plush, reposes a bangle made to bolt about the wrist with tiny screws of gold. A golden screwdriver lies beside it. Usually, Gordon has been told, each of a pair of lovers wears one of these bangles—the pretense is that they cannot be removed. As a physician, Gordon thinks, he can hardly be expected to run around with a bracelet bolted to his wrist. So he has bought just one. Inside the bracelet is a legend of Gordon's devising. "Yessir," it reads, "that's my baby."

Now, as he looks at the bracelet and the words inside the bracelet he is filled with desolation and distrust. The gold screwdriver reminds him of a bundle of rag-wrapped tools he saw that morning when he ran. These tools were strapped to the handlebars of a rachitic bike and the bike itself was pedaled by a man so old, so frail, that only the most coherent need could have forced him out into the dawn to make his slow way to his workplace.

Gordon puts the bracelet back into its box. Perhaps he will give it to Dorinda, when Dorinda surfaces again. He has not seen nor heard from Dorinda for nearly three weeks, but women, he knows, play these games. He is confident of his power over the girl. She is foolish; he is not.

Gordon writes a word on the pad of paper in his clipboard. "Herpes," he writes.

He is sure Dorinda does not have herpes. Can he be sure? Entirely sure?

"C-section," Gordon writes under herpes. He will speak with Dorinda's OB/GYN. He underlines C-section. She is young, she is robust. It will not kill her, probably. And it is safer for his baby.

"Wee Wizards," he writes below C-section. He has heard of a program designed to accelerate the development of gifted infants. He believes it is conducted at the University of Pennsylvania. He thinks the sessions are on Saturdays. He means to find out more about it. He and Eileen will surrender their Saturdays. They will go together to Philadelphia to crouch attentively in little chairs with paddle-shaped armrests. They will watch—what will they watch? His mind supplies only a cartoon sequence of smug, diapered babies chalking theorems on blackboards. He will investigate Wee Wizards. He has already sent for a journal called *Family Affairs* only to discover it is subtitled *The Positive Side of Incest* and not at all what he had in mind.

The thin air tampers with Gordon's thought. He means to focus on the serious legal business of securing the baby's custody, but his mind will not confront it. He has a rich but vague anticipation of dusky paneled offices, decorum, an atmosphere of quiet congratulation. But for all he knows the mechanics of these things are brusque and sordid.

He has tried to put himself in touch with Dorinda's father. He wonders why he did this. The geneticist did not know who he was. He proposed to Gordon an investment in a scheme for training casino employees called Crap Out Careers, and another called BYB—Bequeath Your Body. He tried to sell Gordon a table at a benefit.

Gordon felt orphaned. "Yes, Doctor," he kept saying to Dorinda's father. "No, Doctor. Not just at this time, Doctor. Thank you, Doctor."

Gordon opens the bracelet box and takes out the bracelet and spins it on his finger. Perhaps he will give it to Mick. She is a pack rat and he often gives her the stuff he gets from drug company detail men—digital clocks, mechanical calendars, golf ball–sized globes of the world. He also buys her toys. He will pick up some magic paper figures, little watchdogs, possibly, of the kind they use in Puebla to keep off evil spirits and make the crops grow. If he can find them, he will buy papier-mâché Day of the Dead dolls. He has seen these things in a waiting room copy of *Smithson-*

ian. Soon he will buy them for Mick, and quite soon for his child. He approves of these toys, they are instructive. Though in quite what they instruct, he cannot say.

He has a sudden yearning, senseless and strong, for the company of Mick. When Eileen turned him down he called up Mick. He wanted her commiseration; then he wanted her along in Mexico. A foolish impulse, frivolous, for Mick is agoraphobic and has not left her house and yard in years. She is cunning. She conceals her malady and he helps her to do so, conspires with her. Why not? The world would be a better place if more people pretended there was nothing wrong with them.

He is drawn to the scornful, mocking way Mick treats him and her awe of him. When Gordon goes to see her he brings bunches of zinnias and pig trotters, big red onions for Mick to fry in butter. She teases him; no one has ever talked to him in her way and something about the experience frees him. Ass-in-Pockets, she calls him. Hunger's Mother. Divilskin. Little Father McPriest. He calls her Beulah. Beulah Witch—from a puppet in a half-remembered child's show. He never calls her Beulah when her daughters are around.

Mick cuts articles on medical subjects from her newspapers and magazines. Once she showed him a copy of *Gung-Ho, The Magazine for the International Military Man* with an article on prisoner-survival medicine, dealing mostly with the therapeutic possibilities of urine.

He is delighted and touched by her antics—he thinks of them as her antics—and he sits with colored pens sometimes, showing her how things work: the major organ systems, the circulation of the blood, a protein molecule. He reads all the clippings, even shoves them in his file. He wishes he had been able to bring her to Mexico, buy her a nice mantilla, show her a bit of the world before she dies, which she will do, he thinks, quite soon.

He forgives her for her bad behavior when he first came

to court Eileen, her weeping and raging and starving and vomiting bile. In retrospect, he enjoyed all that, and Mick, though she is primitive, looks as patrician as you like. Sometimes he talks of her to patients. He calls her a character. He feels uncomfortable in doing this, but does it nonetheless.

When Mick and Eileen refused this trip, he telephoned his own mother. A big, virile woman, she has spent her life in her own remanufacture. She wants to be tiny, fluffy, idle, the sort of woman his father and her own much prefer. She couldn't come to Mexico because she was having her nails wrapped. Gordon bores her, he always has and he's always known it. When he is with her he tries to be entertaining. Sometimes, when he thinks of his mother, a pang of futile longing shakes him.

When Gordon came to Mexico the first time he was sullen, he was vile. To avoid the other physicians at the conference he registered not at the conference hotel but at a pretty, shabby inn in the Zona Rosa. He rehearsed his research paper, which seemed less dazzling than he'd thought. He wrote Eileen a long and ugly letter, burned it, flushed the ashes. He decided to ditch medicine and take up something else, take up law. He telephoned Eileen, very late, roused the household, rowed with her. After a few hours' yeasty sleep he rose to run through the Zona Rosa.

Afterward, Gordon was never able to reconstruct the experience so that it sounded like anything. "I saw a man on horseback," he would say—to himself, for he told no one else lest they diminish it. "I saw a man on horseback in gray riding clothes." That was all he did see. Suddenly before him he saw a man mounted on a fine gray horse. The man wore dove gray riding clothes and a flat-crowned hat with a brim, also gray. When he saw Gordon he saluted him, or blessed him, raised his hand. Gordon was unable to say if his hands were gloved or bare. He was to Gordon, breathless, spurting sweat, a vision of achieved perfection.

After a moment, the horseman wheeled his horse and rode away. Absurd as it seemed, even to Gordon, the gray horseman left him changed. All that was vain and dreadful vanished. He felt that he had swallowed a hard knob of grace. It burned and glittered in his gullet, like a diamond, like a star. He resolved to become a Catholic and to marry Eileen.

The way seemed easy and open to him; it was not, but after many troubles, he managed to do both these things. He relaxed into good behavior. He was an ardent husband; he loved to say "my wife"; he was diligent in the discharge of his religious duties; and although his patients died and suffered as before, he no longer felt so slighted by their weakness and mortality.

When months and more months went by and he had not begotten a child on Eileen, he began to be reproachful. "Isn't this odd for Catholics?" he asked her. "It's very odd for *Catholics*," she said, in a way that suggested they were mysteriously less than Catholics.

In time she attended fertility clinics. At first, he encouraged her, insofar as he could do that without himself cooperating, but he finds her intractable fruitlessness an insult. She is guilty when she bleeds; he is sickened. He laughs at her coital logs, her positions, her pills. Secretly, he thinks that his is the flaw, for he sees it as a flaw, an accusation.

As hope for a child departed from them, so did Gordon's faith. His conversion became a bit of party talk. Though he never forgot and never disclosed his experience with the gray horseman, he did wonder in time if it had been some kind of pathology. But he is unable to maintain this view. He no longer entertains the feelings aroused by the gray horseman, but he remembers having them. When Dorinda revealed her pregnancy to him, he felt them flickering again. He is released from some curse of aridity through the child. He will make it Eileen's child, and save her.

Gordon sits at the table skimming his fingers over "Yessir, that's my baby." He has run that morning but he has not seen the horseman. Perhaps he should have prepared himself. Prayer. Fasting. But this conference, so unlikely in Mexico in August, had seemed to him a sign. He felt beckoned to Mexico. He felt it this morning. He ran, but all he saw was the old man on the bike and he is not sentimental about old men on bikes.

Today he will give his paper, tomorrow morning, early, he will run again. The day is already hot. He sees that he has loosened and lost two of the small gold screws that secure the bracelet. He looks on the table and around his feet but cannot find them. The bracelet doesn't work without them. He is momentarily annoyed and then indifferent. He will give it to Eileen and let her worry about it. He puts the maimed bracelet away in its box. His eyes are drawn to the list he has been making.

Under Wee Wizards, there are three words written in an unremarkable but also unfamiliar hand. The words are "Do no harm."

Gordon studies the words. He picks up his initialed gold pencil, warm to his fingers from the sun, and writes "egypt egypt egypt" over each of his entries. Soon the only words on the clipboard that can be read at all are "Do no harm."

Kitty

---◆---

"I'm your child," I say, "I'm going to be out of town for two months. How can you say I can't kiss you goodbye?"

"You may stay where you are," says Mick's voice on the telephone, "for I don't want you." She sounds full of mischief, my mother, very merry, up to something.

"I could come and kiss the dog goodbye," I say, "good God forbid."

"The poor animal is feeling better," my ma says. "Yesterday it passed a serpent. Kitty, you should be more careful."

"Worms," I say. I am heartsick. I have not been easy in my mind about leaving the dog with my mother. But it is Rambeau's dog and I am attached to it by sentiment. "I'll come and get it and leave it at the vet's."

"Not atall," she says. "Worms was not the problem. A big purple serpent it was. Green and purple. An awful-looking thing. The animal was groaning and grunting like a woman in childbed. Your father was tormented by the constipation, too."

"Mommy," I say, "you're not getting gaga, are you?" It worries me that lately she's begun to speak of my father, and in this chatty, offhand way.

"Not atall," she says. "I picked up this snake on the pitch-fork and I plunged it in a pail of boiling water."

"Oh," I say.

"And it was a pair of your pantyhose, Kitty, and you should be more careful."

"Oh," I say. I know what she says is true. I recollect the pantyhose in question.

"I'm leaving Labor Day, you know," I say. "You won't feast your eyes on me for two whole months."

"Knowing you," my mother says, "you'd get a wearing or two from this garment. Would I rinse it out?"

"Oh, goodbye, Mother," I say. "I'll be seeing you."

"I'm just after sudsing the dog," she says. "Its coat is as white as the driven snow and its ears are as red as two coals."

"Watch out for that dog," I say. "Remember, it's the hound of hell."

"So it is," she says, but she's laughing. "It's old Nick."

"I'm your sister," I say to Eileen on the telephone. "If you don't see me now, you won't be seeing me for two whole months."

"My life is opening like a rose," Eileen says. "I have to think things. I can't do things. It's all I can do just to *be*." As always on the phone, she's hushed and urgent, but more than that this time, she is secretive and exalted. At once I conclude that Eileen is in love. "Sissy," I say, "oh, Luna, come on, tell." I don't want her to tell, you know, I don't want to hear a word about it. But I owe her, she's my sister.

"Kitty," she whispers, "it's a miracle. It's a gift from God."

"What is? Talk to me." And all the while I'm thinking, or praying, please don't let her talk to me.

"I'm not ready," Eileen whispers. "Not yet."

"Oh, okay," I say. The truth is, I just want to get away. I

want to do my shopping and my packing. I want to fool with my hideous wig. I want to beat a tattoo on my chest —because I am getting ready to go out into the world and beam strong tender messages to sweet Rambeau.

"Pray for me," my sister says.

"Oh, okay," I say. And I do, a little. But mostly I forget.

"I'm your friend," I say to Mr. Conrad, when he does me the favor of turning up at last. "I'll be gone two months. I should think you'd be willing just to drive me to the airport."

"No dice," Mr. Conrad says. He is masterful. He is shooting me meaningful looks that I don't get the meaning of. He is incubating some plot, I think, he has that look, he is burning with some purpose. Our dinner is thrown together, dollops and driblets I don't want suppurating in my refrigerator while I'm gone. Mr. Conrad looks upon it with disfavor. Yawning, he eats all the best bits. He trots off early, leaving me to wash the dishes on my own.

*T*hings Kitty Learns on the Plane That Flies Her to Iowa

◆

From *Progressive Grocer:*
"Apples are food commodities. They can be marketed as if they were branded products."

From *You Can Be Your Dog's Best Friend:*
"Lapp women sacrifice a dog before childbirth . . .
"A dog that bites its tail is commonly believed to be Satan . . .
"Hill tribes in time of drought torture a dog so the Big Dog may hear and send down rain . . .
"Dogs are often depicted licking the wounds of St. Roch, at the feet of St. Bernard, or carrying a lighted torch in the mouth in representations of St. Dominic."

From *The Search for the Ultimate Apple:*
Some names of old apples—Grimes Golden, Pound Sweet. Winter Banana. Wolf River. Snow.
"Another old-fashioned green apple, well flavored, though not much to look at, is the Summer Rambo."

Kitty

◆

"The quad cities, should anyone ask you, are Davenport-Bettendorf, Rock Island, Moline and East Moline," I say. "I speak to you from Davenport-Bettendorf, I just call it Bettendorf. That's in Iowa."

"Who's this that's talking?" my mother says.

"It's me that's talking."

"Who's me? Who's this that's talking?"

"Me, me, *me*. You'll drive me mad, it's me. So how's the dog?"

"Eileen," my mother says. "How are you keeping?"

"It's *Kitty*," I say. "How are you?"

"I'm as well as I was when last you called, I haven't had time to get worse or better."

"I'm going to call Gordon, and have him go out there and pick up that vicious dog and bring it to a vet where it can bloody well live in a cage until I'm home again. And don't you put your hands on it till Gordon gets there."

"Sure that's ridiculous nonsense," she says. "Nothing of the sort. I rest my two feet on him just like a footstool, so I do."

"You and the Crusaders," I say. "You and the Vikings.

211

You and St. Bernard. Close that dog in the kitchen. I'll call Gordon."

"You'll do no such of a thing," she says. "The dog is feared of me, Kitty. The dog is cowering and cringing. He's a whipped cur, so he is."

"Why is it a whipped cur? It isn't a whipped cur in my experience."

"He's a whipped cur because I whipped him, Kitty. I tore a switch from the tree in the yard and broke it across his back. His whole life long he's been in want of a really good hiding. The little bobbles of fruit on the limb went scurrying all around the kitchen, Kitty. It did me the world of good, Kitty. If God spares me I'll beat him again, so I will. And don't you say a word to me. You do as your own divil bids you and I'll do the bidding of mine."

And she puts down the phone.

So here I am in Iowa, while my mother is crazy in Queens. I don't know what to do so I call my sister.

"Who is this, please?" says Eileen's voice. "Who is this? Please, I can't think, I'm busy."

"Eileen," I say, "it's me."

"Who is this, please? Oh, please, I cannot think, I'm busy."

"It's *me*."

"Eye," says Gordon's voice on the extension. "Eye, it's your sister, Eye, it's Kitty. *Kitty.*"

"Somebody talk to me," I say.

"She's upset," he says. "She's ventilating."

"Just try to say it in English," I say.

"Eye," he says. "Eye." Or perhaps he is saying "I. I." Then he says, "Why don't you leave us alone."

"Because she's my sister."

"I'll take care of your sister."

"I have to talk with her about our mother."

"I'll take care of your mother."

At that moment, I feel an unfamiliar respect for Gordon.

I want him to say that he will take care of me. But he doesn't say that. He doesn't say anything at all.

"Gordon," I say. "Perhaps I should come home." I don't want to go home. There has never before been a time in my life when I wasn't more willing to go home than I was to go anywhere else.

"Do as you like," Gordon says. "It doesn't matter to anyone here what you do. Personally I think you should mind your own business."

"All right," I say. "I'll do that."

These ordinary sentiments of Gordon's release me. It doesn't matter to anyone, really matter to anyone, what I do. How fine a feeling. I have not had it before. I will mind my own business, my own, my business, full of ambiguities and dangers, *mine.*

From Kitty's Confession

♦

When I was a very little girl, my mother told me strange things of an intimate nature—stories, tales. When I was old enough perhaps to understand them, she told me nothing. I have it fixed in my mind, vivid and blurred, that my mother, when she was a girl, was tarred and feathered because my father betrayed her. I believe this so strongly that it seems to have happened to me. I can see rough men come to take me from my house and I can hear their voices. I fall on a cobbled street. A fat coarse-voiced woman takes my arm and shakes me, calls me whore. I am weak and sore and I have lately had a baby, I am quaking with fear for my baby, in a cradle in the house. The cradle has a poker laid across the foot of it. I am called whore and my hair is cropped and stubble on my head is rubbed with tar. I smell the tar. I feel my mother's hatred of my father, who betrayed her. I am she who was betrayed. But how did he betray her? And is the baby that I fear for Eileen? In Queens?

If I asked my mother anything about this, she would say, "Are you not right in the mind? Are you away in the head? Are you sick or what ails you, that is something you have got out of *Life* magazine."

When my father finally died, that night, my mother opened a window. She stopped the mantel clock. She drew the shades. She put a scarf across the mirror. But when I said something of this to Eileen, just once I said it, she said, "Oh, Kitty, *really*. Oh, Kitty, you're out of your mind."

Rambeau

◆

Sometimes, in the mornings, in Atlantic City, Rambeau takes his landlady out for fried-egg sandwiches and cornflakes. They eat at one of the shabby counter places that advertises "breakfast 24 hrs a day."

As they eat, he looks over a racing paper and she reads out the flashier murders, political messes and garden club news. Afterwards, he may stroll on the boardwalk, running his palm over a section of handrail in an area once used mostly by the blind, tilting up his face, eyes closed, as he does so. Sometimes he jogs barefoot on the strand. The beach is not crowded; the season is over, the children are tucked away in schools. It is the children, he thinks, that give this gaming place a character different from any other.

In the afternoons, if he has no business elsewhere, he paces off the casino floors, searching for Dorinda. There is not much heart in his search, for his preoccupation with Dorinda's baby has almost disappeared. The space it occupied in Rambeau's life is empty, which makes more room for his worries about poor Kitty and about the maddening girl called Cherokee, who now, to his horror, claims in her turn to be pregnant.

216

Rambeau doesn't know where to look for Dorinda. She has never spread around much information. But he doesn't want to leave Atlantic City until her due date is past. She may come back to look for him.

He feels restless and temporary, but his music is going well. He is playing better than he ever has. Through many shifts and changes in the group, Rambeau has persevered, and now he has a following. One of his fans, a high roller who writes on jazz for a magazine and a newspaper, has reviewed Rambeau's work so ebulliently that Rambeau feels a little shamefaced. Nevertheless he keeps the clippings with the letter he is writing to Kitty. If he finishes the letter, it will be the third one he has written her and, one way or another, most likely it will be the last.

After the jazz critic's second review, which appeared in a weekly magazine, Rambeau saw Gordon in his audience. Beside him was a big, bored, handsome black woman. Even swagged in flame-colored crepe, she looked to Rambeau like a nurse. When they were introduced, she said she was a nurse; she had once been on a case obscurely involving Charley Pride. Gordon was nervous and drunk. He kept inquiring where the action was "around here," as if he knew where the action was everywhere else.

Gordon sat on through the last set, although the woman slipped away, and Rambeau had to bring him along to a poker game. There the jazz critic took a dislike to Gordon, who insisted on explaining John Coltrane to him.

Gordon, inept at poker, pockets full of fifties in bank wrappers, clung to Rambeau, bellicose, confused and confiding. Rambeau won despite this. Rambeau learned from Gordon's addled mix of hint and history, that Gordon had fathered a child and abandoned its mother. Or perhaps the mother had abandoned Gordon. Apparently the child had not survived. Or perhaps it was the mother who had not survived. Possibly the mother was the splendid, scornful black woman. When any of these things had happened, or if any of them had happened, Rambeau is not prepared to say.

Gordon also told Rambeau that Eileen was pregnant. When he congratulated Gordon, Gordon turned on him and berated him for believing "a classic hysteric" rather than "a board-certified physician." Before the jazz critic could pound Gordon to a powder, Gordon grew solemn and punctilious underneath the alcohol. Soon he hadn't a word to say.

In the early morning sunshine, Rambeau walked him, still unsteady, to the Claridge Hotel and Hi Ho Casino, where Gordon said he had a suite. On the hotel's threshold, Gordon linked his arm and drew Rambeau into the lobby. He tugged Rambeau to a house phone and on it he ordered the woman who liked Charley Pride to bring their bags down. Rambeau was struck by his tone, at once peremptory and pleading. Rambeau tried to take his leave but Gordon detained him, his expression so urgent that Rambeau felt alarm.

But what Gordon said was, "I used to be a cellist, quite a promising cellist. I haven't touched a cello in years."

Rambeau left as Gordon scouted through his pockets for the keys to his red Porsche.

"Enjoyed it," Gordon called after him. His voice was desolate. "Enjoyed it thoroughly."

In these days Rambeau's energy is boundless. He scrapes and paints the trim on his landlady's house and on Mick's. He washes and paints their storm windows and puts them up. He soaks the old brass of their knockers and knobs in muriatic acid, polishes it until it shines like gold.

Mick treats him as though he were doing this work preparatory to moving in; his landlady as though he were doing it preparatory to moving on.

"Just let me show you where I keep the cinnamon," Mick

says, "in case you should be wanting it. Of course, Jock, you may have a mind to make arrangements of your own."

"You don't owe me anything, Jacques," says his land-lady. "It's been real nice, *une bonne chance*, knowing you."

When he stands on a ladder in Queens, flowing fresh paint onto Mick's sandpapered window frames, he hears her brawling with his dog.

"You wouldn't turn your toe where your heel would lie," she barges at the dog. "My heart's nearly scalded with wiping up after your four oul' filthy feet!"

And the dog makes a noise like a rusty gate, moaning and creaking in its throat.

Sometimes what he hears makes Rambeau's flesh rise, for she talks to the dog as though it were a man. "I never did you a wrong turn," she says. "And you give me the worst word in your belly!"

Once he hears her shout, "You cowardly git, if you ever shot a man it was from ambush!"

Once he catches her flogging the dog, though she plays innocent when he confronts her. Her arm is like match-wood and the dog is powerful, not big but thick and stumpy; he feels she cannot do it any harm. Equally, he cannot bear to have her strike it.

"The dog might go for you," Rambeau says. "It's not a reliable breed, they can be vicious." As he says this, he feels a failure of allegiance.

"Oh aye," Mick says with a repudiating smile, "true for you, they can be vicious." She rubs the dog's ears, cleans its eyes with her thumb, pries open its fierce fanged jaws and scrubs at its teeth with a washcloth. The dog grins and shivers.

Late one afternoon, as Rambeau is wrapping wet brushes in foil, Eileen arrives in the blood-red Porsche with BLOOD spelled out on its vanity plate. She is swollen and sloppy in a flapping gum-colored maternity dress. She leaves again

at a sobbing run, throws herself into the Porsche, lurches
and slams so recklessly away that he is worried.

He goes into the house and looks for Mick who is mottled
and trembling.

"I'm after giving out at our Eileen," she says. "I hope she
doesn't do herself an injury. She thinks she's thon way. But
you know and I know that our Eileen is talking through her
hat."

"I don't know," says Rambeau, who wants not to hear
about pregnancies and babies, but is touched by the spec-
tacle of Kitty's beautiful, forbidding sister, ripe and greasy-
haired. "Everyone else is having babies, why shouldn't our
Eileen have one?"

"Hush you," Mick says. "Not Eileen."

Rambeau runs upstairs to shower. As he passes the
locked door of Kitty's old room, now the secret nursery, he
touches the fluted glass knob. He cannot pass this room
without guilt. Mick never asks about the baby they have
made ready for, but she searches his face with her eyes;
startlingly blue, beseeching, they are like Kitty's eyes and
trouble him. He comforts himself with the thought that he
has, in the stead of a baby, supplied the old woman with
an interesting dog.

When Rambeau comes down to the kitchen, Mick, in
her many-colored cardigan, stands by the refrigerator with
her hand on the chromium pull. She looks entranced, frozen; her blue eyes blaze.

Rambeau speaks to her and she answers him, but she
might be speaking in tongues. There are words and they
are grouped in a parody of human discourse; but what she
says makes no sense.

Frightened, Rambeau goes to her and touches her as he
has never done. He is moved by a warm, salty smell that
rises, not unpleasant, from her hair and her skin as he
circles her with his arms. He feels a terror and a chill that
he has never felt. It is what he imagines he should feel for

his child. "You're all right," he says to her, "you're okay, everything's going to be fine. God forgive me," he says, when he hears what he says.

Mick addresses him again and again; she is intent and gibbering. He cannot release her hand from the chromium rod. He sees that her locked grip sustains her; she is swaying, swinging from the hand that is fastened to the wand of chrome. Her left side is feeble, her arm is limp and her foot not properly under her; her mouth is wry.

He drags the kitchen table toward them with his foot. He has some idea of bracing and supporting her, but her face is so anxious and shadowed that he shoves the table away. He stands with his arms around her, trying to take her weight. She feels like a creature half-woman, half-tree; the whole left side of her is stiffened, jammed, blocked, yet loose and useless.

He smooths her hair with his palm. "Don't die," he says. He kisses her brow. "Dear God, do something for me," he says, "this is awful."

He hooks his foot over the rung of a chair and maneuvers it until he can ease her into it. He thinks he must call Gordon. When he turns from her she darts, released. She rushes forward with tiny quick steps, impelled by some force just behind her. He seizes her and lifts her long body and lays her on the couch in the living room, covering her with a bright knitted blanket.

"That was a turn," she says. He is astonished. It is like hearing the dog speak. "What was I doing?" she says. "Was I making your tea? Don't pull any more weeds," she says, "the frost will take them soon enough."

"All right," Rambeau says. It is true that he has pulled some weeds. He is heartened.

"All right," Mick says, "I'm quite all right, I'd be much worse off if anything ailed me. It's hard to get dying."

"Stop it," he says. "I don't want you to think that."

"It's hard to get dying," Mick says. "Wet the tea."

"It's transient," Gordon says on the phone. "Cerebral incident, a little old blood vessel pops, she has them all the time."

"It's a stroke?"

"A little stroke, a small one, nothing special."

"How do you know she won't have a big one?"

"She probably will have a big one, Jack, you know how people die. They have strokes, they have heart attacks, they have cancer. Once in a while they have overwhelming infections, but not so much anymore. My waiting room is full of patients, Jack. She probably won't have the big one right *now*. Maybe she will, but probably not. I don't see a hospital, I really don't. Why put a phobic old lady in the hospital, she'll probably come apart. Her life is so claustral, Jack. She's over this one, anyhow. I don't need to see her. I'll see her when I see her. I drop in now and then."

"You get your ass here within the hour or I'll kill you with my bare hands."

"Look," Gordon says, "she's a nice old Paddy, I like her. What's more she's the mother of the crazy bitch I'm married to. And therefore if she dies not only will the baby Jesus have no grandma, but my wife will deteriorate. Further deteriorate."

"Eileen's not pregnant?"

"My friend, she is not pregnant."

"You be here," Rambeau says. "Within the hour."

Mick is sleeping. He makes some tea. As he does so, he discovers that Mick, assailed as she was making tea, has poured tea into the milk carton. The startling, bewitched brown milk repels him and then it seems brave that she should persevere in a homely task while vessels explode in her brain.

When he brings the tea into the living room, Mick is still asleep. The dog is spraddled over her. He hauls the dog into the kitchen, gives it a feed and chains it in the yard. The dog makes confiding, worried noises, mutterings and clankings.

Within the hour, Gordon does appear. He is driving the crimson Porsche; the nose of the car is newly dented. He looks too grand for the little house in a pale, well-cut jacket of silky suede, a stethoscope looped from its pocket.

"This is damned inconvenient," Gordon says.

"For her, too."

With a minimal change of expression, Gordon conveys his distaste for this sort of talk. He looks down at the old woman sleeping on the couch and curls his fingers about her wrist. His touch is so gentle that she doesn't stir. In a moment he moves his hand away and adjusts the afghan that covers her. He goes into the kitchen and takes from the refrigerator two bottles of beer and opens them and gives one to Rambeau.

"What are you going to do?" Rambeau says. He is impressed by Gordon. Gordon knows what to do and he doesn't.

"I'm going to fix her up so she lives forever," Gordon says, drinking from the bottle of beer.

"Good man!"

"You asshole. I'm going to stick around a while and then I'm going to go away. I'm not going to do a damn thing. Got some cards?"

"*Cards?*"

"Playing cards. To while away the hours."

Rambeau can't find playing cards but he discovers a pocket chess set in the china cabinet. It is very small, the chessmen are tiny plastic pegs, and when he and Gordon play they sit close together. Rambeau is calmed and comforted by Gordon's presence. He calls Irving and tells him to dig up a replacement. He calls his bookie. He and Gordon have a talk about bookies. They drink more beer and talk about golf. Comradely content falls upon them; they are drawn together in time of trouble. They are like brothers. The handsome old woman sleeps on.

When she wakes, Rambeau sees that Gordon's being there frightens her, but she behaves in a way that he has never known her to. She is darling and coquettish, playing up to Gordon's awful teasing, eyes bright, cheeks as rosy as a child's.

"Squeeze my hand, you old devil," Gordon cries.

"Sure I don't want to squeeze your hand, so I don't. Why would I squeeze your oul' hand?"

"Squeeze my hand!"

And she takes Gordon's outstretched hand and squeezes it with all her force, twinkling and flirting as Gordon howls and winces in a parody of pain, yelling, *"Thatta girl."*

Rambeau is happy and uncomfortable.

Mick swings her arms above her head and claps her old hands smartly. "I'm right as rain," she says. "There's nothing wrong with me. I'd be much worse off if anything ailed me."

She springs to her feet and touches her toes. She moves more smoothly than he has ever seen her do. Gordon seizes her and jigs her around a little. Then he sits her down beside him and fumbles with the buttons on her bodice. She slaps at his hands as he tries to place his stethoscope, rocking with laughter and silliness, shy. She slaps at his hands and calls him Doctor Ass-in-Pockets. She calls out to Rambeau to rescue her, she squalls at Gordon, hectic with laughter, "Unhand me, I say, unhand me, sir." Gordon looks up at Rambeau and points with his chin. Rambeau gapes.

"Would you leave me alone with my patient?" Gordon says.

Rambeau drifts off to the kitchen, feeling exiled. He makes sandwiches, dainty ones with the crusts trimmed off, and piles them on a platter. Then he removes them from the platter, puts a napkin on the platter and piles the sandwiches up again. He decorates the pile with some watercress. He makes some radish roses and eats them. He is rooting around in Mick's spotless refrigerator, looking for he knows not what, when Gordon comes into the kitchen. Gordon takes up a handful of trimmed crusts and crams them in his mouth.

"When I was a kid," he says, "they told me that eating crusts would make my hair curly. And I ate them and it did." He washes his hands at the sink.

"How is she?" Rambeau says.

"How is she? She's lousy. On the other hand, she's quite all right."

"Should I stay?"

"Up to you. Can't hurt. Can't help, either."

"I'll stay."

"Bully. You'll wear a starry crown."

"Bugger you."

"Bugger *you*. Call if you need me. I just stare at the fucking ceiling all night long. But you won't need me. I don't think."

When Gordon roars off in the Porsche, Mick stands at the door and waves goodbye. But when Rambeau tries to feed her she won't eat, and when he tries to get her to bed she says she is like an old horse, once she is down she will stay down, once off her feet she will never get up on them again. She is white and tired, and Rambeau curses the doctor who takes his cure away with him.

"The old gray mare, she ain't what she used to be," Mick says to him accusingly. He has a flickering vision of an ideal alternate old woman, biddable and sweetly resigned.

He fetches the platter of sandwiches and the last cold bottle of beer and camps in the living room. Mick roams and rummages, napping from time to time rolled in her motley cardigan or in the colored afghan, rising to roam and rummage once again.

She is not in a very good temper and neither is he.

Kitty

◆

"If you're absolutely sure you're pregnant," Kitty says carefully to Eileen on the telephone, "why would it be so wrong to see a doctor?"

"If you came out in the stigmata, would you call up a dermatologist?"

"Oh I hope so," Kitty says. She is glad to hear some small return of cool argument in Eileen's manner. She has telephoned Eileen from all over the quad cities for weeks now and Eileen has either refused to speak to her or spoken in a way that is strange and ennobled. "There are hysterical pregnancies," Kitty says. "Gordon's been reading up on them."

"Gordon is a dog. I'm leaving Gordon. Gordon says things to me like 'How are you and Philip of Macedonia? How are you and the Infant of Prague?' He's disgusting."

Kitty closes her eyes. "Maybe you should have played this thing a little closer to your vest."

"He says he won't pay child support. He says, 'Take it up with the Holy Ghost.'"

"Luna, you're right, he is a dog. You better come and stay with me for a little while. I'll be home on Halloween.

We'll go to our mother's and eat doorsteps of barmbrack with big knobs of butter. We'll play the game with the Bible on the string and find out the initials of the men we're going to marry."

"I can't go there. She doesn't believe I'm pregnant. You don't believe it either. You think I'm going crazy."

"We have to go there, Eileen. We always go there. Halloween was the first good day we had after our father died. And she's failing. There's a lot of junk in her arteries, her peripheral circulation's shot, Gordon said so. She forgot my birthday, she's never done that."

"She's the one that's crazy. Our mother, she *is* crazy, she thinks she's having a baby, Kitty. At her age."

Kitty makes a low, humming noise.

"You remember those baby clothes we used to look at, the ones she made for us, all tucked and smocked and embroidered, remember them? They'd cost a ransom now, they're wonderful. They look French or something, you couldn't *buy* them. And they're *mine*, after all. Ours, but you don't need them. She won't *give* them to me. She's keeping them for a baby of her own. So she says. A baby of her own. Crazy. Our room is locked. Our old room, she's got it locked. She's going to put her baby in there."

"None of the rooms in that house locks."

"Locked."

"Luna, *is* it Philip of Macedonia or anybody like that? Just give me a clue. I'm trying to get a handle on this thing."

"Don't be stupid, Kitty. It's just a perfectly ordinary little baby. Isn't an ordinary baby extraordinary enough?" She is annoyed with Kitty; she hangs up.

"I'm flying home tomorrow, Mommy," Kitty says into the hot damp phone, "I'll be home for Halloween. All Saints', All Hallows' Eve. Get the barmbrack ready. Put in the thimble and the wedding ring and put in the thruppenny bit. We'll dance around a bonfire."

"That's all ridiculous nonsense, Kitty."

"No, no, we always do it. We have to do it. You always said it was the New Year's Eve on the old Irish calendar."

"I disremember, Kitty."

"We have to play the game with the Bible and the string and see what man we'll marry, we have to eat doorsteps of barmbrack with big knobs of butter and try to tell our futures by our favors."

"You're not children, Kitty."

"No, we won't do it next year if you don't want, but we must do it this time, one last time."

"Kitty, are you all right in yourself? How are you?"

"Oh, yes, I'm all right," Kitty says, and even as she says these words she knows that they are true. "Have you seen anything of my friend, you know, Rambeau?"

"A glimpse I've caught of him, from time to time."

"Do you want me to tell you a story about my competitors, the Peach Creature and the Prune Prince? The Peach Creature wears a suit made of pink velour."

"No Kitty, I've too many calls on my time. Let me get a stub of pencil and a scrap of paper and you tell me the relevant particulars."

"The what?"

"What is your flight number?" Kitty's mother says, who has never seen an airport. "What is your ETA?"

Television, Kitty thinks. She is touched. She reads off the information and her mother takes it down. "Be well," Kitty says to her mother. "Don't worry too much about anything. I'll see you on Halloween."

Rambeau

◆

"It was me that put her up to it," Mick says to Rambeau in her darkened living room. "It was me that poisoned Kitty's mind against him. Not that he wasn't a divil out of hell because he was."

"It was an accident," Rambeau says. He lights a cone of newspaper and holds it in her fireplace while he fools with the damper. He has already heard from her the story of Kitty's father's death. His eyes are gritty and his tongue is thick. He feeds bits of stick to the fire. He is thinking about Cherokee and how passed over it makes him feel to think she might be serious about having a baby. He wonders about the decency of offering Cherry a new car or a few months in Europe as a bribe for not having a baby. Let her have a baby when he is out of the picture.

"I knew Dominic long years before I walked out with him," Mick says. "I knew him when we were bits of bare-footed kids going messages round the doors. I never meant to marry on him, as God is my judge. I did it as you would on a dare. I was a bold piece of goods in them days. I did it to annoy my mother and all belonging to me. I got more than I bargained for."

Rambeau sweeps together small fragments of bark on the hearth. He tries to envision a meeting between Kitty and Cherokee. This fantasy, too awful to pursue, rouses him. He pours a little ginger wine in Mick's tea.

"I was a great awkward gawk of a girl; my father used to say I was tall and straight as a soldier. I was heedless. Dominic was an ignorant lump of a boy not all the way up to my chin. He paddled after me like a wee duck. He made me a mouthpiece, a laughingstock, giving out that he'd have no girl but me. I married him for no reason only badness and to shock my people. The first week we were married, he handed me an opened wage packet. I was insulted. My mother took my father's wage packet sealed. She gave him out of it what would pay for his pint and his tobacco and his wager to put on a horse, and with the rest she did miracles. But she never had from him his wage packet but what it was sealed. I threw the opened wage packet back at Dominic. He threw it on the fire and his wages in it. We went hungry for a week; my few shillings went for coals and the roof above us. My mother was just beyond the wall, our wee houses were attached in a row. My parents could hear every ah, yes or no. One night I roasted an onion so they needn't think we went without our meal.

"Dominic was political. Much of what he said was true. But some of his friends were a bad low crowd; I didn't like them. Indeed I would have been political myself, only to spite them. Not long after we were married, there was trouble in the district. There was a curfew and gunfire and the women were afraid to leave their homes. There was nothing in the way of a larder in those wee houses, sure, every woman went to the shops every day. With the trouble there was soon no food in the houses and the children were famished with the hunger. A man I knew, Dan Murphy was his name, was a baker. He drove his wagon into the street and threw open the doors at the back. He gave a shout and the women ran out and he tossed out the loaves and waved away the money in their fists, their payment. He was famous for it after. I was first out, not because I had a hungry child, I hadn't a child at all for I was newly married. I did it to thwart Dominic for I was in fits of temper and why I disremember.

"The army came into the street and the other women ran into their homes but I stood my ground, just for temper, just for badness. A soldier pushed me to my knees and he tore a bit off the loaf and he thrust it in my mouth. He made a mocking sign of the cross over me. At that very moment someone shot him. They never knew after, say what they might, where the shot was fired from. They never found a firearm. Dominic was lifted and then he was let go. When I asked him did he do it, he wouldn't meet my eyes. Which told me nothing one way or the other. He was very passionate, Dominic, and what had happened made him excited in himself. God forgive me, I was excited by it too.

"Late on in the evening that Dominic was released some of his friends came to collect him. There was talk of America or Canada; Australia, maybe. They said the house was being watched. When it was black dark, Dominic left through the back garden—a friend of his who was low-built like him left the house an hour later. An hour after that the second friend left and so on. I don't know who it was was watching, but whoever it was they did nothing. At full daylight I was all alone. I put on the coat and skirt I stood up to be married in and I went out into the street. I thought I would be shot down dead, so I did. Nothing happened. I felt a fool and came back to my house and made a pot of tea and drank it. I waited. I thought I was well out of it.

"Two years later I was waiting still. I had a postal card from Canada with a picture of a goose on it and no message whatsomever.

"I took against my mother and my sister; I wouldn't touch clothes with them; I wouldn't put my foot across their doors. It was very clear to me at the time but why I disremember. I was ashamed, I think that was the way of it. The soldier did not die and though there was a song about Dominic it was not a tuneful song, not one with an air you would remember.

"He didn't send for me nor he didn't send word. I thought about him morning, night and noon. I got a postal card from Scotland with a thistle and a recipe for haggis on it. I thought he was in tow with another woman and had turned his back on me.

"One night in the small hours there was a rattling at my letter box. My heart stood still in my body—I was afraid it was the army or the police. They had done that to me both before. It was Dominic with his hair colored dark and a bushy big beard sprouted out on him. He was stumpier than ever and his eyes were yellow eyes—the like of them you've never seen except on our Eileen. But in Eileen's head they look a whole lot nicer. He was like an apparition you'd see on the films. He said he had been in South Africa. He said he was on the run, that there were men out after him. He said to get him a drop of tea. I'll not tell you the word of a lie, I was glad to have him in the house. Yellow-eyed and stumpy and liar that he was. For I was sure he was a liar but I couldn't tell.

"We had our whole conversation in whispers of talk, lest my mother hear us on the far side of the wall. I swore before God and his holy angels that I would never tell that Dominic had been there. He said he was on a mission or on a job, whatever he said. I thought he had stolen off to be with me. I thought he had used organization money that was marked for something else to come and be with me. Such was my foolishness and vanity. I never had felt, in the months I had lived with him as man and wife, such a power of emotion. I *was* his wife, after all. I didn't feel easy in my mind about it after so long and what had happened, but he had his rights as well.

"But that is an untruth. I was a young woman and I had been alone with only shame and scorn for companions. I was glad to have his arms around me, Dominic that used to follow after me, pleading for a look or a smile.

"He stayed with me for the day and into the next night and through it to the early light. I stopped a wee girl and sent her with a note to my work that I was that ill I could not leave my bed. You will understand me when I tell you that we barely left it.

"In the dawn Nick pushed me out into the street to steal him identity papers. I thought long after that this was a strange thing to do. Surely to God he had identity papers of some kind and I was not the one to do an errand of that kind. But I did it. I wandered the district shaking with fear until I found an unlocked entry with coats on pegs in it and papers in the pockets of the coats. I took cards and papers. Belonging to a seaman, so I believe.

"Dominic took the papers from my hand and kissed my mouth and left me. He left me in a certain shape and condition. He left me with his child. High and dry.

"I expected that despite appearances word would be passed that I was not a light woman. That I was a chaste woman and true to my marriage vows. No such of a thing. I could not believe that he did not know what he had done to me. But sometimes I would not believe that Dominic had been there. Sometimes the thought of him would work on my mind and my reason. I wore tight stays and went to my work but tongues wagged before and behind me. I hadn't a friend in the street and if anyone had tried to do me a kindness I would have spat at them. I prayed that the child would be a girl and that it would not look like Dominic O'Carolan. Things were said and done to me that do not bear repeating. Rough corner boys had my name in their mouths. I was taken to be a bad woman, disloyal to my husband, the hero. His fame was fresh again.

"It came near time for my lying-in. The child came early,

a seven months' child, a dry birth. The pains came on me unawares. I was kneeling by the side of the bed, my knees was raw with chilblains. I had cleaned the room after my sister's first child and I had washed the cloths and I had seen her bandaged from beneath her breasts down her body like a corset. And I had thought from this that a baby burst through the navel. That is the God's honest truth, that is how I thought a child was born into the world. And I am sure that I was not alone in thinking it. In country places girls may have had a little knowledge, they may not have grown up fools, but I did and it was thought to be a proof of virtue. That birth was a cruel astonishment.

"My son was born on the bare boards. I lay on the floor not to sully the good mattress. He cried out in my womb and when he did that I beat on the wall out of pity for him. I beat with my hairbrush on the wall and called out my mother, my mother, but nobody came. He was a small boy but beautiful in every part and perfect. I thought he would not live and my heart was asunder before he was born on whether it would be better for us both if God should take him. But when he cried out in my womb I loved him and from that day forward.

"I was thought to be a dirty brazen piece with my bastard on my arm and my exiled hero of a husband. I think that is true. I was bold and haughty. I kept myself to myself. I did not have the child baptized, which was wrong of me. I had made the child a baptismal robe, but the child never wore it. Dominic had made me many promises. I believed I would be vindicated. Then I would have the child baptized. That was wrong of me. But Dominic—as well to call on the thin air. My son was a fine child, God love him, and a handsome child—Kitty has his eyes. He was nearly two years of age when he died of nothing atall. He went from sleep to death like a blown leaf and of nothing atall. He was never baptized, never christened. Think of him, denied the light. I suffered agonies. I wasn't twenty."

Rambeau feels a pang of reminiscent longing for Dorinda's baby. He wonders if it is born and who it resembles and if it can be said to be happy. His old specific, intimate concern disturbs him. Mick is looking at him.

"When did Dominic come back?" he asks. He is thinking about babies: Kitty as a baby, Cherokee.

"He never came back. He sent for me out of the blue and I was a woman over forty year of age at that time. He said we should let bygones be."

"Why did you go to him?"

"I don't know. It is hard to know what goes on in yourself. My mother had died and my sister, and I had nursed them. I was on my own and frustrated in my mind. A man two doors down had come rapping on my door and saying we should marry. And me a married woman, as he knew. I thought a lot of the wrong and sorrow of my young days, and of my ruined life."

"Did you think it would work out with Dominic?"

"Indeed," she says, "I never thought that."

"Did you think you would get even?"

"It never struck my conscious mind," Mick says. "I wonder would I be so cute and wily." She smiles. "After my husband died," she says, "I couldn't go into a street where a church stood. Time passed and I couldn't go into a street at all. My last outing was to R. H. Macy's department store and I took a fit in the ladies' toilet over some lip rouge on a wall. I am in a jail here, a hoosegow. That is God's judgment on me."

"What about poor Kitty?" Rambeau says. "Kitty runs around thinking she's a murderess. What's God's judgment on that?"

"You are God's judgment on Kitty," Mick says contentedly.

"It was an *accident*," Rambeau says.

$Kitty$

◆

Kitty answers a page at Kennedy and discovers that her car awaits her in one of the airport parking lots. She thinks at once of Mr. Conrad; it is his act of contrition for two months of silence, for refusing to see her off. She is pleased to think of him, faithful swain, little furry face alight with welcome.

But when she finds Rambeau's limo, Mr. Conrad is not in it. The car is very dirty and WASH ME has been written on it in a hand that resembles Rambeau's. She chides herself for observing this; it is backsliding.

She climbs into the car and settles herself to wait for Mr. Conrad. Her baggage has been lost. She has only the clothes she wears; Eileen's sort of clothes, not hers, but they have served her. She has earned enough money to pay her bills and to keep her mother free of worry for a while. Without baggage, having done to the best of her ability a silly and difficult job, Kitty feels a zany sense of pleasure. She has in her shoulder bag a mare's nest of lined loose-leaf pages. On these are scribbled bits of poems. She also carries the notebook with the marbled cover in which she writes at her confession.

She pulls off her black wig and looks into the rearview mirror as she plucks the pins from her hair, which springs out, livid, around her tired face. She looks aged. She looks, as a matter of fact, like her mother, and below the neck like a mussy Eileen. The idea of this pleases her but the reality does not. She peers into the mirror, poking at her hair. It is Halloween. A cold and beautiful day persists outside the car, with slanting sherry-colored sun. If a girl looks into a mirror on Halloween, she will see the face of her lover over her shoulder. Kitty, who has tried this many times, thinks of it idly now. She has passed her thirty-sixth birthday in the quad cities and no one has remembered it. She peers into the mirror.

Slowly, slowly in the mirror, as if from sleep or death, there appears in the mirror the head of her lover Rambeau. It is joined to the body of a dog. Kitty suffers a captivation of gaze, an enthrallment. She cannot look away.

"God help me," says poor Kitty.

"Boo," says sweet Rambeau.

He throws off the old dogskin lap robe and stumbles to his place behind the wheel.

"I fell asleep."

"That's okay. That's perfectly okay. Don't touch me."

"I have another letter for you."

"My God, stop writing me letters, just come home."

"I can't help it."

"Well all right. I guess that's all right. Don't you touch me, though."

"Kitty," Rambeau says. "I think I ought to touch you."

"Well all right," Kitty says. "I guess that would be all right."

But he doesn't touch her. He sits beside her like a passenger on a bus. Kitty finds her brush in her bag and fumbles it over her tangled hair. Rambeau takes the brush and as he strokes her hair with it, her hair takes life and leaps up crackling to curl about his hand.

"Love me," he says. "If you can stand to after you read that letter."

"This is very scary," Kitty says. "What is this I'm feeling? This is alarming; I don't know what to call it."

"This is called requited love," Rambeau says. "Nobody has much experience in it." Suddenly he locks her door.

"Do you think I'm going to run away?" Kitty says. "Open that."

He releases the lock and holds her against him. His mouth on her forehead is cold.

"I wrote out some things to show you," Kitty says into the neck of his green sweater. "Some things you should have known about me. They're all mixed up and stupid. But they're a sort of confession. That's a little too fancy, but this is something you should have known."

"Oh shut up, Kitty," Rambeau says. "There's nothing you can say about you I don't know in my bones. Just shut up, Kitty."

"All right," Kitty says. "My pleasure."

Rambeau starts the car and drives it to a car wash. The car wash is shaped like a smooth blue stucco whale. Its mouth is wide and amiable. Kitty has never been through a car wash and the prospect delights her.

Rambeau pulls the car onto the track and puts the gear in neutral. Suddenly the car is gliding, slowly gliding with no motive power of its own into the sea-dark cavern of the blue stucco whale. Great sea-creature brushes descend on them, soaping, foaming, covering the car, the windows, enclosing them in froth, in spume. Long streaming strips of hide beat at them, lash them, incessant, rhythmic, steady as the fret of the sea. Kitty and Rambeau are safe and hidden. She is conscious of his seawater eyes, his rosy mothy hair, his voice like honey. His warm hands clasp her body beneath her sober clothes. She feels herself more valued to herself. She is enchanted. She takes him all into her quickly and their union is clumsy and sublime. Clear water sloshes over them, great rivulets of water, torrents, streams, fonts of water rinse them clean. When they move out into the winey sunlight, they are breathless and laughing, separate and blinking in the sun.

Rambeau gets out of the car near the tail of the whale. "I shouldn't have done that," Rambeau says.

"I should think not," Kitty says. "The very idea."

"Read the letter," Rambeau says. "You knob, you knurl, you buttonhead." He stuffs his hands in his sweater pockets and he runs away.

She watches him take his chance and dart across the highway. He looks lean and handsome in the damaged sweater, like a battered, personable alley cat.

In a few minutes, Kitty gets out of the car and reads the directions on the coin-operated vacuum cleaner. She feeds coins into it and wolfs up all the scruff from the car's interior.

As she does this she whistles a song Rambeau sings when he's shaving, when he's not singing "Ten Cents a Dance."

> I'm a rambler
> I'm a gambler
> I'm a long way from home
> And if you don't like me
> Just leave me alone.
> I eat when I'm hungry
> I drink when I'm dry
> If moonshine don't kill me
> I'll live till I die.

When her coins are gone, she gets into the car and takes out the book with the scrappy pages that constitute her confession. She respects these inadequate pages; they were hard to come by. But the important thing, perhaps, is to confess and then to stop confessing.

She looks at the envelope that contains Rambeau's letter

but she does not open it. She examines the cassette he has left. A label on the box says Happy Birthday. In a little time, and without anxiety, she decides to leave. She is eager to get home, eager to get on with things. Eager to begin her future.

Kitty

◆

As I drove to my house, I was in an unfamiliar state of mind. I was happy. There was a tape deck in Rambeau's car, but I never thought to play the tape he had given me. I didn't want to open up and read his letter, either, no matter what the letter had to say. These things were like riches stored up. I don't mean that foolishly. Rambeau seemed to me a marvel and a revelation and I wanted to get all the good of that quickly, just in case it went away, but it is also true that I had never had much to do with anticipation in my life, dread being more my style. And now I felt anticipation. It was delicious, wanting to see what would happen next.

I felt keen and sexy, too. Part of some poem was in my head: "Their mouths so wide / they drank each other from inside / a gland of honey / burst within their throats."

I was glad to be driving to my pretty little house. Once upon a time my little house put me in romantic mind of the half-doored digs my mother grew up in. But then I styled a shoot in some cottages, real cottages, like the one my mother was glad to call her home, and they were dark and cold and comfortless—cold tap dripping just inside the door and a sooty fire and a toilet in the yard where I have beds of roses.

And so I knew it was sentimental folly to make too much to-do about my cozy cot and love nest. All the same I was let down when I saw my too-cute house and concerned that I should feel that way. I was just getting going at being a happy person, I didn't want to tangle up my feet so soon. For some reason, it was my mother's homely lump of a house in Queens I longed for.

When I went into my house I had a sort of three bears feeling. It was messy. An open jar of instant coffee stood on the rug with a crusted spoon beside it. Things like that. Some clothes of mine on a chair that I certainly hadn't left there. Odd, because Mr. Conrad doesn't like mess. On the other hand, he hadn't put a hand to my garden either, so perhaps he'd left me. Taken up with some other squaw; lying in wait for her, trotting along behind her, bringing her baby artichokes and splits of champagne and figs. On the whole I was more relieved than not; he belonged, I thought, to my past. Somewhere a dog was squalling.

I went into the pungent kitchen to find the sink full of foul greasy eggy plates with tea bags clinging to them. Two lengths of green garden hose were taped onto the sink taps. They departed the kitchen by way of the open window. A thick danger-orange extension cord, the heavy-duty kind, was plugged into the light fixture over the sink and accompanied the garden hose on its travels.

In the distance, the dog was miserably moaning. I saw raccoon and possum tracks in a gritty snow of salt or sugar on the kitchen floor. Boxes of cornflakes and gingerbread mix had been pulled apart and thrown around. My enchanted cottage, my little forest friends. I didn't mind so much and then I did mind, once it broke on me that coons and possums don't leave dishes stinking in your sink or steal your water and your power. My next thought, still in the storybook mode, was tramps or gypsies, spawned, I imagine, by my mother's yarns of Ireland.

Then suddenly I was afraid. I knew it was Mr. Conrad. I knew he bivouacked at the mansion, although I pretended not to know, and I knew he had done this. Mr. Conrad had made an unholy, a somehow creepy, mess of my kitchen. I'd often enough made a mess of it myself, but I felt scared.

The taped connection between the hoses and the taps was not secure and water sputtered out, steaming and splashing and puddling on my floor.

I went out of the house and around to the outside of my kitchen windows. The bright synthetic colors of the hose and the cord snaked through the fire thorn planted there. They led up the hill to the mansion; a fair trek, a lot of hose and cord. I climbed the hill, Underneath a window of the big house the hoses were hissing and spurting, churning up a sea of mud.

The window belonged to a room I knew to be a sort of orangery or solarium. The woman who owns the big house calls it the Florida room. The people who own the mansion are not friends of mine, or even close acquaintances, but they expect me to keep an eye on the house; I said I would.

I was sore at Mr. Conrad. I took the key to the mansion from the hollow tree where the owners and I kept it. Mr. Conrad didn't know about the key. The dog was louder. I thought now that it was Rambeau's dog and that Mr. Conrad had it closed up in the mansion. I went in through the mansion's elaborate front door, its creaky portal.

The etched-glass art nouveau doors to the orangery were ajar and Mr. Conrad was in there. He had a crying baby at his breast. Literally at his breast. The wailing I had heard was not the dog's, it was this baby's.

Dear Mr. Conrad, so like a painted gnome holding up a birdbath in some innocent backyard, had opened his shirt and exposed his thatchy chest. On it red nubbins of nipples popped up. He was trying, with one of them, to plug the baby's mouth. I can't tell you how repelled I was. I can't tell you why, either. Perhaps he was engaged in research for *The Mango Cycle*.

I saw that Mr. Conrad had been touching up his ginger beard and hair, because he had not done it lately and therefore was grizzled and piebald. This made him look tarnished and peculiarly untrustworthy.

The room smelled powerfully of baby; a top note of rose-scented powder over milk and excrement. It was, without grounds, a familiar smell and it made me claustrophobic. The baby was crying and smacking and sucking. It wasn't hitting pay dirt on the tit of Mr. Conrad.

I had the sense that someone else had been there and lately gone. The floor was wet with water slopped from a plastic dishpan. Big soiled wads of disposable diaper lay about, near but not in a green plastic garbage bag. I didn't see any woman's clothes. On the windowsill was a baby bottle with thin-looking, blue-looking milk in it. Also an object I think was a breast pump. On top of a case of Similac were piled some fancy baby clothes. The baby, I saw, was wrapped in Rambeau's old blue pleated evening shirt.

The arrangement was so makeshift, so uningenious, that it made me angry. The room was cold, despite a heater plugged into the orange cord; the air was stale; the floor was wet; it was a stupid place to keep a baby.

I saw a little plastic jack-o'-lantern with a big lighted candle in it grinning on the seat of a brocade chair. This chair, now stained, belongs to another part of the house.

I go over to the chair and blow out the candle. The little jack-o'-lantern is soft from the candle's heat.

Mr. Conrad jumps and pulls his shirt together. He stands there with the noisy baby bucking in his arms.

"You are early."

"I'm right on time."

"You have tread like footpad."

"Where is the baby's mother?"

"*You* are baby's *mother*. I have procured for you." Mr. Conrad is holding the baby out, smiling and trying to tempt me. The baby is yammering and struggling. Bound up in

Rambeau's shirt, it can't get its arms and legs free. If it could, it would be signaling for help, or putting out somebody's eye.

"Mr. Conrad, please tell me whose child this is. I promise I won't get angry." True enough; I am already angry.

"I am telling to you repeatedly is now your child. I am giving it you, this child, is it not so?"

"No," I say. "It is not so." I am thinking how happy I had been just a short while ago, and how quickly I have lost the hang of it. I am thinking I must have the habit of misery, it comes so quickly over me.

"You are not natural woman, Kitty. Natural woman says, 'Give to me the child.' " He shifts the baby to smite himself on his collarbone. " *'Give to me the child.'* "

He is repugnant and wronged and I am afraid of him. The baby is getting jounced around.

I take it from him. The weight of the baby surprises me. It begins to gum around on my breast; the poor little beastling is starved. I pick up the bottle from the windowsill and sit down on the dirtied brocade chair. I don't want to feed this baby; feed things, you get fond of them. Look what happened to Rambeau and the dog. Nevertheless, I stick the nipple of the bottle in the baby's maw and choke it. Once the baby and I get organized it settles down and guzzles away.

"Mr. Conrad, I appreciate the thought." I don't appreciate the thought. I can't imagine what the thought *is*, if there is a thought. I want shut of that baby, whoever's baby it might be. "This is a young inexperienced sort of baby and I'm sure it needs its mother."

"It is our baby," Mr. Conrad says. "I have papers."

"No," I say. I am having horrors. I am simultaneously having to keep the greedy baby from strangling on its lunch. The baby has a wobbly head. The baby has teeth. Two tiny front teeth behind its bottom lip, sharp and official-looking. Teeth. Surely teeth came later.

"I am perfectly capable of having my own babies, Mr.

Conrad." I sound prissy. I don't care. I am offended. Also I know I am perfectly capable of taking this baby in and wearing it like a lavaliere for the next twenty years. "I'm sorry, Mr. Conrad, no."

"We are too old for the babies," Mr. Conrad says. "We make monsters."

I am entirely surprised and yet I know at once what he means. What he means is terrible to me. I feel guilty and embarrassed and affronted and sorry and sad. But I feel only little bits of these things.

"No," I say. The imperiled baby weighs across my thighs. "*No*," I say.

"I am sorry you don't like it," Mr. Conrad says. "It is all what I have."

I pull Rambeau's old shirt off the baby and flip the baby over on its belly on my lap and pat its back until it burps. I don't know how I know to do this. Hormones, possibly, or literature. I turn the baby over again. It's hard to feel unfriendly toward a small warm thing that's burping in your lap. I examine its expression. I don't know what to say about it. This is a generic baby; ordinary except for the teeth. It's not very genial at the moment. In fact it commences to cry again. Mr. Conrad comes over and scrabbles bug-leg fingers on its tum.

"Why you can't be nice?" he asks fiercely of the baby.

I push his hand away. The baby, I say, doesn't like that.

Mr. Conrad takes up a transparently antibaby position so as to put me in its corner.

"Is not nice child," he says. "Is constantly micturating."

I slide my two fingers down the top of its diaper. Evidence of micturation. But I don't know how to put a diaper on it and I don't want to learn.

"And the other function also," Mr. Conrad says. Delicately he grips his nose between his thumb and forefinger.

"It doesn't know the ropes yet. It just got here. Where is its mother?"

"Kitty, you are its mother. Is not the best child, is not the worst. I paid with my blood to buy this child, I paid good money for this child, it is not shit."

"*Where is this baby's mother?*" I scream at Mr. Conrad. "This is not a toy, this is not a game, this is a living child it needs its *mother!*" The baby is scarlet and howling.

Mr. Conrad turns with dignity and leaves me all alone. Except, of course, for the baby.

Dreams and Secrets

◆

Kitty lugs the baby all through her house. It is clear to her that she has no surface appropriate to the deposit of a baby. Finally she spreads a raincoat on her bed and puts the baby down on it. She keeps one hand on the baby and with the other stuffs pillows under the sides of the mattress to raise it.

The baby now lies in a trough, but the baby is remarkably mobile. Kitty pictures it ascending the slope and vaulting to a dreadful oblivion. She considers putting the baby to bed on the floor, but she never heard of anyone doing this and it seems irreverent.

On the other hand, no one has mentioned to her what must be an open secret: it is impossible to do anything with a baby around unless the baby is in on it. Kitty rests her arms for a while and then she packs up the baby and takes it into the bathroom. An awkward bundle, bobbly and resistant, the baby is full of objections.

Kitty pads the sink with towels and nests the baby in it. One of the faucets drips, but nothing's perfect. Now she takes a shower with the curtain open, making a sea of the floor. She talks to the baby in a fatuous, monitored-sounding voice. But the baby, much given to girning and greeting when face-to-face with Kitty, falls silent the moment she steps away. Three times Kitty splashes from the shower to make sure the baby is breathing.

She is not up to actually bathing the baby; blotting will surely suffice. She puts the baby back on her bed and blots it. She has brought from the house only one disposable diaper, the nursing bottle and a can of Similac. When she strips off the baby's soiled diaper, she sees to her shock that the baby is a boy.

"You're a boy," she says to the baby. She has not thought at all about the baby's having a sex and to be so incurious seems rude. The naked baby looks remarkably male; there is not a whole lot to it but big head and showy genitals. Kitty anoints the baby with Youth Dew bath oil. Soon it is both redolent and slippery; what's more it spouts straight up in the air, showering raincoat, bed, itself and Kitty. As Kitty slides the diaper underneath it, the baby paddles its hands on its oily thighs and then on the sticky tapes meant to secure the diaper, rendering these tapes unusable. Kitty is exhausted by her own ineptitude.

"I've never had a baby," Kitty says to the baby, "but of course I've worked with them."

The baby caws at her. She is bluffing. It is true that she has worked with babies, but those professional babies were attended by a mother and a nurse. She races down her stairs and races back again with a roll of black friction tape from her kitchen junk drawer. With this she trusses together the baby and the diaper. The effect is odd but serviceable. She wraps the baby up again in Rambeau's pleated pale blue shirt. The shirt is not very clean, but neither, by this time, is the baby.

Kitty gets on the bed with it. She makes some crooning noises at it and caresses its head and its hands with the tip of her finger. The baby's twiddling fingers close on Kitty's nipple and give it a wicked tweak. Kitty captures the baby's wrists and looks it in the eyes.

"Less of that," Kitty says. She kisses the baby, through

the shirt, in the vicinity of its navel. She kisses it small kisses right up to its dimpling chin. "Creepy mouse, creepy mouse, creeping up to baby's house," Kitty croons.

The baby snaps like a turtle, fastening its two small perfect teeth in Kitty's nose. Kitty shrieks and the baby chortles. When Kitty has composed herself, she and the baby go to sleep. Kitty holds onto the baby's shirt with one hand. The other hand she cups to shield her nose.

Kitty dreams of red lacquer apples glowing like vigil lights on emerald trees. She climbs a silver ladder; she wears a gauzy crown; each apple slips from its stem into the heart of her hand. She gives each apple to Rambeau. Wearing the pale blue pleated evening shirt, he waits beneath her on the ground. The green and silver sweater is spread upon the grass, piled with glowing apples. Rambeau and Kitty grow dizzy with the scent of apples. Then Kitty sees that each apple, as it leaves the tree, is becoming in her palm an ordinary apple, knobbed and hail-pocked, wormy, crisp or mealy, tart or sweet or sour. Ordinary and perfect. A joy of revelation suffuses her. "I must remember this," she thinks in her sleep. "How interesting."

Kitty stretches and snorts in her sleep. She dreams of her mother and the wicked dog. Her nose is swelling.

When Rambeau left Kitty at the car wash, he headed into Manhattan. Irving the drummer had given him a message from Dorinda, "Drindy from Vegas," Irving said. Rambeau was to meet her in the vest-pocket park at Fifty-first Street, between Second and Third avenues.

"Bring money," Irving said. "That's only my impression. She put a heavy touch on me. She had the kid."

"With her?"

"With her, no. She says it looks like me. My own kids, none of them look like me. They look like their mother, God rest her. She calls her kid, she calls it Nugget. I ask you, Nugget."

Rambeau sits on a bench in the park, near the waterfall. He turns the collar of his sweater up and looks alert and respectable, though he is soon asleep. He has slept so on many benches.

He dreams first of the car wash and Kitty, he dreams then of the waterfall. He and Kitty play beneath it, sunny and safe, sheltered by water, by light, brightness shields them. He dreams then of an ordinary shower bath, he is soaping Kitty, she is jigging and calling out and her body is warm and slick; he can feel her ribs slide under his fingers. Water runs down his nose and Kitty turns to catch it in her open mouth. He dreams then that he is swimming, Kitty on his back. She steers him like a sled, she rides him like a dolphin, he moves through the water like a blade.

The guard awakens him. Rambeau's neck is stiff and his wallet is missing. He wonders if Dorinda took it. He waits a little longer but Dorinda doesn't show up. "Nugget," he thinks. Dorinda liked the slot machines in The Golden Nugget; it was her favorite casino. "Nugget," he thinks. He has lost a considerable amount of money, which makes him feel like a rube, but amuses him too. He takes a twenty-dollar bill, folded small, from his shoe.

Eileen, who since her pregnancy is always very sleepy, dreams of Gordon. Neither of them sleeps now in their nuptial bed. He sleeps in his study, she sleeps in hers, half-converted to a nursery as it is. Gordon has sent the workmen away and returned some of the furniture but fastidious Eileen now sleeps on a daybed in the midst of disorder; she never sees it.

She means to leave Gordon when she gets around to it, but now she is far too sleepy. She snoozes away the afternoons; she thinks of this as working on the baby.

Eileen dreams of Gordon. Bare-legged, bearded, filthy, Gordon is directing traffic in a dress. He is making a botch of it. Impatient, hooting vehicles jumble and jostle. Gordon's nose is a long prehensile snout. Furling and unfurling as he shouts out orders in a finicking British accent, Gordon's nose grows vexed and bleeds. Gordon's blood tumbles down in hard red glassy beads. One of these impregnates a hamster. It is a new fertility test. Soon bright-eyed beasts, half-Gordon, half-hamster, are loosed in the sacred grove.

Eileen stirs and pats her belly to calm her slumbering child.

"Babykins," she murmurs. "Just a dream."

Mick has been reading, with horror and enjoyment, a newspaper account of a woman who baked her infant daughter in an oven. This woman then telephoned a television talk show and listed what she called her motivations. (The baby was rescued, the heat had been low; offers of adoption poured in and a sort of essay contest was being run—should the mother be pitied or censured? Mick is in favor of extreme and bloody censuring.)

Mick spreads the newspaper out on the table, and arranges on it a cut-glass bowl full of water and a silver knife. She stops to collect herself several times. At last she brings an apple and sits down with it. She peels the apple slowly in a long continuous spiral, catching the peel in the crystal bowl.

She looks at the paring in a speculative way, tilting her head but not touching the bowl. She is seeking the initial letter of the name of her heart's true love. Her doorbell shrills, but she does not stir from the table. The doorbell shrills and shrills again. Mick picks up the bowl and empties it in her kitchen sink. She tosses the pared apple and its peel into a plastic box where she keeps the odds and ends she will chop up to feed the dooryard birds. She washes and dries the bowl and puts it away in her sideboard. She folds the newspaper neatly and puts it with a pile of other neatly folded newspapers in her small back hall. "A lot of ridiculous nonsense," she says aloud. Only then does she open her door.

Gordon is standing on her threshold. He wears a rubber Dracula mask that covers his whole head and under it he is sweating and irritated. In his right hand is an orange and black paper shopping bag with Trick 'r Treat printed on it. The bag is full of Halloween novelties. His right arm encircles a half-bushel basket full of apples, small bright green ones.

"Trick or treat," Gordon says. "Why have you kept me standing here like a damn fool for the neighbors?"

"What is it you want?" says Mick, who has in no way acknowledged the oddity of his appearance. She does not seem to want to let him in. She peers over his shoulder at his insolent red car, parked just so at her curb.

"I have no intention of being dismissed on the doorstep," Gordon says.

Mick totters in an exaggerated way as he brushes past her, pushing him away as he tries to steady her so that they almost scuffle and he feels, for a moment, brutish. Some of the green apples spill from the basket and skip around the room.

Gordon pulls off his Dracula mask; his hair is dark with sweat, his skin is mottled. He wears a foulard scarf tucked into the neck of a thick silk shirt under his pale suede jacket. The scarf is wet with sweat. Gordon puts aside his mask and dodges around the room collecting fallen apples. "I brought you these for the brats," he says. "The ones who'll be pestering your doorbell."

"Those are greenings," Mick says. "Windfalls. Those are pie apples. You can't hand the like of that to a child."

"Nonsense," Gordon says. He bites into an apple and the apple is so sour that his jaws gripe and his eyes fill with tears.

"Bitter as gall," Mick says with satisfaction.

"Make pies," Gordon says. He carries the basket into the kitchen and sits himself down at the table. Mick follows him in with the shopping bag, which she puts on a chair beside him.

"My pie-making days are over."

"You mustn't think like that."

"Why not, indeed?"

"I don't know why not, it's just what one says." Gordon touches a round loaf cooling on a wire rack. "Boxty."

Mick smacks his hand. "Brack. Not boxty. Boxty is made with potatoes. A bad brack, too. I never made a worse one."

The barmbrack she has made is heavy and unpromising-looking, but it smells good. She has had a lot of trouble with it, not quite recalling the ingredients and their proportions, though she has often made barmbrack and makes one every Halloween. When it came time to put the favors in, she could not remember which favors they were. The thimble she was sure of, but she could not find the thruppenny bit and had to use a dime. She has put in her own wedding ring, loose on her shrunken finger. And, because it seemed to her that she was meant to, she put in a rag and a stick. The rag was a small square of well-washed cheesecloth and the stick an end of blessed palm from the frond that Eileen brought her last Palm Sunday.

With all these materials in it, the brack refused to rise, what's more she slightly burned it. But she is too weary now to bake another.

"Let's have a piece of this ethnic object," Gordon says, "whatever you call it."

"I call it barmbrack," Mick says. She is ruddy with anger. "For barmbrack is its name. It is a speckled cake and me and mine will eat it on this eve of the New Year."

"Three witches," Gordon says. "Only teasing, Mrs. O." He begins to haul cardboard Halloween cutouts from his shopping bag. He holds up a hag on a broomstick. "Our

Kitty to the life," he says. He holds up another, "Our Eileen." He is pulling bright paper playthings and candy from the bag, making a show of suspense and surprise to distract her. He is feeling indulgent and professional. Filial, as well. When he hears her voice the sweat grows cold on him.

"Villain!" she says.

"Surely not." He tears open a box of fondants, black and white and orange disks marked out like pumpkins. "Can't you shut up that godforsaken dog?" The dog is keening in the yard. Gordon holds out the candy and shakes the box a little, so to tempt her. "You haven't even looked at your toys."

"I am a woman at the scrag end of life," she says. "I am not a child nor astray in my mind. Why do you insult me?" She is patched with flush, her voice so bleak that Gordon cannot look at her.

He puts a piece of candy in his mouth and smacks his lips. "These are chemical and electrical things you are feeling," he says distantly. "They are not real things."

"These are real things. You are a villain. You have broken that girl's heart."

Gordon is appalled and flattered. A cold power of villainy rises up in him. "See, licorice. You like licorice." He takes in his fingers the black fondant wafer with the jack-o'-lantern on it. He forces the old woman down in a chair; his hand is leaden on her shoulder. "Open your mouth and close your eyes and see what God will send you," he says, it is a childish formula learned from her to announce some little treat.

Mick does not close her eyes; they are blue as gas flame. He sketches a cross in the air between them with the black false host of sugar. He mashes it against her compressed lips.

She does not raise her hands to thwart him, but he must contend with her eyes.

In a moment he lets go of her.

"I've been working too hard," he says. "I'm not myself."

"That is the trouble. You are entirely yourself."

This possibility leaves Gordon weak. In a few minutes, though, Mick pumps herself up in a temper again. She scolds and scandalizes, it is all a jangle: some man did as Gordon did, was shot for it; Mick put her husband on him, or will put her husband on Gordon, or perhaps will loose the dog. Gordon sits at the table, crumbling tarry bits of candy; he does not listen. He hears words scumbled wth age and hysteria.

Suddenly a snakelike thing flings itself around his neck and slides thence to the floor. He cries out in fear. Embarrassed, he sees that the thing is a stethoscope, his, one Eileen gave him months ago, one he'd thought Dorinda had taken.

He stuffs it in his pocket. He likes the feel of a stethoscope in his pocket, though he thinks it a mistake in restaurants; they expect a bigger tip.

"Thank you," he says. He has said the wrong thing, she is breathless with rage. She clatters dishes in the sink.

"Go you home now."

"Well I have an appointment, actually." He has an appointment with Dorinda in a motel near the airport.

"Get out of my sunshine."

"Goodbye then," Gordon says. He picks up his Dracula mask, to amuse or perhaps to frighten Dorinda. "Goodbye," he calls.

Mick does not answer him or turn from the sink.

Gordon comes back into the kitchen. "Goodbye," he says. "Mother."

"Take it with you."

When Gordon leaves this time, it is almost at a run.

Mick washes her china carefully. She thinks of it still as "the good delf," though her daughters laugh at her and say it is not delft at all, delft is something else entirely. The china is some that Kitty bought with her first earnings.

Mick has nicer china now but prizes this because it still shines for her with Kitty's pride in it. She washes it, though it is clean, and keeps, as she does so, a folded tea towel in the sink to protect the china from hard knocks. She has had this china a long time now.

When she has finished polishing the dishes with her old linen towels, she goes to the deep drawer in her sideboard and looks at the catalogs she keeps there. Most of these are Macy's catalogs, some of them favorites two or three years old. She has catalogs from other stores as well as many other kinds of catalogs, museum catalogs and catalogs from companies that make specialty hardware; or cookery gear; or equipment for hunting, fishing, camping out; or dreadful, silly "gifts." Her daughters send off a dollar or two for these; Eileen for those that will improve Mick's taste, Kitty for those that will entertain her. But the best catalogs, for Mick, are Macy's. Macy's catalogs have given her so much pleasure that she cannot bear to throw them away, though she has bundled up and tied with cord her knitting books and quilt patterns, her copies of *Smithsonian*, *Horticulture*, *Natural History*, and put them, together with pounds of other publications, some of them conventional, some of them very odd indeed, out at the curb for the trashmen. Because she maintains fine relations with the trashmen, she knows that magazines in good condition are scavenged by them and resold to scouts for flea markets. She is pleased to know this.

She has, in the last weeks and months, lightened her inventory of possessions. Without a sigh or a moment's doubt she has cleared her closets and her drawers of the accumulation of a lifetime. Always neat, she is neater now; her closets and drawers are almost empty and the trashmen sometimes ring her bell to know if she has loot for them.

Eileen, she thinks, will want nothing of hers and Kitty will want everything. But that is Kitty's curse and Mick will not conspire in it.

The Macy's catalogs are a problem. She knows it is a

foolishness, but she hates to throw them away. Macy's represents to her a last outpost. She reveres the place, though it was there she had her worst panic attack, the worst of those hellish episodes of terror that made her, finally, a shamed and secret prisoner of her house and yard.

She does not hold Macy's responsible. Macy's is ever civil on the telephone and a close study of Macy's news and views keeps her, she feels, abreast of what's current in the world at large. She reads two newspapers every day, but she is not homely with the newspapers as she is with Macy's catalogs. She decides to burn the catalogs in the fireplace.

She is afraid to trust herself with an open fire now, though she lived all her life with open fires on the other side. Now she is forgetful. Her head and neck throb. She sees double. Sometimes she sees two dogs, even three. But they will have a fire this Halloween evening, when the girls are here, and she will manage it: burn the catalogs.

Mick goes to her room and turns down her bedspread. She disapproves of napping, clothed, on a made bed in the daytime, but she is old now; she is an old woman badly in need of her rest.

Mick dreams of Macy's, where a white-tiled wall of lipsticked kisses set her off, years ago. The kiss mouths murmur to her, but her hearing is failing; she cannot make out with certainty what it is the kiss mouths have to say.

Mick dreams then of a great oven door. An oven door or a church door. She dreads to open it in either case, for behind it, she fears, are baked babies. But when she does give a pull to the door it opens on a dream of her childhood, a fantasy in which she gathered together the babies of the world and fed them and warmed them and put them to sleep; this idea fed and warmed her when she herself was hungry, cold and young.

She dreams then of her father's songbirds. Demure brown birds in little wooden cages, they are pegged in insubstantial Irish sunshine to the housefront. She feeds them on cooked egg. She is a child and must be lifted up to do so. The insides of the small birds' opened mouths are yellow as cooked egg. She fetches seed for them. She is proud. She says the names of the seeds. The names are "flax, rape, hemp and canary."

She does not dream at all of her daughters, or of her husband, or the dog.

Her dream veers now; she dreams of the wall she beat on, the wall of the house that was her mother's, when she labored beside it with her first, male, soon-dead, unchristened child. She fights off this dream, she refuses it.

She tries to dream again of the sunshine, and of the singing birds.

Gordon drives to the motel designated by Dorinda. It is a tawdry, hot-sheets place with a neon sign. VACANCY. The streets are already restless with roaming, painted children dragging pillowcases. The unit he books is dingy, but looks out on the parking lot, so he can keep an eye on his car. He has no idea what will happen with Dorinda, no idea what he wants to happen.

He resolves that he will not, despite her pleas, get into bed with her. Well, perhaps he will get into bed with her, but nothing more. She must be nearly at the end of her term.

The thought of her condition arouses him. He is suddenly almost unable to bear his need and deprivation. He sits on the hard wooden chair with his fists clasped between his thighs and his mind moving slowly and sorely. He should call his service, return some calls, check in with the colleague who is covering for him.

He does none of this. He rocks in the wooden chair. After a while he pulls down the shade on the window and takes off his jacket. He lies face down on the bed. He tries to remember the names of the bones of the hand.

He dreams of the numbered skeleton of a dog. A mighty

voice commands him to find the mandible. His hands close around bone after bone, but the bone is never the mandible.

The bone in his hand becomes a telephone. He is phoning a radio psychologist. He recounts in disgracing detail the misbehavior of his penis. All the world is sitting by its radio, listening and nodding. His penis rises and shouts out contradictions. He bats it down, up it bobs, his penis is a dharma doll. The radio psychologist, a lubricious woman, snubs him in favor of his penis.

He is confessing. He is shouting his confession. The confessional is a glass case and in it sits a mechanical fortune-teller—Dorinda. He shouts his confession at Dorinda. With his hands he tries to suffocate his penis. Dorinda does her eye roll, her head loll. She sticks out her tongue and makes a vulgar noise. He cannot tell if this is absolution. With a whirring noise a card advances from a slot. It is his penance. Anxiety pours out of him. He reads the card. He is to enumerate the bones of the hand.

Gordon wakes and stands. He puts on all the lights in the room and in the bathroom. He spends some time there. He picks up his jacket and leaves the motel. As he does so he passes the room where Dorinda is fucking the manager.

Gordon drives back to the city. He puts the car away and goes up to his apartment. Eileen is dressed in a prison-striped maternity sack. Black gloomy bows cling to it at neck and belly. A white choirboy's collar makes her look wan and sickly. She is huge. He wonders if she has a pillow tied around her. Perhaps she has bloated; he knows this can happen.

"Put on a decent dress," he says. "Take some pride in your appearance. That's all that's to you, a pretty face, and it isn't very pretty anymore. Pull yourself together. I mean *try*." He has meant all of this to sound kindly, but it does not sound so.

"Eye," he says, "suppose I go with you to your mother's. Would you like that?" He does not want to be alone.

"Goodbye," Eileen says.

"Take it with you."

Kitty

◆

"You are not natural woman, Kitty," Mr. Conrad's voice comes piping to me from the back seat of Rambeau's car. "Natural woman has craving in her breast. Her womb, her ovary is telling to her, 'Hark! Give to me the child!' "

To tell you the truth, I had hoped Mr. Conrad and I were not on speaking terms. The baby is beside me in a yellow plastic wash basket, bedded on coats and pillows. It is wrapped in more coats as well as a shawl of mine and a blanket from my bed. I have the heat on in the car. The baby is probably stewing. I have bandaged the basket to the seat with some of that black electric tape and wound some over the top of the basket, in case the baby thinks it's going anywhere in a vertical direction.

"You will dress it nicely, so sweet."

"No," I say. I just want to get to Queens, where there's a mother, mine, and a possible mother, Eileen.

"I have so strive to obtain for you this baby. You are too old, forgive me, to make baby. It is costing me cash money, forgive me, I can ill afford."

Mr. Conrad is sitting back there with the case of Similac. He is wearing a Snoopy bomber jacket over a sweatshirt that says OCTOBER IS BONDAGE MONTH. On the top of his head, like a hat, he is wearing a Dumbo mask. Sometimes, to give extra pith to his sentiments, he adjusts the elastic and tugs the mask down over his face so a sappy, sunny elephant confronts me in the mirror. I don't care what he says or what he's wearing, the pixie dust has blown off Mr. Conrad so far as I'm concerned.

"What is this baby's name?"

"Nougat."

"*Nougat?*"

"Nougat. A fragment of golden metal ore. *Nougat.*"

"Nugget."

"Nougat, so I am saying, isn't it?"

I decided to leave the question of what the baby is called for later. I don't, I ardently don't want to know where he got the baby. I just want to get it back where he got it, and soon.

"Kitty, we make life. Together, Kitty."

I am ashamed of myself, but I have nothing at all to say.

"Pah," Mr. Conrad says. "Feh."

The corners of his mouth pull down. The car fills with sourness and disillusion. After a while he fusses with the mask and settles it over his face and I don't know what his face is doing under there. The baby is quiet in his yellow basket.

I cannot say that on that drive to my mother's house I never felt the misery of Mr. Conrad, or the plight of my sister, or the danger I had left my mother in, alone with the dog. But mostly what I felt was an unaccustomed competence. I would make things right. And I would do it quickly, so that I could go away to read Rambeau's letter, listen to his tape. I had guessed what he recorded for me. His music.

I switched on the radio. Already reports were coming in of razor blades hidden in apples and roach paste in candy bars.

It wasn't full dark but children were out, purposeful knots of them: ghost, Mr. T, tutu, clown suit, He-Man, devil, witch, animal with paper tail and whiskers. Little, little children dressed as butterflies and bunnies had flashlight-holding fathers standing by. It had been such a complicated day. My eyes kept filling up with tears at the wheel of Rambeau's car.

Gordon's snotty car, in front of my mother's house, was not so much parked as abandoned. Eileen struggled out of it. The minute I saw my sister, I knew she was padded. I have padded actresses lots of times to make them look pregnant. Eileen had not made a job of it. She was very big, much bigger than she would have gotten since I last saw her. But this was not supposed to be a natural pregnancy. Still, she looked swaddled and stuffed. I felt sick and cold, just to look at her.

"Eileen,"·I called, "come and see what I've got to show you." My voice was careful, cheerful and self-conscious, but I knew it was a stupid thing to say. I wanted to drive right away with the baby. Eileen lumbered over. At that moment it occurred to me that Halloween was no night to have two cars like those two parked in the streets of Queens.

Eileen stuck her head in the car and started to look at the baby. Then she caught sight of Mr. Conrad in his Dumbo mask and she flinched and shouted. She was shaking. I jumped out of the car and put my arms around her.

"It's Gordon oh my God," my sister cried, "don't let him get me it's Gordon."

"It's only Mr. Conrad." I tried to hold her tight. She was a bag of laundry. Soft bulky cloth with Eileen shivering inside it.

"Take off your mask," I said to Mr. Conrad. He looked pretty terrible. His blotchy beard was fringing out all around his grinning elephant. He looked grotesque. Bondage tee shirt and Snoopy painted on him where his heart should be. "Take off your mask." I said to Mr. Conrad, "Get the baby out of the car and bring it in the house. My sister isn't well."

He sat. He didn't move himself. I felt he should take pity on Eileen. "*Do* it," I said. The baby began to cry. I gave Mr. Conrad one of the looks I inherited from my mother, and he did it then, all right. I took Eileen into the house.

An old woman was standing in the hall. I swear, I did not know she was my mother. I'm aware that my mother is old, she's always been at least a little bit old, all my life. But this woman was *old*. Old. She was my *mother*.

"Mommy," I said, I had Eileen by the arm, "Mommy, are you ill? It's me, it's Kitty." I let go of Eileen and went to my mother. My mother shoved right past me.

She moved very oddly, at a kind of skedaddling run, as though if she slowed down she'd tip right over. The bridge of her nose was sharp as a knife and her blue eyes were bright as fever.

She lights on the baby that Mr. Conrad is trundling up the crazy paving path.

"Thank God," she says to it. "God spared me for this hour. God love you," she says. She sinks down and kisses the baby.

My old mother is crying over the random baby. She is kissing its small hands. She is all hunkered down on the cold crazy paving and Mr. Conrad is standing by scowling at the sky. The baby is wailing. My sister is dressed for a play. Small children race across the lawn, screaming, "Trick or treat."

Well, there is a little something missing from this picture, but that is soon remedied, for the dog hurtles out of the open house and makes straight for me.

"Stop," my sister says.

The dog does stop. The dog backs up against her.

"He's his mommy's baby *boy*," my sister sings to the dog, "he's his mommy's dumpling."

"Eileen," I say. "Don't touch it."

"Tum on," my sister says to the dog, "tum on, we go bye-byes." She walks into the house and the dog, bumping into her legs, walks along with her, trailing its heavy chain.

"Don't touch it, Sissy, it will hurt you. Put it in the cellar, shut the door."

"Oh shut up, you," says Eileen. "what do you know?" Her voice was thick with distaste for me, but at least she wasn't moaning and shivering.

When Eileen came back without the dog I told her to help me with our mother, who wouldn't loose her hold on the baby. She was trying to pick it up in her arms, but the weight of it pulled her over.

"You sit down inside," I said to her. "I will fix it in your lap." I took the baby and its basket into the house. The baby had an interested look on its face. I really didn't need that baby. "Help me with our mother, can't you?" I said to Eileen. "Get our mother off the cold street."

"She is not putting those handmade baby clothes on your child's back and that is final," Eileen said.

She came at last to help me with our mother. She was not so very gentle perhaps, but she helped me get our mother up and into the house. I must say that before she did that, I said to her, "You stupid girl. This is no time to be crazy now, please be crazy later." She was giving me looks from those amber lioness eyes. I was afraid of her and for her and I was sweating with fear of the dog. The scars from the last time it bit me were prickling and itching.

We all got into the house in some sort of way and soon my mother was established with her nursling in her chair before the hearth. Mr. Conrad was building a fire. I was dashing up and down the stairs doing everybody's bidding. Eileen was watching me.

My old room, which I unlocked with a key from my mother's apron pocket, had been turned into a nursery. My bed was gone and a crib I had used when we were little was set up in its place. Eileen's bed had not been moved. I was not pleased by the arrangement, apart from its general eeriness. I felt evicted.

I got the things my mother wanted from the room. Baby things, diapers and a shirt and a nightgown thing, a sacque, and a blue receiving blanket. I brought them down to her. I fixed a bottle. I brought her a plastic statue of the BVM from her drainboard. It had holy water in it, I don't know where she got it. Sent off for it, I guess. She made a wet cross on the baby's forehead. She was crying, but very dignified. She was a dab hand at feeding the baby and buttoning it into tiny garments, but something was awry in her head.

"Mother," I said, sitting by her chair and laying my cheek on her knee, "did you miss me? I've been gone two months." I wanted her to put her hand on my hair. Don't tell me I'm a fool, I know that.

"God spared me for this hour," my mother said, hovering over the baby. The expression on her face was hard to bear.

"It's not my baby," I said to my mother. "Not yours, either."

"Hold your tongue," she said. "I want my tea."

I went into the kitchen and put the kettle on. I could feel the dog's presence on the other side of the cellar door. Eileen came in. "The house has been painted," I said to her. It was true and it was something to say. Eileen just squinched her yellow eyes. "It's not *my* baby," I said. "Why does she have a crib up there? What is happening to us?"

"Babies fall out of the trees into your *lap*," said Eileen. "After all I've gone through."

I took hold of a handful of her front. "It's not my *baby*. How could I have a baby, my God, start to finish in two months?" I shook the cloth in my hand.

She squinted her beautiful eyes. "Look at me."

She meant me to look at her pregnant condition.

"I am looking at you," I said. "You don't have to do this. I don't want you to do this, Luna."

"*I am pregnant*," Eileen said. "You and that old woman don't see what's in front of your eyes."

The more I saw of my sister, the less I knew if she was pregnant. She had that incubating look. That look of a cooker cooking, a library with all of its books on its shelves. But she was padded.

"Have you seen a doctor?"

"I am married to a doctor."

"Oh, well. Not him." Suddenly I had what seemed to be a wonderful idea. "You can take the baby home with you. Would you care to take it home with you? On a temporary basis? Till Mr. Conrad works things out with whoever he has to work them out with?"

For answer, Eileen opened the cellar door and let the dog out.

I ran for the stairs, for my old bedroom, but the door was locked; I had locked it to please my mother. The dog was on my heels. I had to double back and pass the dog to get to any of the other rooms. When I did, it leapt at me. I heard its jaws snap as we hit. Its claws raked my breast and tore open my blouse. I slammed the door to the bathroom, catching the dog's foot in it. The dog fell, exclaiming. It hadn't made any noises until then and this wasn't much of a noise.

I slid down and knelt on the bathroom floor with my weight pressed against the door. Fear was like physical pain in me. My tongue was dry and my heart was banging. I could hear the dog patrolling. Its feet made light slapping sounds and its claws clicked. I could hear its intake of breath, more intimate and terrible than snarling. There was no way to lock the door. My father had broken the locks in that house by forcing beads into them. Someone had fixed the lock on my old bedroom, but no one had fixed the bathroom lock.

The dog seemed powerful to me. More experienced and craftier than I was, propelled by motives I would never understand. I had had these feelings before. Then I thought this: if I had become a helpless, cowering person, my father's interests were well served. I stood up and wet my face with cold water. I thought about the car wash and Rambeau. I thought about baptism and penance. These thoughts were flashing through my head. Penance was called reconciliation in the Catholic faith now.

I drank some water. I saw the glass doorknob move. It moved again. I thought the dog, on its hind legs, upright, a mannikin, was moving the knob with its paws.

I snatched open the door and threw the water in my glass on the dog and on Eileen, who'd been standing there, fiddling with the knob. She paid no attention to the water and neither did the dog, which was wooing her, rubbing its snout against my sister's legs.

"He's his mother's angel pie," Eileen said to the dog, but she wasn't heeding the dog. She launched into a list of grievances having to do with my mother and the baby and the baby clothes.

"It's not my baby, Sissy," I kept saying. It seemed to me shoddy to deny the baby. I was beginning to feel that it was as much my baby as anybody else's. I was getting to want another heft of it. "Could you put the dog downstairs?" I said to my sister. "Could you please please put it in the cellar?"

"I can do what I like with him," she said. She walked down the stairs in her pregnant woman getup. The dog kept close to her legs, grinning up at her. Sometimes it threw me a look from its shining eyes.

My mother, doting on the baby dozing on her knees, said the little one was in the Land of Nod. Mr. Conrad doled out pennies to a pirate child and went back to feeding paper to the fire.

I made more tea. I didn't know what else to do. Perhaps Rambeau would show up, perhaps he'd know what else to do. Perhaps, on the other hand, Rambeau would never show his face again. I cut the barmbrack. There wasn't any butter. The brack was dry and hard to swallow. I got out the bottle of ginger wine. The dog kept its eyes on me and so did Eileen.

I used to love barmbrack. The currents and sultanas and the fruit peel. And the favors. The dog escorted Eileen to and fro. She seemed to me aimless in her wandering.

"Do you remember all those wonderful Halloweens?" I ask the company. Nobody replies. "We never eat meat," I say. "It's a fast day." I want to hear my mother correct me as she always has. "You pagan," she should say. "It is a day of abstinence."

She does not say that, or anything. She is with her baby.

"We never eat meat," I say. "But we used to have those dumplings. Apples and potatoes, and butter and sugar under the top, all melted together and delicious. We used to have boxty. We used to have colcannon. We used to roast hazelnuts right on the hearth to see if our lovers would be constant. We did the thing with the Bible and the string."

"Shut up, Kitty," Eileen says and the dog makes a rumble of agreement. "That's tomorrow, that's All Saints' Day. This is only Halloween."

"I *love* Halloween," I said.

I loved Halloween because the first Halloween I remember was the one my mother made for us the year my father died. He died in October, on the feast of St. Francis, my birthday, October fourth. After our father died, we were numb and scared.

My mother began to brace us up a bit. She told us we were descended from the kings of Ulster. She said we were the people who invented the horseshoe and the wheel. She said Halloween was really the last night of the old year on the ancient Irish calendar, and so a new year was coming that would be better. And after Halloween would be All Saints' Day and then All Souls' Day, when special intercession is made for the souls of the dead, and we would pray then for the soul of our father.

She prays still, I think, for the soul of our father; she has Masses said for him on All Souls', or so I believe. I do.

"Shut you up," my mother says, making me jump. She is talking to the dog. "You divil out of hell," she says to it, leaning forward over the baby, "I'm sick of the sight of your bulgy oul' eyes. I'm sick of the gravy on your jollers. Get you back to hell where you belong."

She is red as a beet. The baby is squalling. Eileen is saying, "Oh, really, Mother," and closing the dog in the cellar. Mr. Conrad, who has been stuffing packets of papers on such a pretty fire and darting out to look at the sparks coming out of the chimney, darts in again to say that the house is burning.

Eileen stamps her foot like a child and sobs. She has broken a tooth on the hardware in the barmbrack. It's no wonder, she's got the piece with all the hardware in it: coin, thimble, wedding ring. I have got a piece with some sweepings.

Mr. Conrad insists that the house is on fire.

Eileen is crying as though her broken tooth, actually a broken crown, were a broken heart.

I dial the fire department and run around throwing sweaters at people.

Suddenly a truck is there, crackling radios and whirling carnival-colored lights. I wrap the baby in a blanket and then in Rambeau's dirty shirt, for luck. I shout at my mother, who will not leave the house without the handmade baby clothes, or putting on a nicer cardigan or sheerer stockings.

Somehow we are all on the street. So are the tiny

Chinese neighbors. My mother is enthroned on a kitchen chair, flirting with the firemen who trip and scramble in their big black coats, laying down coils of flat hose.

Eileen holds out her porcelain crown and scolds at my mother.

"Oh, so," my mother says dismissingly. "You lose a tooth with every child."

Eileen is triumphant. "Do you hear what she says? She *knows* I'm pregnant."

"There's your pregnant," my mother says. She reaches up under Eileen's dress and gives a yank and Gordon's silk monogrammed drawers, stuffed with Gordon's silk monogrammed other things, fall down on the sidewalk around my sister's ankles.

Eileen begins to scream at our mother.

"You are not fit," our mother says. "You are not able. I am fit and I am able." She reaches up and tries to take the baby from my arms. "Give it me," she says. "Give me my child." I won't let the baby go.

Eileen runs toward her car. Gordon's underpants hang onto her leg until she kicks them free. I give the baby to Mr. Conrad and try to catch my sister.

The windshield of Eileen's car is covered with smashed eggs and spray paint and shaving cream. As she swings out from the curb, I know she cannot see.

She drives up onto the sidewalk at high speed, reverses, up again, back, up and into a wrenching turn that skins the fire truck and takes her, fast, out of there. I snatch Rambeau's shirt off the baby and run to his car to wipe off some mess. I open the windows to help me see. I don't want to leave my old mother on the sidewalk with a chimney fire and a baby and only Mr. Conrad, but I know I have to follow my sister. The car is blocked by the fire truck, then suddenly it is clear. I have never handled it so well. Pulling away, I see the dog. It is squirming out of the cellar window, squeezing and struggling until it slips free. It pelts

across the lawns and then I lose it. I think it is trying to
follow me.

A few minutes from my mother's house, I have an accident. Rambeau leaps into the beam of my headlights, wearing his blue pleated shirt. I wrench the wheel and it spins
from my hands. The car shoots off the road onto gravel,
then it stalls. It comes to a stop nudged up against an
ornamental gate. I have no idea where I am. When I
can, I back up and find the road again. Rambeau was not
there of course. The shirt he'd been wearing was the
one I'd mopped the car with. Filthy with egg, it lays on
the floor beside me. There is no one around at all—a
yew with a pennant of muslin on it, part of some child's
costume.

The next thing that happens is this: I hit the dog. It darts
out of the darkness to run across the road in front of me. I
brake and swerve the car, but I hit it. The dog is not spec-
tral, the car hits its body with a solid, sickening smack that
tosses the animal in the air. The dog screams. When its
body lands, it rolls and then, to my astonishment, the dog
regains its feet and runs away. I am badly shaken. I have
never hit an animal before. I feel sick and worse, I feel a
tiny repellent trill of power.

I drive up and down some side streets, looking for the
dog. When I get my bearings, I stop at the precinct and
leave my number.

I know there is no use at all in my chasing my sister. She
will be crossing the Fifty-ninth Street Bridge. She will have
whomped along Utopia Parkway in the blinded, insolent
car. Sped past Northern Boulevard, past the fish place
where we stop to go to the bathroom, through the ware-
house area she hates. I know she is crossing the Fifty-ninth
Street Bridge.

Before I ever get to the bridge, traffic is backed up and
honking. I am imagining awful things, preposterous things.
The usual things. I am weeping. I am imagining the car,

skewed across the bridge, slammed across the bridge and Eileen dead in it.

I am not wrong, you know.

The car is there, saucy and lethal. Egg on its windshield, foam on its windows. BLOOD it says on its license plate. That will be in the paper. She is not in the car though. They have taken her away. She is gone.

*K*itty

◆

I have dinner with Gordon in a restaurant:

"I THINK THE SERVICE WENT RATHER WELL. I SAY, I THINK THE SERVICE WENT RATHER WELL. IT WAS AFFECTING."

"How many funerals are you going to give her?"

"SURELY YOU DON'T OBJECT TO THE MASS?"

"The Mass was fine."

"EVERYBODY LOVED EILEEN. I KNEW HER FRIENDS WOULD WANT TO GATHER AND SAY A FEW WORDS IN MEMORIAM."

"Twice?"

"NOT EVERYONE COULD MAKE THE FIRST OCCASION."

"Knock it off now, will you. Neither you nor I can stand any more."

"I WISH HER MOTHER COULD HAVE BEEN THERE."

"My God, I don't. Why would our mother want to be at Eileen's funeral? Funerals."

"SHE WON'T LAST LONG NOW, KITTY. I GIVE HER PERHAPS SIX WEEKS."

"I know you give her perhaps six weeks, shut up about it."

"JACK RAMBEAU WAS IN TO SEE HER. NOT THAT SHE KNEW HE WAS THERE. HE PLAYED A LITTLE WHISTLE FOR HER. IT MADE QUITE A STIR ON THE FLOOR. IT WAS AFFECTING."

"Who was that woman who read the excerpt from *Marriage Without B.S.?*"

"Did you like that excerpt?"

"I was just crazy about that excerpt."

"I asked you to write some verses, something, and you wouldn't do it."

"Right."

"Did you like the Pindar?"

"How could you stand up there and say that was Eileen's favorite poem when Eileen never heard of Pindar? How could you do that?"

"What was Eileen's favorite poem, what was it?"

"Eileen didn't have a favorite poem. Eileen didn't know a thing about poetry and what's more she was better off for it."

"Was she?"

"No. Eileen liked Hazlitt."

"That's news to me, if Eileen liked Hazlitt. She certainly kept that to herself."

"Just stop having funerals for her."

"Services, not funerals. Just gatherings of friends. Jack Rambeau refused to play today."

"Good for him."

"Kitty, I don't suppose you'd care to marry me."

"Gordon, I couldn't do that."

"I suppose it's in terrible taste, my asking."

"Just don't have any more funerals for her, Gordon, let her alone."

"A one-centimeter tear in the aorta. Not a mark on her. Not a mark on her body. A one-centimeter tear."

"Let her alone a little bit. It's all so awful."

"Two months pregnant. She could hardly have known. She certainly didn't show. The way her cycles were, she couldn't have known."

"She knew all right, you bastard."

"SHE COULDN'T HAVE KNOWN. I THINK YOU SHOULD GIVE THE MATTER SOME THOUGHT, THE MATTER OF OUR MARRYING. WHEN YOUR MOTHER GOES, YOU'LL BE ALONE, OR WON'T YOU?"

"Gordon, is she suffering?"

"WHO AM I TO SAY WHO SUFFERS? I DON'T THINK SO. SHE LOOKS SO AWARE, DON'T YOU THINK? SHE LOOKS SO PERSPICACIOUS. THESE INDIVIDUALS OFTEN DO."

"She could talk when I first got there, got to the hospital. She was trying to tell me something. Tell me everything."

"WHAT WAS SHE DOING AT THAT CHURCH? THAT CHURCH WAS A FAIR BIT FROM THE HOUSE. FURTHER THAN SHE'D BEEN IN YEARS."

"She was having a baby christened. She was praying for the soul of my father, murdered father. Maybe she was having some banns posted. Maybe she was thinking of marrying Mr. Conrad."

"LEVITY. COME TO MEXICO WITH ME."

"Take Mrs. Wainscott."

"MRS. WAINSCOTT IS MY OFFICE NURSE. NOTHING MORE, I ASSURE YOU. SHE'S QUITE BROKEN UP ABOUT EILEEN. IT'S AFFECTING."

"Take her to Mexico, why not?"

"NOT UNTIL YOUR MOTHER DIES."

"Gordon. Thank you."

Kitty

◆

Eileen was, at the time our father died, a very pretty girl.
She loved being pretty, but she feared it too. Boys, older
boys, began to tease her. They drove by the house, or biked
by, even, shouting things. They threw beer bottles on our
lawn, with notes in them. Notes and drawings. Our mother
was frightened. Girls who were jealous of Eileen left notes
for her too. These notes said the girls would cut off Eileen's
hair, things like that, said her hair was bleached, said she
wore mascara.

These attentions kept the house roiled up. My mother
was suspicious of Eileen, she was accused of inviting the
boys to notice her. I don't know that she did. She was just
so pretty. All the commotion bothered Eileen and it bothered me and it bothered our mother a lot.

Eileen was more bothered than I knew. One day she and
I stayed late at school for field hockey. I was never any
good at field hockey, but Eileen was superb. It was that
same year that my father died, late autumn, what my
mother called "the fall of the leaf." I don't know what we
were doing, we were dawdling around, either we were glad
not to be home where our mother was grieving or Eileen
was meeting a boy later and I was along because she pre-

ferred to have me along. Anyway, we were in the locker room, in the showers.

We were fooling around, celebrating; Eileen had got a hat trick—three goals.

We started soaping the walls of the shower and sliding down them on our bare backsides. It was fun. We were noisy and nobody cared and nobody would ask us anything about our father's death or how our mother was doing. We soaped and slid, skidding on our rumps across the slippery tile.

Eileen broke a tooth, a front tooth. She cut the inside of her lip and it was bloody. I picked up the broken piece of tooth.

I was frightened of our mother and frightened of hurting Eileen's beauty, which was like a family possession, but Eileen was more than frightened, she was hysterical. I had an awful time getting her out of there. We had soap and blood all over us. Eileen was wailing and clinging to me. She thought she'd had a miscarriage. She knew she hadn't, but she thought she had.

I don't believe Eileen knew any more about boys than I did at this time and I knew nothing. Maybe she'd done some little something, but I'm sure it was nothing much. She was full of incoherent horrors. Blood and little babies. Perhaps it was the business with our father.

Talk went around school about Eileen O'Carolan and blood in the shower room. Kid talk, but awful. Eileen stayed out of school for a while, and then my mother made her go back.

From then on, although she knew that there had been nothing wrong with Eileen but a broken tooth, my mother didn't trust her. As if she believed the schoolyard gossip, she checked every month to see that Eileen menstruated. She had to see the bloody pads.

Years later, Eileen referred to this period as her first nervous breakdown. Her doing that used to annoy me.

When nervous breakdowns stopped being interesting things to have had, Eileen never talked about the broken tooth. She and my mother and I pulled along together. It was hard. We had a bad time in a lot of ways. Eileen was a beauty and a belle but nobody suited her. She went out with all sorts of boys and they liked her, even loved her, she was good and sweet and loyal and rather pious. She was cool and responsible.

I was angry when she said she was going into the convent. In the first place, it took me by surprise. I never had seen any sign in Eileen of religious vocation. I knew it was arrogant to feel that way, but I did. Actually, I wanted her to earn some money first, get our mother on her feet.

My mother said that our Eileen would never stick it, that she fancied herself in the finery. That she would stay long enough to have her picture taken in the clothes. Later Eileen told me that before she entered a room in the convent she tightened the cord around her habit to show off her small waist and bit her lips to redden them and slapped herself to give her cheeks a glow. It was innocent. Eileen began to think a lot about our father in the convent. She thought the secret we have lived with was getting buzzed around in the convent. She said she felt it everywhere. She had confessed it, but nobody believed her. Everyone is so enlightened now.

I thought Eileen went into the convent because I had taken a lover.

This was Pauli, the photographer. I worked for him while I was still in high school, as a model, a little bit, and then a stylist.

Something happened to Eileen in the convent. I don't know exactly what. Another episode of blood and babies. Not her blood, not her baby, another girl's.

But pretty soon they wanted Eileen out. That was no disgrace, although my mother took it so. People were popping out of convents and writing books about it. But when

Eileen came home to Queens, my mother wouldn't let her sit on the doorstep. My mother was ashamed. I was discreet, very cautious, so as not to upset my mother, but she thought I was no better than I should be, nonetheless. And now Eileen, the good girl, a failed nun.

That was Eileen's second breakdown.

Her third breakdown was Gordon and she married him.

Rambeau

◆

Rambeau finds Dorinda in a stadium before a rock concert. She and Mr. Conrad are selling hot dogs and soft drinks, or setting up to do so. Mr. Conrad is clean shaven, right up to the top of his head. He is jaunty in a mint green fleecy jumpsuit like a baby bunting, with a black band of mourning on its arm. Dorinda wears a bunting, too, yellow, so she looks like a Cranshaw melon. She has two babies on her lap, one of them nursing greedily, the other making mewling, mumbling sucking noises and smacking its lips on air. Dorinda obligingly hauls out her other dug and stuffs it into the second infant's mouth. They are robust, handsome children. Neither of them looks at all like Irving.

"How's Nugget?" Rambeau says.

"She's fine."

Rambeau looks at the babies. Droplets of rich milk trickle from the corners of their muzzles. Surely Irving had said she'd had a boy. One baby, a boy?

"Two?" he says. Not that he cares.

"Had one, found one," Dorinda says. "I got two tits."

"*Found* one?"

"Well, you know. The way people leave things laying around, they deserve to lose them, am I right?"

"I doubt it."

"Listen," Dorinda says.

"Just take the money, now, and we'll say no more about it."

"I told you, BoBo, I don't need your money. Me and Connie have got a very good scam. I got guys hitting up on me all the time."

"I'm not hitting up on you. I'd just like to see that you have this money. I'm not using it. It's for Nugget."

"Oh, well, the Nuggets," she says. "They don't need much. They're not hardly any trouble."

"They look like a lot of trouble."

"No. Moderate." The pearly luster of her skin has dimmed. Her hands are chapped and her nails are broken. She looks fine.

"Watch this, it's cute." She has two plastic pails and in each of them she plunks a baby. They are fine fat human pups and torn from the breast they howl. Dorinda is unruffled. She takes up a length of wooden pole with a hook at either end and depends from each hook a big bucket of baby. Then she gets her shoulder underneath it and hoists. She shows him how she can walk with the pole on her shoulder and a baby dangling fore and aft. It is a most unhandy and uncomfortable expedient. It has no utility at all. "Cute?" she says. She is very pleased with it. "Watch this." She maneuvers the pole so it lies like a yoke across her neck and shoulders. To hold it in place she keeps her arms cocked. Now a baby hangs down on either side of her. "Adorable?"

"It makes you sort of wide. I mean, wider than the aisles. And it might not be so good for selling hot dogs. You haven't a free hand."

"I like it." Dorinda does her eye roll and head loll. "The refinements Connie is working out." Her great maternal breasts are bare and one of her nipples is bright with blood.

"My God, Dorinda," Rambeau says, "you're bleeding."

Dorinda puts down her yoke and seizes a howling baby. "You're a selfish pig," she says to it. "What about *my* rights?" She plunges her breast in the baby's mouth and the baby stops mid-howl and chuffs with pleasure. "One of them has teeth," she says, "hurts like a bastard. Did you know babies can digest blood?" She grabs up the second baby and puts it to her bloody breast. She holds each baby so that most of it is in her armpit, cradled like a bagpipe. The babies suck and burble, when one of them loses the nipple it utters an urgent, commanding bleat.

He sees that the babies wear evening clothes: footed suits of black and white, appliqued to look like tuxedos. He further sees that Mr. Conrad's fleecy costume and Dorinda's are meant to suggest baby clothes. Just noticing this makes his head ache.

"I'll say goodbye, Dorinda."

"Wait a minute, you didn't get the dress. The dress is why I wanted to see you. It's on my diaper bag." She points with her thrusting, foxy face. "Go get it."

A cardboard box is balanced on Dorinda's bulging diaper bag.

"It's cute," Dorinda says.

In the box is the christening dress that Mick made long ago for her son, who never wore it. Eileen wore it, Kitty wore it, and Nugget wore it, one of the Nuggets wore it, when Mick and Mr. Conrad took that Nugget to be christened. When Mick went down in the street with the stroke that will kill her, Mr. Conrad waited until help arrived, then he picked up the baby and disappeared.

"I'm glad to have this," Rambeau says.

"Yeah, it's cute."

"You washed and ironed it."

"Nah. Who has time for that garbage. I sent it to this

French dry cleaner where they clean like wedding dresses if you can believe it. They guarantee your wedding dress for a hundred million years. It's vacuum-packed. My sister had three. All vacuum-packed." Dorinda sniffs at the babies. "God, this kid has shit itself again. This kid's shit stinks worse than any shit I ever ran across." She is proud. "Connie," she shouts. "This kid has shit itself again."

Mr. Conrad runs over with a diaper. "Why you can't be nice," he says reprovingly to the baby.

"Give him a card," Dorinda says. "Maybe he'll throw us some trade."

Mr. Conrad produces an oversized business card, oddly Persian in appearance, covered with tiny intricate drawings Rambeau can't make out. The print is large, though. Drindy. Rebirther. Diplomate University of Mind. And a phone number.

"I took this course. Connie took a course in how to be a detective which he already knew, thank you very much. I took a course in rebirthing. You lie on a mat. I take you back. You get to do it over. Take it from the top. Get rid of your trauma, get rid of your shit. It was a short course but like intensive."

Mr. Conrad grips Rambeau's hand. He brings together his fleecy heels and says, "Goodbye, my friend."

"Nursing babies aren't supposed to stink," Dorinda says contentedly. "But mine stink."

The card that Mr. Conrad has given Rambeau:

"Shouldst inclemency intrude on love
Be gracious.
Vile guests instruct and
Learning's efficacious!"

Fragment from *The Mango Cycle*, a work-in-progress by "Connie" Conrad
New Jersey, 1985

Kitty

◆

They kept telling me to communicate with my mother.
They meant talk to her, rouse her, get her to respond. I did
all they told me to, but dread was in my heart. I didn't want
my mother to respond.

I want my mother to miss her dying. I don't want her to
know where she is, or be frightened. I don't want her to
know that Eileen was pregnant and is dead, or that the
baby was not her own baby returned to her. Perhaps she
knows these things despite me; she is calm now.

At first, when they took her to the hospital, she was wild
then. They put her in restraints. She was trying to tell me
something. Not one thing, everything. She was so agitated
when I was around that they made me stay away from her.

That's not entirely true. I could not bear to see her as
she was. I was always there, but sometimes I stood outside
her door and watched her. I kept myself away from her.

She looks grand now, haughty and fine. She is calm. She
is silent and aristocratic. Gordon says she is ready. I was
surprised to hear him say that, but he did say it and he said
he sees it all the time. People compose themselves, people
in comas, even, if that is what she is in. Her blue eyes are

286

open, and follow me. She is attentive and noticing, groomed and scented like a queen in fine nightgowns. Her hair is dressed. She is speechless.

I have nurses around the clock. Gordon says it is foolish, since I am by her all the time. But I want her to have the nurses. They are matter-of-fact, they make death seem more ordinary. They have nothing much to do but wait for death to come and so they brush her hair and cream her skin and manicure her nails.

Last night I put my arms around my mother. I do that every night; the nurse was in the bathroom. "Goodnight, Mother."

And she answered me. "Goodnight, Mother."

It astonished me and wrung my heart. I thought it was some brain trick, just an echo. "Goodnight, Mother."

But she said to me, so happily, so safe, like a contented child, "Goodnight, Mother."

I bent there with my arms around her, tucking in her blanket. She had not spoken for weeks. And she met my eyes. "Are you leaving now?" she said. It's what she wanted. "Are you leaving now?"

"I am," I said. "I'm leaving."

"Good," she said. I was holding her hand but she wasn't holding mine, it was her good hand. I held her bad hand too. "Kitty," she said, "safe journey home."

Kitty and Rambeau

◆

Rambeau takes the christening dress out of its sealed plastic envelope, out of its blue tissue wrapper, off its padded hanger. He arranges it in the crib in Kitty's girlhood room. Kitty catches him doing this, which annoys him. The house is full of music, his music, the music he wrote and taped for Kitty and gave her in the car wash. It is lovely; he is tired of it. She plays it night and day.

"I thought you were going to fold up that crib and put it away," says Kitty. There is an edge to what she says.

"For Christ sake," he says. "I'm run off my feet. I'm blowing my ass off in Atlantic City. I'm whipping up to Westchester to doll up that house for the broker. I'm still not done pointing this chimney you let that fool set fire to. You want a crib folded up and put away? Fold it up and put it away, why don't you?"

"I can't quite bring myself to do that." She says this with a little sniff.

"Dry your eyes."

"My eyes aren't wet."

"The possums have been in the garbage. Why do you leave the garbage on the porch in plastic bags for the possums to spread around maggoty chicken bones? There's grease on the floor of that porch that'll never come off."

"Possums aren't what they once were, though I like possums."

"I like possums, too, that's not the point."

"Every possum scrabbling after roots and berries, that's what made this country great. Every possum pulling its share of the load. None of this standing around, waiting for the Rambeaus' garbage."

"With its hand out."

"With its little possum hand out, right."

"I think we should leave this crib. We maybe could use it."

A cold wind blows along the hollows of her bones. She ignores it.

"I had that thought myself," she says. Frances, she thinks, brightening—she declines to call Cherokee anything but Frances—Frances will be fit to be tied. She kisses Rambeau and strokes his head. "In years to come," she says, "my hero, you'll be bald as a perfect apple."

Rambeau's Third Letter to Kitty

◆

Dear Kitty,

When I got out of the Marines I could play alto and baritone and tenor sax. I could play clarinet and flute and piccolo. I could play drums. I could play blackjack and poker. I had a feeling for that sort of thing. I thought I was hot stuff. I was hot stuff. I had read what I could get my hands on, I had been a Marine, I was a musician and a gambler and my hair was red and I had money in my pocket and I was young.

I had a mixture of personal hatred and affection for the Marines. When I went in, my idea of dissipation was a game of craps and a quart of ice cream to eat all by myself. The Corps opened vistas to me. I got into every scrape I could, but I got out again. And I learned all the things I told you.

When I got out, I had the money and I wanted to go to school. I wanted to meet a girl, too. I had known a lot of girls and I liked some really well, but now I wanted to meet a different girl. Also, to tell you the truth, I was a little bit lost.

I went to Saratoga to show myself off, which was a fizzle,

290

and I met a Skidmore girl. I liked her right away, we just jammed, just had some natural things together. Her name was Frances but they called her Chinky on account of the set of her eyes.

She was a girl with a lot of life to her. She had more daring, crazy daring, than any girl I ever knew. I liked her. I keep saying I liked her, of course I liked her, I was in love with her I think. But I don't remember her very well. I nearly broke my heart over Chinky, but I can't recall a lot about her. She had tilted eyes, I said that.

She was a girl who had never had anyone say no to her. Her parents had some money, her father was a judge. They lived in a little town outside of Albany. Chinky thrived on trouble. Not real trouble, mischief she stirred up. I am trying to think of things about Chinky to tell you. I can only think of foolish things. She drank straight whiskey. Nobody did that. She dived off way high rocks.

I was a sexy little bugger and I wasn't getting much and we went crazy, spending my money I'd won and I'd saved.

We decided to get married. I'm a widower, Kitty, you didn't know that.

We decided to get married. Her family couldn't see it. I was a pretty raw boy and what could I do but play instruments and poker. And I had too much money. I bought her mother a present, a watch. Her mother hated that. I wasn't what they had in mind for Chinky.

We were very charged up, very sexy. Sex in the Marines was a whole other story. Chinky said we would get pregnant and they would have to let us marry. There was more of that in those days. In a little while Chinky was pregnant and we thought we'd done something no one else could do. We had plans. We would buy a boat and sail it around the world with bells on the ankles of our kids so we'd know if they fell overboard. We were crazy about justice and sex and getting married.

So we did, we got married. Her parents' lives were ruined, you could see they thought so.

One night I was lying in bed with her and my hand was on her breast. I don't even know if we were happy. My hand was on her breast and under my hand I felt like a lump of coal, sharp edges. And I never heard of such a thing but I knew right off what it was. It was cancer. She was a healthy young girl, it seemed impossible. But it was possible. The hormones that fed the baby were feeding the cancer, too. They cut and cut on her.

From the day she was diagnosed she turned against me. She never looked full at me, never again.

She became the daughter her parents wanted. She was docile and refined. They adored her. In a way they were never happier in their lives though it was killing them. She never looked me in the face again. We never fought. She treated me like I was somebody she remembered dimly from high school. I was wrecked. She was in and out of the hospital, at her parents' place. She never came home to me after she was operated. They never asked me to stay with them.

I tried to keep myself straight because of the baby and Chinky. I was twenty, twenty-one. I was doing a little drugs and drinking and playing a little music in a jazz place in Saratoga. There would be six people in the place and four of them would hate me and one of the other two would be drunk. Chinky was in the hospital in Albany, or at her folks' place. No car, no cash. I was gambling. I wasn't hot stuff anymore. I called up Zeke and got a stake from him and won a lot of money on a horse. I lost that. Poker. Sometimes I couldn't seem to lose and that made me crazy. Sometimes I couldn't do anything but.

When the baby was ten months old, at her parents' house, Chinky died. There was no other way. She knew it, they knew it, I knew it, nobody let themselves know it. I had been planning to win a lot of money and pay for a miracle cure. I had to hitch to Chinky's house the night she died.

Chinky's parents took the baby. I didn't want that baby, I didn't want any part of it, I didn't have an iota, not a speck of feeling in me for it. But I should have found a way to take the baby. They had documents. The judge was a great man for documents, things Chinky had signed. The truth is, I wanted to kiss that baby goodbye and get out of town forever. They called the baby Frances, after Chinky. They never asked me, but I would have called her Frances too.

I got myself together, went to Juilliard on Zeke's money. Most every weekend I took the bus to Albany. I went to Chinky's house. Her parents never made me welcome and they never turned me away. I stood and looked at the baby. I looked at it like it was a dead baby, like I was paying my respects. This is my daughter I'm talking about. I always bought the baby presents. The presents were always wrong. Too noisy or too old for her or too young for her or dangerous. Vulgar. Dull. Needed batteries. I bought toys and presents in every state in the Union and places in Europe and I don't think I ever once hit it right. I thought things would get better when my daughter got older, I thought I would have more to say to her, feel more for her, know how to be a father.

It has never happened. I never see that child two times in a row that I could recognize her. She never got used to me, as far as I can tell, and I never got used to her. Not so as to say, this is my child. I am the father of this child.

When I was on the road I sent her postcards with pictures of shells on them. I don't even know if Cherokee likes shells. (I call her Cherokee after a piece I used to play.) Shells were like a thing a father ought to do. I watched that girl go through changes. One time she was pudgy, then she had acne. Then once she was sick and I was scared. She got all right again, I was still scared. Things she'd do would trouble me. Everything she'd do would trouble me. I never liked the books she was reading, or else she wasn't reading any books. I never liked the way they dressed her. I thought her way of speaking was affected. When she was an adolescent girl she had a sort of crush on me and I thought I'd go insane from it. She danced too close to me, she hung on me, she kissed me with her mouth open. I thought she was some kind of monster, I wanted them to take her to a doctor, but I didn't know how to bring the subject, if it even was a subject, up.

My father was a bad father. I never hurt or humiliated Cherry, I say that after due consideration, but I am a bad father too. The old judge, at least I'm sure he knows how he feels about Cherokee.

It was a relief to me when Cherokee got married. I think it was, I'm not exactly sure. I never know how I feel about anything Cherokee does until a long time after she's done it.

This is the shame of my life, Kitty, my failure as a father. And I think I should tell you, I have thought long and hard about this, I think I should tell you I don't think you and Cherokee are going to hit it off.

But she is married now. Did I say that? I said that.

You are an awful handful, Kitty, but I have a yen for you that won't die down. I will do my best if you will have me.

Jacques Rambeau

$\mathcal{K}$itty

———◆———

Sometimes when I am alone at night, I hear the distant barking of a dog. Sometimes it is a baby crying. Sometimes I hear a saxophone. Sometimes I think of the worst thing that almost happened to me. I think of the Halloween when Rambeau in his pale blue pleated evening shirt appeared in the road before the heavy car.

This is one of my poems. If you run around hinting you're a poet, sooner or later you have to deliver a poem.

THE BAD FATHER

I fear you in the ordinary ways
Your arm at my throat
Your fist at my skull
Your face outside my blackened windows
Your breath behind my half-closed doors

More than that
Your shouts and stillnesses
Inhabit my places
Fill up my pot closet

295

And the space where I keep
My ironing board, my cans of chili
Fuses, that ax

You are my driver in foreign cities
The dog I struck on the highway
Most often a man
Sometimes a woman
One terrible time
A child
Most terrible of all
A rag
On a hedge.

Kitty and Rambeau

◆

Rambeau is upstairs painting constellations on the ceiling of the bedroom where I slept for so long with my sister.

He is whistling and singing and generally goofing around.

Sometimes he does a little tap routine, setting my mother's good delf to dancing too, in the cupboards.

Every once in a while he calls out his next selection.

"Red Nichols and His Five Pennies," he calls. "Blue-Eyed Baby."

"Hit it," I call back.

We sing together. Of course I can't really sing at all. We don't care. Rambeau just sings a little louder. His voice is the color of honey. "I'm tickled pink with a blue-eyed baby," Rambeau sings, pasting stars up. "And she's tickled pink with me."